Lucky
Town

Lucky Town

james brown

harcourt brace & company

new york san diego london

Requests for permission to make copies of any part of
the work should be mailed to: Permissions Department,
Harcourt Brace & Company, 6277 Sea Harbor Drive,
Orlando, Florida 32887-6777.

"Lucky Town" by Bruce Springsteen,
copyright © 1992 by Bruce Springsteen (ASCAP).

Library of Congress Cataloging-in-Publication Data
Brown, James, 1957–
Lucky town/James Brown.
p.   cm.
ISBN 0-15-100067-0
I. Title.
PS3552.R68563L83   1994
813'.54—dc20   93-38749

Designed by Camilla Filancia
Printed in the United States of America
First edition
A B C D E

In memory of my father

DONALD   BROWN,

and to my boys,

ANDREW and LOGAN.

Here's to the loaded places we take ourselves
When it comes to luck you make your own
Tonight I got dirt on my hands
But I'm building me a new home
Down in Lucky Town
Down in Lucky Town

—Bruce Springsteen,
  "Lucky Town"

Lucky
Town

MY FATHER picked me up in a stolen car the day after he was released from the state prison in Salem, Oregon. It was an old Ford Falcon with no heater and cold vinyl seats that never seemed to get warm. He would've liked a Mercedes or Jaguar. But there are a lot more Fords on the road, and the smart man, as my father used to say, must weigh his priorities accordingly. One way or the other, it made little difference to me. I was sixteen at the time, and for the last three years, since my father's arrest, I'd been living in a foster home in Portland as a ward of the state. The woman who cared for me was nice enough, and though she could be strict at times I never had to worry about my next meal or whether I'd be wearing the same socks for a week. She liked to call me her child, just as she did her two other wards, but I knew full well that despite her good intentions she wasn't any closer to me than the last month's check from the state of Oregon.

The fact of the matter was I missed my father terribly. Despite what the child welfare authorities had said of him, and none of it was kind, despite, say, having to skip a few meals here and there, or sleeping in the car when we hit a streak of bad luck, if given the choice between living in a foster home or with my father, he'd win hands down every time. It wasn't always rough, though. From time to time we found ourselves in some nice apartments, some top four-star motels, and once, for a year, in a house on the outskirts of Portland with open land as far as you could see. All that, however, depended on how long my father held a job and if he had the sense to stay clear of the bars, back-room poker and craps. While he was away, as I preferred to call it, I wrote him once a week, sometimes twice. He generally returned my letters, and we grew to know each other in ways we never could've realized had the circumstances been different. As far as I was concerned we were both serving time, paying our debts, wiping the slate clean so that we could begin anew. I'm thirty-six years old now, and I've long since forgiven my father for getting us into the predicament that first divided us, a night years past, down along the bank of the Willamette River. His name is Floyd Barlow, and though not many people have heard of him, the police in Portland, Seattle and Las Vegas certainly came to know him well enough.

As for myself, I came quickly to bide the days when we would be reunited.

The last time I saw my father, that is, before his arrest, he was driving a big Cadillac Eldorado. Back then we were living in anonymity in the River Towers on the west side of town. This was the late sixties, and it was one of those luxury apartment complexes that blight much of California, though for Portland it was a proud new addition to the city's sense of modern architecture. Moving here was my father's idea of stepping up in the world. The red banners outside the main entrance boasted We're More Than Just an Apartment. For the first and last month's rent, and a hefty security deposit, you got a small one- or two-bedroom with shag carpets, a built-in dishwasher and a breakfast bar. You also had full use of the community spa, an Olympic-sized pool heated year-round, a clubhouse and exercise room, two tennis courts and the barbecue pits in the courtyard, which had to be reserved at least a week in advance during the summer months. But what really sold my father on the place had little to do with its country club features. It was teeming with women.

What first tipped off my father to the Towers, as it was known to the tenants, was a full-page spread in the sports section of the *Portland Times*. He was a compulsive man, and it just so happened that at this point in time he was at the tail end of one of his six- to eight-month cycles, and he was itching to pick up and move again. It was a Saturday morning, and we were eating breakfast when he showed me the ad. It featured a picture of a beautiful dark-haired woman in a bikini lounging next to the pool with her arms stretched above her head. Beneath her it read, "Come Home to the River Towers."

"What do you think?" he said.

"About what?" I said, though I knew damn well what he was getting at.

He rattled the paper.

"This place here," he said. "It sounds nice."

"But we just moved," I said.

"That what I asked you? Who pays the bills around here anyway?" He took a sip of his coffee and set the cup down hard in its saucer, so they rattled. "We could *use* a change of scenery. Besides," he said, "this is a crummy neighborhood."

There was nothing crummy about the neighborhood or our apartment, for that matter, but there was no point arguing. Time and again I'd pleaded with him. Time and again I had tried to convince him that switching schools whenever we up and moved was tough on me. I hated making new friends. I hated trying to figure out the new teachers. I hated the label of newcomer and having to battle the school bullies for my place in the pecking order. But my father, who had left school in the ninth grade, showed no sympathy for my plight, and when he got it into his head to do something he simply went ahead and did it, regardless of the consequences.

To justify the move, he'd begin finding things wrong with our latest apartment, house or motel room. The water pressure was too low. The rooms suddenly seemed too small, and the landlord, who at first my father might've thought a decent, fair sort, quickly became a "greedy slumlord" bent on stealing our last dime. But moving cost, and it was during these times, when the fancy struck my father, that he worked his hardest. When he had a goal in mind, I've known few more determined. He'd take on two jobs, on this occasion he already had a good one at Pacific Lumber, and he soon took another for the next couple months, as a night clerk at Al's Liquors. He'd save like a miser. And when he had a full wallet, for he didn't believe in putting his money in banks, he would empty all but a few dollars into an envelope and hide it beneath the refrigerator in a dark space beside the motor, the cobwebs and dust. Sometimes late at night, when he came home from work, I'd wake and go to the kitchen and find him there with a beer and all the cash fanned out across the table. Fifties. Twenties. Hundreds. He'd count and recount them, then separate them into neat piles, lean back in his chair, look at me and smile.

"We ought to hop on a plane and blow this place," he'd say. "Tahiti. Hawaii. Mazatlán. Or maybe we should hit Vegas. We could double this money in Lucky Town. Seriously, go pack your bags."

And I'd stand there in the doorway in my pajamas, knowing there was nothing for me to say. The linoleum at my feet felt cold.

"Got to dream," he said.

"It's late," I said. "You better get to bed."

"But you *got* to dream. Without dreams, Bobby, we're nothing."

Norma Tucker and her husband Frank managed the River Towers. Before that they had looked after a trailer park on the

Pacific coast near Hobsonville. They were a gentle couple, in their sixties I would say, and the first time I met them I thought to myself that they deserved better. I pictured them growing older in a small house in the woods, on some real land, not in this big apartment complex full mostly of loud young people.

"As of now," my father said, "you're on your best behavior. Let me do the talking."

We parked down the block, so they wouldn't see our car and get the wrong idea. It would be a while before my father found himself behind the wheel of a Cadillac Eldorado, and in the meantime he was driving an old Buick Riviera. The fender was dented, and the windshield had a crack in the middle that spread out from its center, like the legs of a spider. We walked up to the entrance. The banners above it hung limp in the still air. The day was hot, and my father had on a tie. I wore a good white shirt and a pair of slacks.

Both of us were sweating.

"Tuck in your shirt," he said. "And quit slouching. First impressions are generally the last. Don't you forget it."

I did as I was told, and we passed through the doors. In the middle of the courtyard was a fake river, and beyond that the pool. All around it lay wonderful young women in various types and colors of bikinis, their skin bronze and slick with suntan oil. There were men, too, but not many. My father leaned over and whispered to me.

"Those aren't your everyday locals," he said. "Those girls have class. You can tell just looking, by the way they carry themselves. By the walk."

But they were all relaxing on lounge chairs or towels spread on the concrete. Few even moved, except to lift a can of soda to their sun-glossed lips, or to turn the page of a paperback, or to work more lotion into the soft, smooth skin of a leg. My father cleared his throat and knocked on the manager's door. Frank opened it, though at this point in time I didn't yet know his name. He was wearing carpenter overalls, and he had a pair of channel-lock pliers in one hand and a plastic sprinkler head in the other. My father introduced himself, told him our business, and Frank called to his wife, who appeared a second later from down the hall.

"Honey," he said, "you want to show Mr. Barlow here and his boy around?"

"Can do," she said.

"They're interested in a one-bedroom."

Then she disappeared again and came back with a set of keys attached to a ring with a white tag on it. She walked quickly, and I found myself, as we followed her, having to double-time it. She wore the kind of nylons that only came to the knee, and beneath the sway of her skirt I saw the dark elastic bands cutting into the pale skin at the back of her legs.

We climbed two sets of stairs and walked down an open hallway to apartment seventy-three. My father reached to loosen his tie, then thought better of it and let his hand drop back to his side.

"What is it you do, Mr. Barlow?"

"I work at the mill," he said. "For Pacific."

"Year-round?"

"Yes, ma'am," he said.

"It's just you and your son?"

"My wife," he said, lowering his voice, "we parted ways before the boy took his first step, and I'll tell you, it hasn't been easy. Sometimes he's the only thing keeps me going." He slipped his arm around me. "Bobby's had to grow up pretty fast, but he's a real gentleman. They don't come any better."

She slipped the key into the lock.

"You know," she said, "we don't have too many children here."

Mrs. Tucker opened the door and we went inside. The smell of carpet deodorizer was overwhelming, and I wrinkled my nose. Another sharper odor lingered in the air: cat, I thought. Definitely cat. But my father didn't notice, or else he simply didn't care. He didn't comment on the small bedroom, either, or the dripping faucet in the bathroom, or the broken door on the kitchen cabinet. None of it seemed to matter. What counted was our view from the living room. A moment after we'd walked in, Mrs. Tucker pulled the drapes back and cranked open the window to let in some fresh air, and he saw what his money could buy. If it wasn't a trip to Tahiti, then at least he could afford a glimpse now and then of some of the prettiest, most eligible women in Portland. As he stood before the window, and it was only for a moment, because he had better manners than to stare, I put myself in his place. The apartment overlooked the pool below, and I imagined he saw himself down there, surrounded by all those women. I imagined he had on a pair of trunks, that he had a cool gin and tonic in one hand, and I saw him laughing. It was over someone's joke. But I couldn't see myself there, though I tried.

"If you don't mind," he said, "I'd like to leave a deposit."

Mrs. Tucker smiled at me.

"You won't be lonely?" she said.

I shook my head.

"You can always come talk to me or Mr. Tucker," she said. "You can pester that man all day long and he won't blink an eye."

My father put his arm around me again.

"What do you say?"

I shrugged.

"Think you'd like it here?"

"Sure," I said.

"Nice pool and everything," he said. He looked at Mrs. Tucker. "How about the schools around here?"

"The best," she said.

"I guess that settles it then," he said.

There was still the routine matter of a credit check, but I don't believe the Tuckers did a thorough job of it. Either that, or they simply chose to overlook my father's shaky employment record. In the last few years he'd worked as a cook, a salesman, a handyman, a clerk, a carpenter, a bartender, a lineman for the telephone company, and once, for three months, as a fisherman. It also could've been that she liked children, that her heart had gone out to this man trying to raise up a boy on his own, and she believed we needed a break. But more likely it was the rent, which was high, and they hadn't had all that many takers. The River Towers was less than a year old, and out of a hundred and twenty units a third of them were still unoccupied. There's a good chance that the real owners of the place, whoever they may have been, saw less risk in people in my father's situation than they did in their original investment.

Two

*I*T WAS AT the River Towers that my father met Melinda Johnson. She worked as a receptionist in the firm of Schwartz, Simon and Hansen, and at night she attended the Career Institute of Law and Nursing at Rollins Mall. Though I mean no harm by generalizing, in terms of that ugly thing called social class, Melinda, like my father, was trying her damnedest to move from one life to the next. Some of this I learned long after the fact. Some of it came from Roger Dunlap, another bachelor, whose overtures had been met with an icy reception by just about every good-looking woman in the complex. He lived in the apartment two doors down from us.

On weekends Roger donned a pair of Bermuda shorts and put on his Portland Bucks cap, our local minor league team. With a portable radio and a six-pack of Schlitz at his side, he settled into a lawn chair on his patio and studied the women sunning themselves around the pool below. He pointed out Melinda once, when he noticed my father looking at her as we passed in the hall. We'd just come from the grocery store and each had a bag in our arms. Melinda lay on a towel near the edge of the water. It was early afternoon, and the sun beat hot overhead.

"Now there," Roger said, "is one fine looker."

"No doubt about it," my father said.

"Trouble is, she knows it."

My father stopped to switch the bag of groceries from one arm to the other. The radio blared. The Bucks were down two runs. Roger let out a long sigh, but it wasn't for Portland.

"Twenty-four," he said. "Twenty-four and going to law school. Pretty soon she'll be taking home more in a year than I make in five. Look," he said, "just *look* at that girl."

Instead he looked at Roger, and it wasn't kindly.

"I don't imagine she appreciates being stared at," he said.

"A guy has to enjoy himself a little now and then," Roger said. "And in this case looking's about as far as you or me will ever get."

"Speak for yourself."

Roger laughed.

"The girl's untouchable. Besides, she already has a boyfriend. I'm only trying to save you a lot of sweat, grief and time, buddy."

It was the sixth inning and the bases were loaded for the Bucks. A guy named Delbanco was at bat. Roger took a drink of his beer and leaned forward to listen more closely. My father glanced at Melinda again, then drew a deep breath and cradled the groceries to his chest.

"No woman," he said, "is untouchable."

I'm only guessing, but I think the kind of work Melinda did said a good deal about her character, and that what she saw on the job gave her even greater insight into the psyche of those of us born less fortunate. She was tall, she was thin. She had long dark hair and big green eyes. She carried herself, as my father once remarked, with "confidence," and yet there was something tentative about her walk, something that suggested both restraint and skittishness. I don't think she felt comfortable in a bikini, and I'm sure, as my father had said, that she didn't like being stared at any more than I would've, if the roles were reversed. On her left thigh, where it curved smoothly into her hip, was a mole about the size of a dime.

My father had learned her last name from the tag on her mailbox, and the first by her subscription to *True Detective*, which the mailman deposited in the community bin once a month. She lived on the second floor in the apartment across from ours, and every Sunday morning, before the pool got crowded, she slipped out of her room in a terry-cloth bathrobe and a pair of rubber sandals that slapped the soles of her feet as she walked. Her hair was pulled into a ponytail, she had a towel slung over her shoulder, and a paperback in her hand. My father, who liked to sleep in on Sunday, had taken to rising early once he'd caught on to her routine. But several weekends had come and gone before he actually worked up the courage to join her. I accompanied him the first time out. This was toward the end of summer, the days were growing shorter, and the pressure was on. If my father didn't act soon he might well lose the opportunity.

"C'mon," he said. "Let's go for a swim."

I was belly down on the living room floor watching cartoons, and I didn't want to be bothered. Wile E. Coyote had dug a pit for the roadrunner, and it looked as if this time he might get him.

"Not right now," I said.

He stood in front of me in his trunks and tennis shoes, which I noticed had a hole in one toe. His legs were pale, muscular and hairy.

"I'm not asking," he said. "I'm *telling* you. Run put on your trunks."

In Portland there's as much sun as fog, and generally more of the latter. Today was no exception. I nodded at the window.

"You're kidding," I said. "It's freezing out there."

"What are you?" he said. "Some kind of sissy?"

"No," I said.

"Then let's move it. Turn that idiot box off," he said. "It'll ruin your eyes."

My father saw fit to save me from myself and turned off the TV. The screen went dark just as the roadrunner leaped safely over the pit. I didn't have to see the rest to know that Wile E. Coyote, in hot pursuit, was a split second away from becoming his own quarry. Even though I was only thirteen years old at the time, I still made the connection between the coyote and my father, and it brought a smile to my lips, then as it does now.

"Grab some towels while you're at it," he said as he turned to go. "I'll meet you downstairs. Don't diddle around, either, or I'll throw your ass in the deep end."

I put on a pair of trunks, though I left my T-shirt on, for two reasons. One, it was cold. And two, I didn't like my body all that much. In my fantasies I saw myself like my father, tall and muscular, with meaty forearms, a broad chest and a sharp cheekbone, like, say, Clint Eastwood, whom my father resembled in stature, if not complexion. He had thick black hair that he combed back with Brylcreem, pale blue eyes, and except for his nose, which had been broken a couple times so that it now slanted to one side, he was an extraordinarily handsome man. In my case, however, despite my fantasies, one look in the mirror and I knew different: reflected in it was a scrawny little guy with no hair on his chest, skin pale as the dead, a mop of limp brown hair and no real muscles yet to speak of. I grabbed the cleanest of our towels, a couple sour ones that were draped over the shower stall, and joined my father on the steps at the shallow end.

Wisps of steam rose from the surface of the pool, and from somewhere came the soft hum of a motor. The drain dams slapped against the sides and made a gurgling noise. I moved my feet back and forth and watched Melinda Johnson glide beneath us. She wore a black one-piece, and when she reached our end she did a somersault, pushed herself off the wall of the pool with a smooth thrust of her legs and returned to the deep side. I counted three lengths underwater, back and forth, and always with the smoothest of strokes before she finally rose for air. Then she did laps, the first five slowly and gracefully, so her body hardly made a ripple in the water. The second set she did quickly, as if she were in a race. At the deep end again, she pulled herself to the edge, planted her hands and lifted herself from the pool, all in one motion. There she sat for a while to catch her breath, her chest rising, then falling, as she wiped water from her eyes.

"Go on," he said. "Go introduce yourself."

The idea seemed as sudden as it was inappropriate.

"No way," I said.

"What do you mean?"

"I mean *no* way."

"You know that pocketknife you've been wanting? With all the gadgets?"

"It's called a Swiss army knife."

"Whatever," he said. "You want it, you go introduce yourself. Show her your manners."

I wanted that knife badly. I had wanted it for a long time, since I'd first seen it in the glass case at Walbee's Hardware. I sighed and started to get out of the pool, intending to walk around it, when my father grabbed my arm.

"For Christ's sake," he said, under his breath. "Swim over there. Make it look natural. And hurry, before she takes off."

I waded into the water and swam across the pool, took a detour to the side once, and then surfaced a few feet from her. She was staring at the bottom, at what I didn't know— the drain maybe, a rock, a penny? I took note of her legs, and they were marvelous, long and perfectly shaped, shining with water.

"You lose something?" I said.

She raised her fingers to her left earlobe.

"I think my earring," she said, "and I'm blind without my contacts."

At that she laughed, and it was a pleasant laugh, not forced or false. I looked into the pool, but I didn't see anything.

"What's it look like?"

"It's gold," she said, "with a diamond."

I dived under and came up a dozen seconds later, short of breath and empty-handed. Again I dived. Again, as I dragged my hands along the rough concrete bottom, I found nothing. When I surfaced, my father was standing beside her. There was a look of concern on his face, but it was too strong, too overdone. He ran a hand through his hair and shook his head.

"The boy bothering you?" he said.

I glared at him as I treaded water. But he ignored it.

Melinda smiled.

"Absolutely not," she said. "He's trying to help. I lost an earring."

He squatted on his haunches. He stared into the pool, long and hard, as if he were concentrating on a tough problem. He rubbed his chin between his fingers. He shook his head again. But if I couldn't see it, how could he? I resented him for even considering the possibility.

"Don't worry," I said. "If it's down there, I'll find it."

"I'm sure you will," she said.

She smiled at my father in more than a casual way. He was, after all, a very handsome man. Then she slipped on her robe, her rubber sandals, picked up her book and left us. My father watched the gentle swing of her ass as she walked around the pool and disappeared up the staircase. He took a deep breath.

"See the way she swims? I bet she was on her high school team, I bet she was the best, too." He motioned me to come closer, and I did. "Tell you what," he said, "you find that earring, you got yourself a BB gun."

"A pellet gun," I said.

"Fine."

"A Crossman. No Daisy."

"Just find the goddamn earring."

The sun had broken through the fog, and soon after my father had rounded the staircase back up to the apartment, I looked again into the soft blue water. I lifted my foot. It was there, curled between my toes. The glint of metal, small as the point of a knife, with an edge that could cut glass.

Three

THE EARRING provided my father with the perfect excuse to call on Melinda Johnson the next evening. He knew full well that etiquette required some kind of recognition, if not dessert, then at least a couple drinks. But to be on the safe side, he stopped at the grocery store on his way home from the mill and bought a bottle of Lancers. He showered. He shaved. He put on his best cologne. We had pork and beans for dinner that night, and twice, while we were eating, he thought he heard a door slam somewhere in the complex. He rose from the table and went to the living room and looked out the window. Melinda's apartment was still dark and the drapes were drawn.

"She must be working late, or else she's in school. I admire that," he said. "Ambition. The girl's trying to do something for herself." But he wasn't talking to me, so I said nothing. He paced for a while, then returned to the kitchen and looked at my bowl. "Eat up," he said. "You got a long way to go." We ate pork and beans no less than twice a week, and to this day the smell of them makes me nauseous. I dipped my spoon into the bowl and raised it partway to my mouth. Surrounded in syrup and beans was a slick chunk of pig fat.

"Quit staring at it," he said.

"I'm full," I said.

"Don't give me that."

My father rolled up his sleeve and showed me his biceps—round and hard.

"Look," he said. "Muscle. All muscle. You think I got this starving myself to death? No way. There's not a damn thing wrong with those beans. Eat," he said. *"Eat."*

The trick was to hold your nose, and though it annoyed the hell out of my father, it was only the way I could get them down without gagging.

"You want that knife," he said, "you want that pellet gun, you better clean your bowl."

"That wasn't part of the deal."

"It is now."

"No fair," I said.

"What's fair?" he said. "There's no such thing."

I ate the beans, though I did so begrudgingly. We'd made plenty of deals before, and generally he lived up to his word. But there was no telling about my father. "What I give," he sometimes said, "I can also take. Just like God."

Around eight, after we'd finished the dishes, and just about the time he'd given up hope and resigned himself to another evening of TV, a light flashed on in Melinda Johnson's living room window. "Let's get a move on," he said, "before she gets dinner going." He combed his hair in the bathroom mirror, grabbed the bottle of Lancers, and we walked over to her place. The earring was inside a matchbox, tucked safely in my father's shirt pocket, but he patted it once to make sure. Then he knocked on the door, and we waited there in the open hallway, two floors off the ground. I stared at the pool below. The light was on, and the chrome drain cover at the bottom shined. A man swam from one end to the other. Somewhere in the complex, music played.

She opened the door, a carton of vanilla yogurt in her hand. A speck of it clung to her lip, and she wiped it off with her thumb, licked the tip of it and grinned. If my father wasn't already in love with Melinda Johnson, he was now.

"We found your earring," he said.

She looked puzzled. I don't think she remembered.

"What?"

"Your earring."

Then it came to her.

"Fantastic," she said.

My father smiled.

"You're one up and so am I. I landed a promotion today. That seems reason enough to celebrate." He held up the bottle of Lancers. "Got a corkscrew?"

Hesitation showed on her face, and for a second there I thought she was going to decline the offer. It could've gone either way. But she surprised me, just as the news of my father's promotion had. He introduced himself, they shook hands, and he held onto her fingers a few moments longer. I suppose it was her neighborly duty to invite us in, considering how *we'd* found her earring and had taken the trouble to return it. I imagine, too, that it all seemed harmless enough with a thirteen-year-old there, and I have no doubt whatsoever that my father brought me along for exactly that reason. Melinda took the bottle of Lancers. She was in her stocking feet, and they brushed the carpet as she crossed the room to the kitchen. She wore a conservative-looking black skirt and a simple white blouse. A matching black coat hung on the back of a chair at the kitchen table. We heard her rummage through a drawer of silverware.

I stepped closer to my father and whispered.

"What do you mean *we* found it?" I said.

He jabbed me in the ribs.

"Keep your trap shut."

I sat on the couch while he wandered around the room. There were books on the coffee table. Magazines on the floor. Beside me were a pair of jeans and a couple blouses, and in the doorway leading to her bedroom, resting in a heap of other clothes, lay the bathing suit she'd worn the day before. It was as if she undressed in stages, tossing her clothes over her shoulder as she went from one room to the next. Melinda peeked around the kitchen doorway.

"Congratulations on the promotion," she said.

"It's nothing. I'm just down at the mill," he said. "A foreman now."

"Don't be modest."

"You don't have to worry about that," I said.

He gave me a dirty look.

"I'm sure he's only teasing," she said.

There was a lull in the conversation. My father continued to wander around the room.

"But I'm thinking of going back to school," he said, "and finishing up my A.A. In business management. Those boys make the real money."

I wanted to believe him about the promotion, but common sense told me otherwise. He'd been fired or laid off too many times before. And in his mind, it was never any fault of his own. Once he came to blows with his boss, and for weeks he was more sore about losing the fight than his job. That was one of the times, when his unemployment ran out, that we ended up living in some motel, not a four-star, either.

On top of the TV rested a picture in a wood frame. My father picked it up and examined it. It was of a man considerably younger than himself, say in his early twenties, with short blond hair and a round, plump face. His neck was as thick as a linebacker's.

"This your boyfriend?" he called out.

"In the picture?"

"Yeah."

"That's Bo," she said. "He's a cop in Seattle. Before that he was on the Portland PD. We're thinking of moving in together, but I've got my doubts. I've only dated him a year."

"What about law school?"

"How'd you know that?"

"A good foreman," my father said, "has to keep his ears open."

Melinda peeked around the doorway and smiled. She seemed flattered that he knew, or that people had been talking about her.

"It was mostly because of Bo," she said. "He's got this idea of opening his own detective agency and having me handle the legal end. But the school's not exactly Harvard." She paused. "You don't need much more than money to get in. Passing the bar though, that's not easy. I'm studying criminal law."

My father glanced at the picture again and set it back on the TV.

"Just keep on doing what you're doing," he said. "Don't let anybody get in your way. I know how that goes. I've been there myself. You have to watch out," he said, "or before you know it you lose sight of the things you wanted to do."

"You sound like my father," she said.

That didn't settle well with him, and for a while he was quiet. Melinda worked the cork loose on the wine and it made a popping noise. "They have law schools in Seattle, but I know what you mean," she said. "If he gets the milk, why buy the cow? I think we should at least be engaged." She came into the living room then, with two glasses of wine, and a can of 7-Up for me. She raised hers to toast.

"To your promotion," she said.

But the act had come to end. I saw it in my father's forced smile the moment she mentioned the word "engaged." The stakes had shot up, and his confidence suffered a blow strong enough to knock the wind out of him. Boyfriends could be exchanged easily enough, and my father had known plenty of married women. But a woman on the cusp of marriage was another matter altogether. I thought to myself, as they touched glasses, that he couldn't have wished them the best any more than he could've impressed Melinda Johnson that evening, with all his bravado and lies.

He finished his wine. He took the earring from the match-box, gave it to her and started for the door. Melinda seemed confused.

"What's the hurry?" she said. "I thought you wanted to celebrate."

"I'm not feeling too good."

"You look a little pale," I said.

And it was true.

"It's his stomach," I told Melinda. "My dad's got a bad stomach."

"Thanks," he said, "for the diagnosis."

"Any time," I said.

He gave me another one of his dirty looks.

"What's that they say about children? To be seen and not heard?"

"I'm no child," I said.

"Just be quiet. I'm not in any mood."

Melinda touched his arm.

"How about a shot of Pepto-Bismol?" she said.

"I'll be fine," he said. Then he glanced at me and added, "Maybe."

That got a rise out of Melinda and she laughed. We said our good-byes, but he had trouble looking her in the eyes, and when they shook hands he didn't let it linger this time.

On the way back to our place he looked at me and wagged his head.

"Bo," he said. "What kind of name's that?"

I shrugged.

"The picture, you see it?"

I said I had.

"He's a punk."

"You don't know," I said. "You never even met the guy."

"Cops and punks," he said. "It's been my experience that generally there's not a great difference between the two."

We walked down the open hallway to our apartment. It was maybe nine o'clock now, a Monday night, and the man in the pool had left. The music that we'd heard earlier was gone; there was only the hum of the pump motor in the pool and somewhere, further down the hallway, the faint sound of laughter. My father put the key into the lock, and it made a tinny, hollow noise.

"You believe I'm a foreman?"

"Yeah," I said. "Sure."

"That's good," he said. "Because believing's half of it."

We shared the bedroom, though we had our own separate beds, and late that night I heard him get up. He wandered out of the room. I waited ten or fifteen minutes for him to return, and when he didn't, I got up and looked for him. I found him in the living room, staring through a crack in the drapes, in nothing but these tight, red jockey briefs. It was only in the last year or so that he'd taken to wearing those kinds of shorts, and for a man his age I thought they looked silly. "Can't sleep?" I said. He didn't say a word, he just stared out the window. I don't think that I could've understood how he felt at that moment, not as a thirteen-year-old kid. But I'm older now, and I wonder if he felt that he'd somehow made a fool of himself that night. I wonder if he was embarrassed for falling in love with a woman more than ten years his junior, and "untouchable," as Roger Dunlap had said, or if he even had the presence of mind to consider it.

"Hey," I said, softly. "Hey, Dad."

Again he didn't answer.

"C'mon," I said, "you got to get some sleep."

The refrigerator clicked on and made a whirring noise as if it were breathing. On the street outside I heard a car pass. I put my arms around my chest. I shivered and hugged myself.

"In a minute," he said. "Her light's still on. I want to know she's safe in bed."

From that night on our lives took a turn for the worse. I believe it had less to do with Melinda Johnson than it did with my father's general discontent with the world at large, and what he called his "personal deadline." By thirty-six he'd expected to accomplish a whole set of goals, among them a job he liked working, a stable home for myself and above all a woman he could love with the certainty of his own death. I believe in an afterlife, and in that next world, when the time comes, I hope my father and I meet up again. I hope to toast a drink or two. But I've run ahead of myself here, for we were a long way from being dead, though my father did have a serious brush with it the day after we returned Melinda's earring.

I wasn't present for this, but I know the physical details well enough. I know the layout of the mill and how it likely happened. He'd brought me there twice before, just to show me around and meet some of the men he worked with, and maybe I'm exaggerating, but it seemed that about every other man's hand I shook was minus a finger or two. The mill was a huge building with rows of windows at the top, near the ceiling, and walls made of thin weathered boards, like an old barn. Mountains of sawdust dotted the landscape around it. Inside, the noise was incredible, with the floors shaking under the weight of the great and old trees. Steel arms lifted them, pine and redwood, some as big around as the trucks that hauled them, and fed each slowly into a spinning ripsaw twice the height of an ordinary man and with a breadth no greater than your smallest finger. From there they went on to smaller, though no less ferocious saws that sliced them into more manageable lengths. The smell of fresh cut wood and hot, smoking grease filled the air.

It was my father's job to make sure the machines were well oiled and that every tooth on every saw was sharpened to its finest point. The bandsaw blades had to be removed for the filing, and some of them stretched the length of a room. It took two men to get the blade off and onto the floor so that they could roll it into another room where they did the sharpening. Probably the most important rule in the saw filer's trade is this: if a blade ever gets away from you, you jump. You don't try and catch it. You don't try to keep it from falling. The weight of the blade alone can take your leg clean off. But when you've got two men working, it's sometimes hard to coordinate your moves, and that's exactly what happened to my father. He and another fellow, an old man named Lou, had just finished sharpening a hundred-foot length of steel bandsaw and had begun to roll it back to the motors when it tipped. That sent a slight ripple through the blade, which was all it took. Once it starts, you've got to jump. There's simply no stopping it.

My father was generally pretty quick, for most of his life he'd made his living with his hands, and it had kept him in excellent shape. But this was one occasion when, maybe because he'd missed too much sleep the night before, he reacted a split second too late.

Lou jumped back and hollered.

"It's *going*."

My father turned. He stumbled, he fell, and before he could pick himself up and scramble clear of the blade, it came down full force on two fingers of his right hand and sent them flying across the room. He later told me that at first he didn't feel any pain. They had done a fine job sharpening. Even a moment later, when he looked down at his hand and saw the bloody stumps and the gnarled white of bone, he was in as much rage as he was in pain.

"My fingers," he screamed. "Where's my *fingers*?"

He picked himself up and began looking for them. The

machines continued to whir and thump, and the floor shook
with the thunder of the redwoods. Of course he was bleeding
heavily, and wherever he ran a trail of blood followed. He
combed the room. He searched beneath the workbenches and
tool lockers. He ran from one end to the other, scouring the
floor, while old Lou chased after him.

"Damn it, Floyd," he shouted. "You'll bleed to death, you
don't stop."

But my father had his heart set on finding his fingers and
taking them with him to the hospital, where in his confused
state of mind, though he could not recall the source, he had
read somewhere that they could sew them back on. But if it
was to be successful, it had to be done quickly, this much he
was absolutely sure of, and time was running short.

"Shut up," my father screamed, "and *look*."

Lou was up there in years, getting close to retiring, and
not only was he physically weaker than my father, so it
would've been hard to overpower him, but his eyesight was
also poor. He wore glasses with lenses thick as the bottom of
the old Coke bottles, and he moved slowly. Still, he made the
effort for a dozen seconds or so before he came to his senses
and realized that his first response was the right one. My father would soon bleed to death if something wasn't done.

"To hell with the fingers," Lou shouted.

And he jumped on my father, who by this point had
grown light-headed from loss of blood. He was no match even
for an old man. Lou took him to the floor and straddled his
chest.

"Listen now," he said, "you ain't going to need *any* fingers, you don't lay still."

He pulled an oily rag from his back pocket and pressed it
to my father's hand and ordered him to hold it there, "good
and tight." Then he worked off his belt and strapped it
around my father's arm, just below the elbow at the pressure
point, and cinched it up. By then a crowd of burly men had

gathered. Most of the saws had wound down, and it was close to something quiet.

Lou glanced up at them.

"Don't just stand there like a bunch of idiots," he hollered. "Call an ambulance."

My father later told me that shortly before help arrived, as he lay bleeding on the floor in the sawmill, he had a near-death experience. He felt his body grow light, lighter and lighter, and soon it lifted out of itself and rose above him. His field of vision narrowed to a pinpoint, it blurred for a moment, and when it cleared all he could see was the long, white tunnel of death. He told me that it wasn't scary. He told me that he could've gone there if it wasn't for me, and I believed him.

"The last two things I remember thinking," he said, "was 'Oh shit, what a way to go, over a couple lousy fingers.' And the second thing, the thing that really pulled me back to the earth, was 'Who's going to look after my boy?' "

When he woke up he was in the hospital, and I was there to nurse him. The doctor told him if he hadn't run around like a fool, he wouldn't have lost so much blood and come so close to death. He also credited Lou with saving my father's life.

"If that man hadn't tackled you," he said, "there's a good chance you wouldn't be here."

My father, however, didn't see any reason to thank old Lou.

"They should've retired him ten years ago," he told me after the doctor had left. "He's the one who got the damn saw to shaking in the first place."

The only consolation was that my father's insurance company, Quality Life, now owed him somewhere between five and eight thousand dollars. The reason for the spread had to do with how the company interpreted the claim. He'd lost one finger below the second knuckle, but the other had only been severed at the first knuckle. Quality Life contended that he hadn't lost two fingers, but one and a half, and therefore he was only entitled to a partial claim for the second. Half a finger was half a finger. It was not a complete dismemberment, according to Mr. Oates, the insurance officer in charge of claim disputes.

Complete or not, my father was determined to collect every cent of the full claim on both fingers. It was a matter of pride. Quality Life was out to screw him. "And I'm not going to take it lying down," he said. "These jerks got a thing or two coming if they think they can mess with Floyd Barlow and not get a fight." Of course the settlement was delayed, and in the meantime we had to make do on his disability checks, which amounted to less than a third of what he regularly brought home. Bills piled up. We fell behind on the rent. Though he could've gone back to work after a month, on lighter duty, to do so before the settlement meant certain defeat.

"I know damn well what they'll say," my father said. "Any lawyer in town would tell you the same. If the man can work, who cares how many fingers he lost? He'll settle for next to nothing."

I don't know if his argument was a sound one or if he simply didn't want to go back to work. But one thing is clear: I had never seen my father more depressed. He used to rise before the sun, but since he returned home he had taken to sleeping long hours and napping in the afternoon. He drank more and started earlier. He went days without shaving or ever leaving the apartment. He spent hours on the phone to the insurance company, threatening to sue if they didn't get their asses in gear, but the secretaries generally put him on hold, or told him Mr. Oates was out to lunch or in a meeting, or else they kept transferring him until his call was lost somewhere deep in the bowels of the Quality Life office building in downtown Portland. This, of course, always left my father frustrated and angry, and, in turn, short-tempered and quick to criticize.

"You call that plate clean?" he'd shout. It was my job to do the dishes until his hand had completely healed; he wasn't supposed to put it in water. "Do the job right," he'd say, "or for Christ's sake don't do it at all. There's enough half-assed people in the world already. We don't need another."

Yet I was confident that his foul moods would pass, and during those days I forgave him a good deal. After all, he had spent the better part of his life working with his hands, and the loss of two fingers was certain to cause more than simple grief. To add to his problems, Melinda Johnson was preparing to move to Seattle, and once again he felt the pressure of time, more acutely than ever before; that is, if he planned to pursue Melinda he'd have to act soon or not at all, but since the accident he could hardly bring himself to go outside, let alone muster up the courage to approach her. However seriously he'd entertained the idea of her falling for him, however tenuous that possibility, it must've seemed all the more remote the moment that saw sliced through his fingers. Minor as that loss may have been, it had a devastating effect on his self-confidence, at least temporarily, and his sense of spirit, daring and boldness took on an odd form of expression bordering what some might consider obsession.

At night, when Melinda got off work, she brought home empty cardboard boxes and spent her evenings packing. She tended to leave her drapes open until she went to bed, and my father liked to sit in our living room and pretend to watch TV when, in fact, he was watching her. Observing Melinda's simplest actions brought him pleasure and accounted for the few times during his convalescence in which I actually saw him smile. He enjoyed watching how she walked through her living room, with a slight bounce to her step. He enjoyed watching her cook, though generally it involved nothing more than taking a TV dinner out of the freezer and shoving it in the oven. He enjoyed watching her reading her magazines, with her feet up on the coffee table, popping chocolates into her mouth, then licking her fingertips. He liked her in the big T-shirt she put on before she turned out the lights and went to bed. He liked her in the ratty terry-cloth robe that she wore in the morning, her hair mussed and wild from sleep, or all wound up in curlers, and we both especially enjoyed those rare but much anticipated occasions when she rushed through the living room, fresh from her shower, with nothing but a skimpy towel wrapped around her. Once, late at night, when we all should have been asleep, I woke up, rolled out of bed and found my father on the phone in the kitchen. Our apartment was dark, hers was brightly lit, and through the window I saw Melinda cross the living room and pick up the receiver, the sound of her hello at first faint in the darkness of our kitchen, then louder as she repeated herself while my father, on his end, remained silent.

She had to know it was him, I don't see how she couldn't, considering all the staring he'd been doing. And considering that they had once been, if nothing else, at least on speaking terms, I felt compelled to explain, if not apologize, for my father's odd, even perverse behavior when our paths converged in the laundry room a few days later. She was doing a load of whites, and after some small talk, while her clothes were in the rinse cycle, she asked me point-blank, "So what's going on with your father? He hasn't left that apartment in weeks."

"I guess you didn't hear."

"About what?"

"His accident," I said. "He lost two fingers at the mill."

I went on to tell her the whole story, how it happened, how he was depressed and all, how it was making him weird, withdrawn, and later that night Melinda came by with a bottle of Lancers. But my father spotted her as she made her way up the stairs.

"Tell her I'm not here," he said. "I don't feel like talking."

And he hid himself away in the bedroom.

Those were tough times for my father. He was feeling sorry for himself. He was angry over the settlement battle; he was worried about the bills. He was worried about the things you worry about when you think too much. And if he still held any hope for Melinda Johnson, it had to be as small as that pinpoint of fading light when he looked beyond himself and saw his body rise above him.

Then, suddenly, there was change.

four

MY FATHER left the apartment early one morning and came back that afternoon in a Cadillac Eldorado. "The sons a bitches finally settled up," he said. "One lump check. I told you if we held on they'd break sooner or later, and it's sooner." We were down in the carport; he had run upstairs only the minute before to get me, and now we stood staring at the big Cadillac. I shook my head in amazement. It was long and white and if you leaned over the hood you could see yourself in it. He slipped behind the wheel, sat back and grinned.

"Isn't she a beauty?" he said.

He patted the seat beside him.

"Get in," he said.

The upholstery was leather and the same color as the car, though a slightly darker shade.

"It's not exactly brand-new," he said. "There's close to ten thousand on the odometer, but listen to this." He fired up the engine. "Smooth as a kitten's purr." We sat there for a while and listened to it idle. Then he gunned it and the engine roared.

"Now that's *power*," he said. "A V-8, fully automatic. Ever think we'd be driving a car like this?"

"No," I said.

"Well," he said, smiling, "we are. Go ahead and pinch yourself."

I was pleased to see him happy again, but I was also concerned about the price.

"How much it cost?" I said.

"What?"

"How much you pay?"

"Worry wart," he said. "Knock it off. I already told you it was a deal."

"The last thing we need is a goddamn Cadillac."

"Don't be cussing. How many times I gotta tell you?"

He put the transmission into gear and backed out of the carport.

"Where we going?"

"Who knows? Maybe we'll take a little trip to Vegas. I'm feeling kind of lucky today. Of course," he added, "if you'd rather sit home by yourself, that's fine by me."

As we headed down the driveway, a cherry red stepside Chevy with a U-Haul in back pulled to the curb. Behind the wheel sat Melinda's boyfriend. His hair looked shorter than in the picture. He rested one arm outside the window; the sleeve was rolled up and his biceps had to be as big around as my thigh, and solid. It was clear enough that he'd come for Melinda's things.

"Looks like a goddamn bodybuilder," my father said. "You know, that kind of muscle slows you down. And I'll tell you something else, too." He rubbed his chin between his fingers. "You can't build this up. No sir, lift all the weights you want. I just hope the girl comes to her senses before they tie the knot." My father made a clucking noise with his tongue. "A cop," he said, "a muscle-head cop for the Seattle PD."

The Cadillac rode wonderfully, particularly when you're used to something more along the lines of an old Buick Riviera. My father maneuvered it smoothly with just his palm on the wheel, like he'd been driving it all his life. His other hand rested in his lap. The bandages had come off a while back, and the stubs, where there used to be his fingers, were pink and shiny, as if the skin had been polished with a thin sheen of oil.

Our first stop was Walbee's Hardware, where he let me pick out a Swiss army knife and a pellet gun, the pump type that looked almost exactly like a long-barreled .38. "You be careful now," he told me as he opened his wallet at the register. The billfold was fat with cash. "I don't want to hear about any busted windows. I don't want to be running you to Emergency, either. God only gives you two eyes, you know. You keep the damn thing pointed away from you or to the ground. Never, *ever* look down that barrel." I stared him square in the eye as he spoke and I nodded at his every warning. He was serious and so was I. But an even bigger part of me couldn't wait to get that gun alone, far from my father's control. I pictured myself hunting blue jay and squirrel on the outskirts of Portland, creeping through the woods, maybe even squeezing off a shot at some quail or pheasant.

I appreciated that my father had finally made good on his promise, and I was on my best behavior for the rest of the day. We drove to the Willamette River, ate hot dogs and french fries and blasted my father's empty beer cans full of holes. Then we rode back to the apartment and took showers.

"How about we go out to dinner?" he said, as he toweled himself off.

"Sure," I said.

"Someplace nice," he said. "I think we owe it to ourselves, don't you? When's the last time you had a big, juicy steak?"

He put on a neatly pressed white shirt, European cut, a pair of slacks, then tied his white cardigan loosely around his neck. He looked at himself in the dresser mirror, rubbed his hand along one cheek, then the other, tilting his head this way and that to be sure he hadn't missed any spots shaving.

He winked at himself and smiled. He winked at me, drew a comb through his thick hair slick with Brylcreem, and then we left.

In the car again, as we turned the corner outside our apartment complex, we spotted Melinda Johnson. She threw a cardboard box full of clothes into the back of Bo's pickup truck, slapped her hands clean, then continued down the block. She walked fast and heatedly, and at first she didn't notice us driving alongside of her.

My father tapped the horn. He lowered my window and leaned across me.

"Hey," he said, "you need a ride?"

"No thanks."

"You and Bo have a little difference of opinion?"

"Something like that."

She kept right on walking.

"Anything I can do to help?"

"I'm fine, thank you."

"You don't look it."

"Leave her alone," I said. "Let's just get going."

She turned a corner. We followed.

"We're headed into town for a bite to eat," my father said. "You're welcome to join us."

"Maybe some other time," she said.

"I don't see when. It looks to me like you're moving out."

"I thought so, too," she said. "Up until about five minutes ago."

"That bad, huh? It might help to talk about it."

"I doubt it."

"C'mon, let me buy you a drink."

She stopped and stared down at the sidewalk for a few seconds. She was thinking. She was seriously considering the offer, and my father knew it.

"I probably shouldn't," she said.

"I don't see Bo." He nodded at me. "Do you?"

"No," I said.

He gave her his best smile.

"After the way you walked off I'd be worried if I were him. Let me tell you something, you want to break that boy in right you better keep him guessing."

She had on Levi cutoffs and this big baggy denim shirt with pearl snaps. It was probably Bo's, I thought, and it was dirty from all the moving they'd done, and by the way she just stood there, tired and angry and sad, she was a pitiful sight, beautiful as she may have been.

"Hell," she said, "let him finish loading the truck by himself. Or unloading it. At this point I really couldn't give a damn."

"That's the attitude."

My father opened the door for her, then looked at me.

"Show some manners, Bobby, and hop in back."

But Melinda would have none of that.

"Stay right where you are," she said. "There's plenty of room up front for all of us, honey."

Her legs, as she scooted into the Cadillac, were enough to make me dizzy.

I glanced back at the apartments as we drove off, and there was Bo, stepping to the curb. I don't know if he saw us or not, but I didn't say anything. I just watched him look up and down the block, and soon, as we put the distance between us, he faded into the background. I saw my father's eyes in the rearview mirror. He'd noticed him, too. But by then he must've felt on top of it. There behind the wheel of a big, fat Cadillac with a beautiful young woman. This was the life, the one he imagined for himself, and he wasn't about to turn around, play the nice guy and cut it short. There was also the risk of a fight, and though my father was tough in his own right, I wouldn't match him against Bo.

"The way I figure," he said, "it's your last night in Portland and you might as well enjoy yourself now. I don't suppose you'll get much chance later."

Her thigh rested against mine and it was warm and more
than comforting. I smelled her perfume, taking a deep and
silent breath.

"When did you get this car?"

"Today," he said. "You like it?"

"It's nice," she said. "I won't even ask how much it cost."

My father laughed.

"Two fingers. But I've paid a whole lot more for some
things." He turned on the radio. "It's got stereo. Four speakers. What do you want to hear?"

She sat back in the soft leather seat, and when she spoke
I smelled spearmint gum on her breath.

"Anything country," she said. "Or rock and roll. Some really loud rock and roll."

He spun the dial. Hendrix played. He turned up the
volume.

"Sometimes the best thing to do is just put your problems
out of your mind."

"Ignoring something," I said, "doesn't make it go away.
Sometimes it does worse."

"As I recall," my father said, "I knew everything at
thirteen, too. It's amazing how stupid a man gets over the
years."

"Some guys never grow up," Melinda said.

"Ain't that the truth."

"There I am packing up the truck and Bo's down at the
pool putting the moves on some blonde. Like I wouldn't notice? I mean, like I wouldn't care? And we're supposed to
move in together. Hell of a start, wouldn't you say?"

"He's a fool," my father said.

"I'm the fool," she said. "How old are you?"

"Where'd that come from?

"Just wondering."

"Guess."

"Thirty-two, thirty-three maybe?" she said. "It doesn't matter. I used to date a guy in his forties and that's when I was twenty and living in Vegas. You know," she said as we drove on, "I'm already beginning to feel better."

"Good," my father said.

Then she elbowed me in the ribs, as my father often did, and laughed.

"I bet all the girls in school are after you," she said. "I just hope you treat them better than guys like Bo."

My cheeks suddenly felt hot, and I knew I was blushing. I stared out the window.

"Why so shy?" she said. "I don't bite."

All I could do was smile.

We cruised downtown Portland, we cut from Third Street to Main and circled again. It was quiet, there weren't many people walking about, and most of the stores were closed. I don't think we were on the road ten minutes when a Portland patrolman pulled in behind us after we made a left at the light. Melinda and I had no idea what was going on. My father glanced in the rearview mirror, then made a hard right at the next corner.

The patrolman followed.

A moment later he flashed his high beams.

"You better pull over," I said.

"I'll let you off," he said. "Both of you. Soon as I can."

"What's the matter?" I said.

Melinda looked back.

"Sit straight," he said.

"This isn't your Cadillac?" she said.

"Not exactly."

"Oh shit," she said. "I knew it. I knew I should've stayed with Bo."

Then she did something that I thought was pretty damn

odd, and it forever changed my opinion of her. She put her hand on the back of my father's neck and massaged the muscles.

"Relax," she said, "there're really only two things you can do. Pull over now and get busted. Or try and outrun them. I tend to procrastinate myself, especially when I know it'll just get ugly. How many horses you got under the hood?"

"She's crazy," I said. *"Pull over."*

My father put his hand on her knee and squeezed.

"The way my luck's been running, I don't imagine it can get much worse. Bobby," he said, "climb in back and put on your seat belt. I don't want anybody getting hurt."

Then he punched it.

And the sirens came on, and we were off.

At the edge of town he turned onto a two-lane blacktop and really hit the gas. The Cadillac shot forward into the darkness, and we gained some distance on them. I looked out the back window. There were dips in the road, and every now and then I saw their headlights rise then disappear for a moment. One time we rose so high off a dip that the rear end scraped the asphalt when we landed and spilled a shower of sparks into the night. Pastures lined both sides of the road and the fence posts were nothing but a blur.

"You don't pick it up," Melinda said, "they'll be all over you."

"I got it to the *floor.*"

My father was sweating.

"Can you see 'em, Bobby?"

"Not right now," I said.

Then the headlights appeared again.

"There they are," I said.

"Damn it," my father said, "I'm not so sure this was a good idea."

"You pull over now, honey, and those boys'll beat the living hell out of you."

Melinda pointed ahead.

"There's a crossroad coming up, say a mile," she said, "about twenty seconds at ninety. A little dirt road swings back to the Willamette. You get there before they cut you off and we might stand a chance. The river's running high this year, and I know a nice spot you can dump the car. We could walk back," she said. "It's a beautiful full moon tonight."

True to her word, we came onto the crossroad in about twenty seconds.

"Take a sharp left," she told him. "Hit the lights and keep your foot off the brake. You don't want to advertise us."

My father turned to her and half smiled, half frowned. He drew the back of his hand across his forehead and wiped away the sweat.

"You're really something," he said. "Where'd you learn all this?"

"I've known some cops in my day," she said. "How do you think I met Bo? He's one of the few who gave me a fair shake."

Soon the road forked, the pavement ended, and we found ourselves bumping up and down in our seats, on account of all the deep ruts and potholes. Near the river, my father veered off the road and drove into some weeds that brushed against the fenders and made a ticking noise on the hubcaps. He parked under the trees on a downhill slope and killed the engine. For a long while we just sat there, listening to the crickets and the soft rush of the river. Then they got out of the car, and I knew better than to follow. My father called to me just before they disappeared into the brush.

"Stay put now," he said. "We'll be back in a minute, Bobby."

That minute turned into an hour, then two, and it occurred to me as I sat beside the river that someone might spot the Cadillac. The chances were slim, but we'd taken more than our share for one night. I climbed back up the bank.

He'd left the keys in the ignition, so all I had to do was turn it a notch, slip it into neutral and let the emergency brake off. The Cadillac rolled through the weeds and missed, by a foot on either side, the trees around it. I expected a loud noise, but it went down quietly. The water rose up around the hood, swirled into the cab, made a gurgle, then sucked it under. In the moonlight, I caught the glint of chrome, the small wreath of the Cadillac emblem shimmering just beneath the surface in the slow ripple of water that passed above it. Then it disappeared. I'd done my best to help that night, but come dawn, while I slept in the weeds, the county sheriff paid us a visit.

They found him a little ways up the river, and myself, a few minutes later. I woke to see my father, his shirt unbuttoned and his hands cuffed behind his back, as two young deputy sheriffs led him up the bank. Bo was there, too, waiting beside the squad car in the thin morning light. He had on a loose madras shirt that hung past his waist and a pair of snakeskin cowboy boots. His eyes were puffed and heavy as if he'd been up all night, and his face was pink with exasperation. I can't say that my father looked much better.

The two deputies brought him to Bo.

"Let him go," he said, though it wasn't as if my father had been struggling. He was as dazed as he was scared, and I don't believe there was any fight in him. Still, the deputies left the cuffs on.

Bo got right in my father's face.

"Listen, asshole," he said. "I'll fucking kill you. I'll bury your ass right here."

I certainly believed him, and I suspect my father did, too, but Bo was an asshole in his own right and took it a step further. He reached under his shirt and pulled out a snub-nosed .38 and jammed it under my father's chin.

"The girl's been through a lot of shit and johns like you

just keep dragging her back down. Look at her again, I'll blow your head off.''

And there he was, little more than an old trick from Melinda's shady past, caught in the very position that only the day before he'd so sternly warned me against: staring straight down the barrel of a gun.

"Put the gun away," one of the deputies said, who had just now spotted me. "There's a kid over here."

Melinda, however, was nowhere in sight.

five

WHETHER MELINDA used my father to somehow punish Bo, or she simply wanted to make him jealous, I don't know. It could've been both. Or neither. It could've been that she saw something in my father that she saw in herself and it was something she liked and something she found missing in Bo. Again I can't say, and I doubt if my father could, either. There were all kinds of things that we didn't know about Melinda Johnson, including the details of her former life as a working girl, and it would remain that way at least for several years to come. It was certain, however, that my father was arrested that morning on the Willamette, and that Melinda, while he'd slept, had hiked back to town in the lingering moonlight. As for Quality Life, contrary to what my father had told me, they weren't even close to settling up; that possibility was nothing more than a hopeful act of imagination on his part. And his wallet, fat with cash like I'd seen at Walbee's Hardware earlier that day, turned out to be the last of our savings.

They booked him on grand auto, kidnapping, assault and resisting arrest. The latter charge came as the result of a beating administered by Bo with the blunt end of his pistol to the side of my father's face. It nearly crushed the cheekbone. To justify the blow, both deputies swore that he'd taken a swing at them. Of course his hands had been cuffed behind his back, but then fact in these kinds of matters rarely plays a role. It was his word against theirs, and right now he wasn't in any better position to protest than he had been down on the river. Twice in as many months he'd seen his life almost pass before him.

Regarding the kidnapping charge, it involved an earlier episode. He had stolen the Cadillac—that much was true—but it wasn't a simple case of grand auto. My father had gone to the offices of Quality Life that morning and demanded the full compensation for the loss of his two fingers. He told Mr. Oates, the unfortunate soul handling his claim, that he was fed up, that he wanted his money and he wanted it now. To show he meant business, he went so far as to sweep his hand over Mr. Oates's desk and send all the papers on it flying across the room. Mr. Oates immediately phoned security and had him escorted out of the building. It could've ended there and I often wished it had, but as I've said before, my father was a stubborn man.

When the guards left, he sneaked around to the parking lot, one of those subterranean types, dank and poorly lit, and waited for him. The space was reserved in his name, which was painted on the wall facing his car, this new Cadillac Eldorado. I believe that my father was prepared to stay there all day if necessary, but shortly before noon Mr. Oates took his lunch. As a claims officer for a major life insurance company, he must've been aware of the dangers of the underground parking lot. Too many people had been robbed, stabbed, raped or murdered on their way to their cars, if not in this particular lot, then in another. Certainly a claim or two along those lines must've crossed his desk at some point in his career. So he may well have feared for his life when he encountered my father sitting on the hood of the Cadillac in the concrete bowels of the parking lot, all silence and darkness. This was the man, after all, who had phoned him countless times, often drunk and belligerent, and who now had gone so far as to throw a tantrum in his office. Who knows what he might've done if security hadn't booted him out. But now there was no one to phone. It was just Mr. Oates and my father, and if I were in his position I think I would've been scared, too. He tried to run but Mr. Oates, though still a young man, wasn't much of a runner. He was overweight and slow, and my father collared him before he could take more than a few steps.

"You son of a bitch," my father said. "Now you're going to listen." He held up his hand, the one minus the fingers. "Take a look, a good hard look, and see if you can't tell me how many are missing."

I doubt if he wanted anything more out of Mr. Oates than for him to acknowledge the loss and to pay up accordingly. But from Mr. Oates's point of view, my father must've seemed out of his mind. The upshot of the scene was that he convinced Mr. Oates that they ought to take a little drive and discuss this matter in greater detail. Once inside the car, as they were headed out of town, my father began to play with the power windows. Up and down. Up and down. Which made Mr. Oates, who was already frightened and nervous, even more so.

"You have power brakes on this Cadillac, too?" my father asked.

"Yeah."

"Power steering?"

"Yeah."

"Power antenna? A big V-8, I bet. Am I right?"

"That's right."

"You must enjoy all that power."

"It's a company car, Mr. Barlow," he said. "I don't exactly own it."

"I'm not talking about the car, I'm talking about power. Power and convenience." He sat a little closer to Mr. Oates.

"I'm talking about somebody calling and having his secretary say the big man's out to lunch, or in a meeting, he'll call you back. Only he never does. And in the meantime," my father said, again scooting closer to him, "this guy's got bills piling up, he's sweating, just like you are now, and sooner or later you know he's got to settle up for next to nothing, whatever you offer, just to save his ass." Here he paused to smile, take a deep breath and look out the window at the passing splendors of the countryside, for that's where they were now, on a quiet road running through the forest, and my father had always appreciated the solemnity of Mother Nature. "And it's all to your convenience," he said. "Isn't that how it works?"

If Mr. Oates wasn't sweating heavily before, he must've been now.

"Listen," he said, "if you're strapped for cash, I have three hundred in my wallet right now. Let's just consider it an advance on the settlement. We'll work out the details later."

"I don't want your money. Give me your hand."

"What?"

"Your *hand*. Give me your hand."

When he hesitated, my father lost his patience, grabbed Mr. Oates's hand, pressed it flat on the dash and then pulled out a knife. On his ring finger was a diamond as big around as the head of a sixteenpenny nail, and my father put the blade to the first knuckle and applied a generous amount of pressure, though not enough to break the skin.

"If I cut it off here, would you say it's a full dismemberment or a half?"

Mr. Oates groaned.

"You look like an educated man," my father said. "I'm sure you can figure it out." He brought the knife to the second knuckle. "Or say we cut it there. We're both in agreement that's a full finger. How much is it worth to you? Five thousand? Ten? Times two makes twenty. I'd settle for half that." He took a deep breath and let it out slowly. "I got a policy with Quality Life, Mr. Oates, and I've never missed a payment."

Likely fearing more for his life than the loss of a finger or two, Mr. Oates hit the brakes, threw open the door and, with the Cadillac still moving, leaped out, rolled several times, clambered to his feet and ran off into the woods, leaving my father to take the wheel. When he had it under control, he slammed the transmission into reverse, backed up to the spot where Mr. Oates had jumped, and hollered out the window.

"Hey, I was only trying to make a point."

Silence.

"Hell, if you want, we'll forget the whole damn thing. Just call it even."

But Mr. Oates was gone. And the brush was thick, the forest dense. It would've taken a pack of hounds to flush him out.

My father cursed under his breath.

"Stupid son of a bitch."

At this point he had the choice of leaving the car and hiking back to town, which would've been the smart thing to do, except he'd never driven a car like this and it rode wonderfully smooth and had a full tank of gas. Maybe he only planned to take it for a quick spin. Maybe, given the circumstances, he felt that the very least that Quality Life owed him was a night on the town in a brand new Cadillac Eldorado. Whatever his rationale, it was all downhill from there.

My father already had two priors on his record, one a dozen years back for passing a bum check in Montana where it's considered a felony offense, and another, when he was a young man of eighteen, for stealing two cases of beer from the coolers at the local Elks lodge. The charge was breaking and entering, as he'd had to jimmy the back door to get in. He sold the beer to some varsity football players, who in turn got drunk; the driver wrecked his parents' car, and they ratted on my father when the police arrived. The judge presiding over the latest charges felt that although the earlier crimes seemed minor in light of the new ones, they nonetheless suggested, at the very least, that he'd gone from bad to worse. There was also a strong possibility that he'd committed quite a few other crimes for which he hadn't been punished. In a sense, my father paid not just for the laws he was known to have broken, but for those he might have broken earlier in his criminal career, if not in this life, then maybe some other, possibly the next.

The judge sentenced him to five years hard time at the state prison in Salem, Oregon. He'd be eligible for parole in three. The money he'd fought so hard to claim went directly to Mr. Oates's auto insurance company, as the Cadillac was considered totaled. I blame myself for that, but at the time I thought I was doing the right thing. Where my father had failed to convince Quality Life of the validity of his claim, the auto insurance company succeeded; they received the full compensation on the loss of his two fingers without so much as an argument. Mr. Oates bought a four-door station wagon and pocketed the difference. The only real losers in the deal were my father and me.

No relatives came to my aid. I knew of only two, my father's brother, Luke Barlow, "beautiful, beautiful Luke," he called him, whose death at the age of eighteen contributed, if not directly, then at least emotionally to my father's own reckless sense of life. Then there was his sister, Mary Ann, who like my mother simply seemed to have disappeared. I'd never met Mary Ann and I had no desire to change that. My father seldom talked about her, or my mother for that matter, and when he did it was always in guarded terms. Before he was actually sent up to Salem, a woman from the child welfare authority consulted him about what to do with me, and I learned that aside from his sister he had an uncle in Idaho and an aunt in Georgia. But my father hadn't spoken to any of them in ten years or better and he seriously doubted that they wanted to hear from him now. Still, the social worker told me that she'd try.

"I understand your Uncle Luke passed on and that your mother's missing," she said. "And according to your father, he's not very close to your other relatives. But I can always ask. I don't want you to give up hope."

I didn't have a whole lot to start with, so it wasn't hard to give up a little more. For several days she made phone calls all over the country, trying to locate Mary Ann and my mother, but none of them panned out. She reached a dead end in Great Falls, Montana, at Mary Ann's last known address. The uncle in Idaho had emphysema and could hardly care for himself, let alone a thirteen-year-old boy. The aunt in Georgia wanted nothing to do with my father or anything at all close to his blood. She didn't even know that he had a son. While the search dragged on, I stayed at the Cooper Youth Center downtown with some boys in a situation similar to my own, and with a few who had committed crimes considerably more grievous than anything my father had ever done.

A month later I was placed in a foster home under the care of Mrs. Helen Watson, a stout, middle-aged woman with a growth behind her ear that pushed it out some, so that she looked a little strange. She was neither mean nor nice. The state paid her to do a job and she did it. She'd had five kids of her own, all grown and gone now, and with some assistance from the state and some odd jobs under the table, she'd raised them well enough without a husband. Children were her business. Literally dozens had passed through her door, some just toddlers, others on the cusp of adulthood, who may have only stayed a few months. Quite a few had serious problems, and if she couldn't straighten them out, she sent them back. It was that easy, or something very close to it. Mrs. Watson had no patience or time for those things she didn't understand or chose not to understand. The world was black and white and it had a clock. If you didn't like the rules, such as when you should be home, when you should bathe, and always to watch your mouth, you simply packed up and left. There were too many others in need of a place to stay and you'd damn well better be grateful.

"Because, honey," she used to tell us, when one of us got out of line, "it's here, maybe another foster home if you're lucky, or jail. Take your pick. It doesn't get any better, and it's likely to get worse."

All this is to say that she treated me and her other two wards as she treated herself, with respect and decency; and she expected no less from us. There was myself, Bonnie Walker and Todd O'Sullivan, a half–Klamath Indian. Mrs. Watson offered us the basics: a room with a bed, clean clothes, two hot meals a day and a pair of eyes to see that we stayed out of trouble. But that's not warmth. That's not what it was about. There were many nights when I lay awake in bed wishing for more, though I suppose I had no claim to it, given the circumstances. I lived with Mrs. Watson for three years, attended school on a regular basis and went to the Baptist church every Sunday. I shared a room with Todd, the oldest of us at seventeen and already the manager of a hot dog stand called Rocket Dog, across from the University of Portland. Todd never talked about his past or how he'd come to live with Mrs. Watson and I didn't press the issue. Of the three of us, however, he'd been with Mrs. Watson the longest, and if she had a favorite, as I believe she did, it was definitely Todd.

He always brought home straight A's. He belonged to the German Club and the Model U.N. Club at school, and twice he ran, both times unsuccessfully, for student body president. "You don't know how far he's come," Mrs. Watson used to say, "especially for a little Indian boy. You could both learn a thing or two from him." He even handed over some of his money to her once a month, which she slipped into the pocket of her apron. When he left the room, after she'd thanked him, she would turn to Bonnie and myself, smile and say, "It just goes to show what a little hard work can do. That boy's going places. You watch and see." I don't know if she was aware of it or not, but all her talk about Todd didn't help Bonnie or me like him any better. In fact, it had just the opposite effect.

One Sunday, only a month after I'd arrived, he accused me of stealing his baseball mitt. Rocket Dog had a softball team, and after church they were going to play another group from the Pizza Hut. Todd rummaged through his closet; he was running late. I was stretched out on my bed, writing a letter to my father. The more he looked, the angrier he got, and pretty soon he was throwing stuff around, making a hell of a racket.

"Okay," he said, "where'd you put it?"

"Put what?" I said.

"My mitt," he said. "What do you think."

"I didn't touch your mitt."

"Sure you didn't, you're perfect. That's why you're here."

"Fuck off," I said.

My language shocked him, he was that righteous, and he just stood there and stared at me for a moment. I returned to my letter.

"If I find out you stole it," he said, "I'll kick your butt."

I looked up at him.

"Say it right, say it like you mean it," I told him. "You don't want to kick my butt, you want to kick my *ass*. If you're trying to scare me, Todd, you got to put more heart into it."

"I wouldn't waste my time on a piece of crap like you."

He stormed out of the room, and from down the hall I heard him tell Mrs. Watson that I'd cursed something "unmentionable." A few seconds later she came in and reprimanded me.

"I give everybody two warnings," she said. "You just got your first."

On the few occasions when Todd tried to act like a big brother to me, with his pep talks about the importance of school, hard work and religion, I turned away. I was already a serious-minded kid in my own right, and in terms of my report card it generally boasted at least C's. Although Todd and I shared the same room for three years, he kept his hours, which were long, between school and his job, and I kept mine, so that we rarely saw each other. That schedule suited me just fine, as it did Bonnie. In three years, I did take a strong liking to her. She turned fourteen the month before I left, and even if I didn't yet understand women the way my father had known Melinda, my feelings for Bonnie were as real and strong as anything else in my life. Unfortunately, I could never work up the courage to tell her that, and so our relationship remained at a polite, friendly distance from the beginning to almost the end of my stay. It was just as well. There were only two years between us, but at that age the difference seemed vast. She was a shy, pretty girl, with no mother and a lout for a father, who molested her when she was barely ten.

I wanted to spend more time with Bonnie, but I generally stuck to myself. I kept my side of the room clean. I always did as Mrs. Watson told me. I wrote my father regularly, and we struck up a pact: we agreed to remain on our best behavior until we both qualified for early parole. I upheld my side of the bargain.

And my father did the same.

In December I sent him a letter, and with it a photo of myself, Bonnie, Todd and Mrs. Watson huddled around a white-flocked tree on Christmas Eve. Perched at the tip was a plastic star that blinked on and off every few seconds. On the mantel behind us hung pine boughs, four stuffed stockings with the traditional candy canes peeking out of the tops, and a string of Christmas cards that reached clear to the floor. Mrs. Watson had taped them together, end to end, just for the photo. We all smiled into the camera, though for me it wasn't by choice. Todd was taking the picture, adjusting the lens, setting the timer.

"Everybody move in a little," he said. "Mrs. Watson, you want to put your arm around Bonnie? And Bobby, how about a smile for a change?"

"Just take the picture already," I told him.

"C'mon, everybody else is smiling. Give me a smile, a big, big smile," he said. "It won't kill you."

I gave him one, all right, if only to get it over with, and that's how the photo was sent, me with my foster family and this fake smile plastered on my face.

My father wrote back soon afterward, and in his letter he told me that he'd been granted parole, two years shy of his five-year sentence. They were giving him his ticket, as he called it, on the first week of February, and he said he needed to see me. He said we needed to talk. I wrote him that same day, and we set up a time and a neutral place to meet. This was just between my father and me, and neither of us wanted outsiders around to waste our time on small talk, awkward smiles and introductions. I spent my last weeks at Mrs. Watson's wondering what I'd say to my father when we met again, how he might look now, if he'd lost or gained weight and what plans he had in store for us. I slept fitfully. I couldn't concentrate on my studies anymore. Todd sensed the change in me, and several times when he came in late from work and found me still awake, he asked if there was something wrong, if there was any way he could help. Was I in trouble? Was my conscience bothering me?

"Did you steal something?"

"No," I said.

"You know you can always return it."

"Return what?" I said.

"Whatever you stole," he said. "I know you steal but you can stop."

"I didn't *steal* anything."

"Bobby," he said, "you need to talk. We've been living in the same room for practically three years and I don't know you any better than when you came. You can't keep holding it all inside."

Wherever he came up with this stealing business, I had no idea. But I told him nothing. I told no one about my father's release, and if the proper authorities had informed Mrs. Watson of it, as I expected they may have done in cases like these, she never let on. She might've thought that he wouldn't come for me, and that it was better for all involved that I remain in the dark. My father and I had agreed to meet outside the minimart in downtown Portland at seven o'clock at night. It was a short walk for me, and early enough so that I could tell Mrs. Watson that I needed to use the encyclopedias at the library before it closed. This was February, there was a couple feet of snow on the ground, but I figured that would work in my favor. Only the most determined student would fight that kind of weather, and Mrs. Watson was sure to be impressed. I couldn't eat much dinner that evening, though I made a show of it, and afterwards I returned to my room.

My suitcase was already packed and stowed under my bed. I had no intentions of coming back. All I had to do now was wait, and when the time came open my window, drop the suitcase into the snow beneath it, then grab my schoolbooks, my backpack, and deliver the lie as I headed through the living room for the front door. I had it all worked out. But as the time to leave drew closer, I began to wonder if I ought to leave Mrs. Watson a note. I thought I ought to thank her for taking me in, and for being, in many ways, a good mother. I pulled up a chair at Todd's desk, found a sheet of paper and a pen, and set myself to the chore. As I was trying to think of something to say, something I could believe myself so I'd mean it, a knock came on the door.

I hid the stuff in the drawer.

"Who is it?"

"It's me," Bonnie said. "Can I come in?"

I unlocked the door and she stepped past me to my bed. She sat on the edge of it and folded her hands in her lap. Her hair was long, like Melinda's, and fell in thick strands around her shoulders. She had on a long, plain cotton dress tied at the waist with a sash, and her shoes were scuffed and worn. She bowed her head.

"I just wanted to say good-bye," she said.

"What're you talking about?"

"I know."

"Know what?" I said.

She raised her head, and I had to look away.

"I saw your suitcase," she said.

"You had no right to snoop."

"I'm sorry," she said. "But I had a feeling something was up, and I needed to know for sure. It was more for me than you." Bonnie rose to her feet then and came over to me. She put her hand on my shoulder, and for a moment there I had trouble swallowing. "You know, if they catch you," she said, "Mrs. Watson won't take you back. You know what happens then."

"They won't catch me," I said.

Why she chose to open up to me at this particular juncture in our lives, after three long years of a purely platonic relationship, could only be attributed to my leaving. It was poor timing for both of us, and there was a part of me that wanted to stay on and get to know her a whole lot better. I wanted to touch her hair. I wanted to taste her neck. I was sixteen, and though those feelings weren't altogether new to me, they were more intense than I'd ever felt them before.

"I'd run too," she said, "if I could, except it's different for girls."

I knew without asking what she meant, and it angered me in the same helpless way it did when I thought of what her father had done to her. Though I still had time, I could see that it was going to get emotional if I stayed, so I put on my jacket and told her I'd better get going. She gave me a smile and an awkward hug. Then I pulled my suitcase from under the bed, opened the window and dropped it out.

"So you're going, just like that."

"Yep."

"And leaving me here with Todd."

"You'll be okay," I told her, "just don't let him give you any shit."

"That's easy for you to say," she said. "Want me to keep Mrs. Watson busy?"

" 'What's My Line' is on. Nothing'll bother her now."

I grabbed my backpack and my books. I slipped by her, passed through the living room where Mrs. Watson was watching TV, told my lie and that was it. "Don't be late," she called as I closed the door behind me. I hustled around the side of the house, retrieved my suitcase and got on my way. It had begun to snow again, and as I headed down the side-walk flakes of it landed on the back of my neck. I shivered, stopped to pull up the collar of my jacket and continued on. The streets were empty and quiet. I passed an old woman at the corner, but we both looked the other way. I thought of Bonnie. I thought of Mrs. Watson and the note I didn't write.

At the minimart I waited outside under the eaves. I jammed my hands into my pockets and hopped from one leg to the other to keep warm. The snow was really coming down now, it showed no signs of letting up, and I worried that my father might be delayed. I worried, after a half hour had gone by, that he might not come at all. Every few minutes I looked at my watch, and every time a car pulled up I felt my heart lift. The clerk inside stared at me suspiciously through the glass. Finally, at a quarter to eight, a beat-up Ford Falcon pulled into the lot. The tappets were loose, the engine pinged. The windshield wipers slapped back and forth and until he actually stepped out I didn't know it was him. But there he was, my father, standing in the middle of the parking lot. His hair was considerably shorter than I remembered and he was smiling. He had on a pair of black leather gloves and he rubbed them together. Then he glanced down at my suitcase. His smile wavered.

"Well," he said, "what're you waiting for? Hop in, unless you want to freeze to death."

I picked up my things, threw them in the backseat and climbed in, but the cab wasn't any warmer. My father cocked his head and looked me up and down. "Jesus," he said, "you must've grown two feet." He smiled again. "What's that on your face?" He reached out to touch my cheek but I batted his hand away. "Those real sideburns or just peach fuzz?"

"They're real," I said.

"Must be all that Italian blood on your momma's side. I couldn't grow 'em until I was nineteen."

"I'm just ahead of my time," I said.

"Wolf-boy, you mean," he said. "I raised a wolf-boy. You'll be all covered in hair before you're drinking age. Won't be able to see your eyes. It isn't catchy, I hope. C'mere."

He put his arms around me, there in the car, and we hugged good and hard. I felt the ribs in his back, even through his coat; he'd lost weight, too much. The odor of tobacco clung to his clothing, and his breath smelled faintly of whiskey. He leaned back and looked at me again, started to say something, then seemed to change his mind. He slapped the dashboard.

"How about a cup of coffee? You drink coffee yet?"

"No," I said.

"Maybe a piece of pie then," he said, "with some hot chocolate to wash it down."

My father put the Falcon into gear and we backed out of the lot. The pavement was slick with snow and it took a moment, when we hit the street, for the tires to catch. The heater didn't work, so neither did the defroster, and we had to drive with both windows down. Now with the wind it was even colder. I knew what was coming. I knew what had to be said and I didn't want to drag it out over pie and hot chocolate in some damn restaurant with everybody staring at us.

"Dad," I said, "I'm not going back to that house."

"Hold on now," he said.

"I mean it," I said.

The cold wind continued to blow through the cab, and the snow fell faster now, so that the road was hardly visible.

"Seems to me you got a good thing going there. A real family," he said. "I'd hate to see you lose it."

"I want to be with *you*."

"I don't know," he said. "You looked awfully happy in that Christmas picture."

"That was bullshit and you know it. I'm not going back there."

"You'll go back," he said, "if I tell you to, and I'm telling you."

I wanted to hit something, not my father, but something. The windshield, the dash. Anything. But I only sat there. "Don't be crying," he said. "You're too damn old to be crying." The snow passed through the white beams of our headlights in a flurry of even greater whiteness. "Listen," he said, "first of all this car isn't exactly mine. You get caught with me again and they won't send you to any foster home. I have a hundred bucks to my name, and in about a minute I got to spend half of it on a set of chains just to get the hell out of this town. And when I cross that state line I break probation, there's no coming back. Now you tell me, you go ahead and tell me how I'm supposed to take care of a boy?"

"I'm not a boy anymore. I can take care of myself just fine."

"I'm sure you can."

"If that's the way you want it."

"Damn it, Bobby, you know it's not."

He pulled into a gas station and put the Falcon into neutral. The snow fell lightly on the hood and all around us it was white. My father sighed and closed his eyes for a moment and for a long time we said nothing. I stared out the window at the falling snow and the sign of the gas station as it turned in the night. There was a loose piece of vinyl on the seat between my legs and I picked at it. My father reached for my hand.

"Don't touch me," I said.

He sat back and again, for a long while, neither of us said a word.

"It doesn't mean I love you any less, it just means you damn well better hang on to the family you got now. Because I don't believe," he said, "I don't believe I can do a good job of it anymore."

The cords in my neck were tight. I kept staring out the window at the snow, all the snow.

"I don't care," I told him. "I'm going, with you or not. Either way I'm going and there's nothing you can do."

Then the gas attendant came up to the window and looked in. He wore a parka, his hand at the throat of it, and I couldn't see his face.

"What's the problem?"

"Everything's fine," I said. "Couldn't be fucking better."

My father smiled sheepishly at him.

"The boy's just upset," he said, then he turned to me. "There's no call for that. You watch your mouth or you'll be walking home."

I opened my door, took my pack and got out.

"Get your ass in here," he said. "I'm not finished talking."

"Buy your chains. I'll be back."

Up the street was the Rocket Dog. Todd closed at nine, but probably earlier on a night like this, so I had to hurry. It was a small place tucked between a shoe store and a tailor's, and it was all but empty when I got there, just as I'd hoped. But first I looked through the window. Inside, a teenager had placed an order to go; he collected the bags of burgers from Todd and headed for the door. I waited until the guy hopped into his car at the curb and drove off before I reached into my backpack, took out the pellet gun and went inside.

Todd stood behind the counter wiping it down with a rag. He had on an apron and a T-shirt with Rocket Dog stenciled across the chest.

I pointed the gun at him.

"What're you doing?"

"Gimme the money."

"Come off it, that's a dumb pellet gun."

"It's one-seventy-seven caliber," I told him. "About the same as a twenty-two. It'll drop a rabbit at fifty yards."

"If you hit it in the head maybe."

"Where do you think I got it pointed? I'm a good shot. I'll pop your eye like a grape."

"You would, wouldn't you?"

"Damn right," I said.

"Your own brother," he said. "I can't believe it, Bobby."

"Just because we shared a room together doesn't make us brothers. You want to keep that eye," I told him, "you best move."

I tossed my pack at him and he went to the cash register and opened the drawer.

"I always knew you were no good," he said.

"That's right, nothing but a thief."

"Just like your old man."

"Shut up and give me the money. Change, too." He put the bills and the coins into the pack and started to hand it over. But I shook my head.

"All of it," I said, "including the cash under the drawer."

Todd glared at me, but did as I'd ordered. I grabbed the pack out his hand, and as I backed up toward the door he hollered at me.

"I'll get you for this, asshole."

Then I was outside, running through the snow as best I could, up the street and back to the gas station. My father had just gotten the chains on and was putting the plastic case in the trunk.

I jumped into the front seat.

"Let's go," I said. *"Now."*

"What's the rush?"

He slipped behind the wheel, and I unzipped the flap on my backpack. At a glance I'd say we had a couple hundred dollars, but all mixed up like that it looked like plenty more.

"Oh shit, what did you do?"

"You needed money," I said. "We got it. Quit bitching and let's get the hell out of here. I can't stay in Portland now anymore than you."

Todd spotted us as we dipped down the driveway and into the slow-moving traffic.

"Hey," he hollered. "Hey!"

Then he lit out after us. With the chains on, and in the traffic and the blinding snow, we couldn't go all that fast, either. He was right at our heels, his apron flapping at his legs, his hands grabbing for the rear bumper as we slogged down the road.

"I'll get you. I swear it, Bobby."

I leaned out my window and hollered back.

"Faster, Todd. Faster. Gotta pick it up."

"Fuck you."

"Smile when you say it. Smile, Todd. Give me a big, big *smile*. It won't kill you."

We picked up speed and soon Todd faded into the blizzard, for that's what it was now, and my father yanked me back into the car.

"How's that kid know your name?"

"He's part of that family," I said, "the one you like so much."

The chains rattled against the asphalt, and the windshield wipers moved slow against the snow, hardly able to brush it aside. Beneath the seat my father had a bottle of whiskey, and he reached for it, uncapped it and took a long drink.

"You fool," he said, "I ought to whip your ass." But I knew he wouldn't, as he'd never so much as raised a hand to me before. Instead, he struck the steering wheel with the side of his fist. "Here I wanted to make Seattle tonight and now we got to stop and find us another car."

I felt bad for Todd, because I didn't really have anything against him other than that we didn't much like each other, and I knew that I'd done wrong by him and myself. But I also felt that up to this point my life had somehow been placed on hold and that now, suddenly, it had finally begun. I counted the money as we drove, the edges of the bills fluttering in my hand in the cold wind. Three hundred and sixty-two dollars, not including change, and all in no more time than it took to strap on a pair of snow chains in bad weather. Despite my guilt, I couldn't help feeling a sense of accomplishment.

"Pass that whiskey," I said.

"You got enough bad habits already."

"Me?"

"Yeah, you."

"C'mon, I deserve a shot."

"You deserve a hell of a lot more for pulling a bullshit stunt like that."

I closed the pack.

"Anyway," I said, "if we have to get another car, at least find one with a heater this time. It's freezing in here."

We found it a mile up the road, in the parking lot of a Safeway, a Chevy Nova with the chains already on it. My father had learned to wire a car in prison, from under the hood or beneath the dash, and it didn't take but a few minutes to get us back on the road. It surprised me how easy it was; the diagram is on the back of the ignition, on the female connector, so that all you have to do is join a wire between the starter and the hot line off the battery. We stopped again at a roadside diner, just before we reached the Oregon border, and switched plates with a Buick from California.

The stakes were considerably higher now, for as my father had said, he was on probation and under court order not to leave the state, and transporting stolen goods across the line was a felony in itself. But at this point I don't suppose any of that made a great deal of difference. In less than twenty-four hours he'd stolen two cars, while I was a bona fide runaway who had just robbed his foster brother at gunpoint. The police weren't likely to make a distinction between a pellet gun and the real thing. The picture was bleak any way you looked at it, and it was bound to get a whole lot bleaker. For now, however, the storm had finally let up, there was nothing ahead or behind us except the long stretch of highway, and in its emptiness there had to be promise.

My father reached into his coat pocket as we crossed the Columbia River. He shook a cigarette out of the pack and lit it.

"Since when did you start smoking?"

"Three years ago."

He'd often warned me against it, so I gave it back to him.

"Speaking of bad habits," I said. "Those things'll kill you."

"That's the least of my worries right now. Do as I say, don't do as I do."

I stared out the window. Somewhere below us, in the

darkness, was the Columbia River. I couldn't see it, but I heard the powerful rush of the water, running high this time of year, running hard and fast and taking with it the smaller weaker trees, the brush, just anything that lived too close to the edge.

Six

WE TOOK A ROOM in a cheap hotel, and my father set about looking for Melinda Johnson. The place was called the Royal Arms, and though we had no view of the Puget Sound, as our only window overlooked the tar and gravel roof of the warehouse next door, we weren't far from it. Often we heard the sound of foghorns as the different ships arrived or left port, and often, late at night, they woke me. Other times it was the whir and thump of the cooling unit on top of the warehouse, when the fan motor kicked into gear. All night long it clicked on and off, its cycle so regular and frequent that I could predict, almost to the minute, when it would start up again and when it would cut out. The same held true for the old sailor in the room next to ours, who smoked too much and who regularly went into a coughing fit in the early morning hours.

My father and I shared a Murphy bed. It was a pain to pull it out of the wall every night and push it back during the day, just so we could walk around. Our room was that small, and the mattress was lumpy and smelled vaguely of the oils and sweat of the others who had slept here. Sometimes, while I lay awake, I tried to picture just who they may have been. An old man, say, down on his luck, or an old woman in a nightgown, curled on her side. I tried to keep my face from the mattress, to always sleep on my back, so that I wouldn't have to breathe in the smells and envision these others, but it was hard. The walls had an odor, too one of dampness and age, of mildew and stale tobacco. My father generally slept through the noise, snoring, with his lips slightly parted and the faint smell of whiskey on his breath.

How prison had affected him, I can only guess. It wasn't an experience that he liked to talk much about, and clearly for good reason. I doubt if there were many pleasant memories, and of those I'm sure that he would've gladly forsaken them in return for the years he'd lost. Although he seemed able to put that part of his life behind him, at least well enough to sleep through most of the night, there were occasions when I'd wake and find him standing at the window. Of course I couldn't know what he was thinking about, and because on those occasions I sensed that he didn't want to be disturbed, I said nothing. I feigned sleep. But I imagine, as he stood there looking out the window, that he had Melinda on his mind. I imagine that he had thought a great deal about her while he was in Salem and that he often found himself unable to sleep and that he went to the window of his cell and looked out over the prison yard. Or maybe he remained in bed, maybe he just stared at the ceiling. But he had to think of her beside him. He had to want her. He had to want her badly and it had to grow and keep growing until it became something greater, more volatile than ordinary lust. It was her memory that kept him hoping against hope, when the days just dragged on, one into another without shape or design. I imagine that he saw his life wasting away in increments small as minutes and that he measured the loss in regret and self-loathing. I imagine that he thought of me, too, and of our lives together and where we were headed. Outside, on the streets below or in the prison yard, it had to be quiet. It had to be dark.

Once, when he was hogging my side of the bed, I made the mistake of jabbing him in the ribs. My father threw up his arms as if to protect himself and strike out at the same time, as if, maybe, somewhere down the line he'd grown to fear the most vulnerable moments of sleep. He awoke a second later, bolted upright and switched on the light.

"Don't," he said, "don't *ever* touch me like that when I'm sleeping."

That was a side of him I'd never seen before, and it frightened me as much as it probably did him. On still other occasions, while he slept and I lay awake, I thought of my mother and what our lives might've been like together if she hadn't run off and left us. I knew little about her, and except for the picture that I carried in my wallet, one from her high school graduation with a crease down the middle, her hair long and her shoulders bared in the black gown, we had no connection, no history, and for my part not even a memory. What disturbed me more, however, for I was sixteen now, and in the picture she couldn't have been but a year or two older, was that I sometimes found myself looking at those shoulders, those lips and her long hair in something other than motherly terms.

Her name was written on the back. Angie. Angie Carter. It was in this flowing, dramatic hand that had to be her own. Beneath it were the words True Love, and they were underlined twice. I'd always figured they were directed to my father, though he'd intimated once that there had been other boys in her life, many of them perhaps, and I had my doubts. She was, like the things my father had stolen from others, and the things he would steal again, just another part of our past far beyond reclaim.

Between Melinda and my mother, though, the likeness was considerable.

————

The first thing he did was check the phone book. Bo's last name was Stenovich, and there were three in Seattle and one in Bellevue. My father wanted me to do the dirty work. We were in a coffee shop at the time, just down the block from the Royal Arms, and most of the customers looked like they'd had a rough night—a rough life, for that matter. The majority were unshaven, the majority wore shabby, mismatched clothes that didn't seem to fit right. One poor lady was talking to herself at the counter.

Before we went to the phone booth, over ham and eggs for myself, the same but with a coffee and a roll for my father, he leaned across the table and whispered to me.

"These gentlemen," he said, "you can bet they've been in the navy, the merchant marine. Probably seen the world twice over before they ended up here. Hell of a trade-off, though." He snapped his fingers. "Don't blink twice, Bobby. That's how fast you can slip, and once you hit bottom it ain't easy to get your footing again. Most people would just as soon stomp on you as give you a helping hand. My old man," he said, "he never was sober enough to know the difference."

I pictured this deep pit, all darkness and fear, and at the bottom it was full of people. They were feeling along the sides of the walls for some kind of handhold, but the walls were made of rock, slick rock, and there was just no way they could get out. I promised myself that my father's advice wouldn't go unheeded, as I certainly didn't want to find myself in some run-down restaurant twenty years from now, hunched over a lousy cup of coffee, wearing worn-out clothes and counting my pocket change. It was a real cause for concern. Nonetheless, we *were* in that coffee shop, and the only saving grace, the only thing that separated us from those around us, or in that pit, was the belief that our current situation was nothing more than temporary. We were destined for a better life. It was "in the cards," as my father put it, and I took refuge in hoping that he would, in the end, deliver us.

The phone was back near the bathrooms and the cigarette machine, and it was here that my father thumbed through the phone book.

"If you get Bo," he said, "hang up."

"I don't know why you even bother. She's nothing but trouble."

He deposited a dime in the slot.

"Just do it."

"Why me?" I said.

"It's not so suspicious."

That didn't make me like the idea any better and I was in no rush to find them, not after what they'd done to us. It was my belief at the time that Melinda had informed on us that night; I didn't see the logic in any other explanation. And as for Bo, in my estimation, he was nothing more than a psychopath best left to his own devices. I blamed them both for all the time my father had lost in prison and for myself in a foster home. I told him that, too, but it didn't make much of an impression.

"Don't be jumping to conclusions," he said. "We don't know what went on. There just might be another side to the story."

He dialed the first Stenovich, then handed me the receiver. It rang three times before an older woman answered, much older judging by her voice, and if she was any relation to Bo she would've had to have been his grandmother. Still, I asked for him and she told me I had the wrong number. I apologized and hung up.

My father dialed the next.

Another woman answered, and as far as I could tell it wasn't Melinda. A baby screamed in the background.

"Is Bo Stenovich in?" I said.

"Sorry," she said. "No Bo here."

An operator for a message service picked up the third call, for Gerald Stenovich, a mortgage broker with Seattle Title, then she put me on hold.

"Is Bo in?" I said.

A pause.

I cupped the receiver against my chest and nodded to my father.

"Jackpot," I said.

"Jesus," he said. "Hang up."

But I returned the receiver to my ear.

"Hello, Bo," I said. "It's Bobby Barlow, and my old man wants to kick your ass."

"Gimme that thing."

My father grabbed it out of my hand.

"You got a warped sense of humor," he said. "You know that. *Warped.*"

Again my father dialed, then gave me the receiver.

"Hello?"

"Mr. Stenovich?"

"Yeah, what do you want?"

I recognized the voice immediately. Deep and full of confidence. Years alone couldn't make me forget. This was the man who had put a gun in my father's face.

"Is the missus in?" I said.

"Who's calling?"

I put on my best salesman's voice.

"Mr. Stenovich," I said, "I'm trying to earn enough to go to camp next summer and I'd really appreciate your help. I can promise you the best deal on any magazine you want. *Sports Illustrated. Soldier of Fortune. Good Housekeeping* for the little lady."

"Sorry," he said, "we're not interested."

He hung up.

I did the same, then turned to my father.

"It's him, all right," I said. "Notice I asked for the missus, too."

"What'd he say?"

"She's there," I said. "Either that or he's found somebody else."

My father cuffed me affectionately on the back of the head.

"You're a sharp one, even if you are a smart ass sometimes."

He tore the page from the phone book, shoved it in his pocket and headed for the door. I followed a few steps behind. As we passed our table he took a five-dollar bill out of his wallet and slipped it under the plate. He may have been hoping against hope, hoping just to hope, but those were odds enough for my father, and it had put him in a generous mood. Still, to leave a five-dollar tip on less than a ten-dollar tab seemed a bit steep for our budget. I let him go on ahead of me, and when he reached the door I reached for the bill.

The waitress caught my eye.

"Thank you," she said.

"Anytime," I said.

Instead, I took a napkin from the dispenser, as if that had been my intention all along, smiled sheepishly and continued on my way. My father was waiting for me at the curb, and he'd seen it all through the window.

"Don't be such a cheapskate. What's a few bucks?"

"It was a *five*," I said. "It's not like we got it to spare."

He put his hand on my head and messed up my hair.

"Quit your worrying. This city's full of money. And besides," he said, "I got this feeling, this feeling our luck's about to change, Bobby."

But this particular part of the city certainly didn't look full of money to me, and as for luck I didn't much believe in it. This was the last stop for a lot of the people in it, and even at my ripe old age I knew that a dollar here was worth a great deal more, simply because there were fewer to go around. Some were mugged for less.

"Let me handle the money," I said. "For safekeeping. I'll give you some when you need it."

My father, he only laughed.

"Penny-wise, pound-foolish," he said. "C'mon, tightwad, we got a bus to catch. Or maybe you want to save a few quarters and walk it."

Walk where, I didn't know, but I followed him down the street.

We were on foot this morning, and it would remain that way for a while yet. Night before last we ditched the Nova in the parking lot of a stationery store, no worse for our use, excluding mileage and normal wear and tear.

Dwayne Washington had spent most of his adult life in prison. My father met him at Salem where they shared a cell, and where they struck up an almost immediate friendship. He was released a year before my father, and several months later he sent him a present of Hershey bars, a couple cartons of Marlboros, a heavy wool blanket and some thermal underwear.

"Believe me," my father told me, as we walked down the street that morning, "it was a welcome gift. Salem gets cold as a bitch come winter. It's not like they keep the thermostat cranked."

Along with the gift was a note, and in it Dwayne wrote that he'd be glad to help my father out should the need ever arise.

"The old geezer even offered to put us up for a while," my father said, "until I got back on my feet."

Dwayne had settled in Seattle, and when I first met him he was living in an old boardinghouse. His skin was the color of coffee mixed with cream, and for all his years behind bars he'd kept in excellent condition, mentally and physically. He'd read books on the theory of mathematics, communism and world religion, and like Melinda he had a keen interest in law, particularly prisoners' rights, which he'd made a study of. He lifted weights, played basketball and boxed; and his arms, like my father's from manual labor, were thick and strong and the veins protruded around the muscle. One struck me as grotesque. It ran straight down the middle of his biceps to his wrist, it was large and purple, and there was a dogleg in it just below the bend of his arm. You couldn't have drawn a sharper, more defined line.

My father and he also shared a similar taste in clothes. Although Dwayne had to be pushing sixty, he still wore his slacks tight, his shirt opened at the throat, and the style of shoe for them both was a slip-on made of blue suede. He liked his hats, too, in particular an old gray fedora with a feather tucked in the band. I doubt, however, that my father and he were able to compare fashions in prison, though I'm sure they had plenty of time to discuss the more important matter of crime. Dwayne, I learned, had been strictly big time. He had specialized in fine jewels, safecracking and cash, and among thieves he was considered an aristocrat. But his glory days were long behind him, and now he worked as a cook at Fanny's Bowl and Dine and spent his evenings drinking in the lounge. There wasn't much reason for him to rush home, for he lived alone, and his room, like ours, was small and depressing. He had a single bed, a desk and a beat-up Laz-E-Boy chair, which was piled with old newspapers. He had a kitchenette, too, the same as ours, with a Formica table, and on top of it was a hot plate with a frayed cord.

My father looked around the room.

"Nice place you got here," he said.

"Cut the crap, Floyd. It's a dump."

"At least you can come and go as you please," my father said. "Can't knock that."

On the desk was an old Remington typewriter, and beside it a manuscript thick as the Sunday paper. Dwayne picked it up and felt its heft.

"My life story," he said. "A tome. It'll sell a million."

"A book?"

"So you got eyes."

"What makes you think you're so special? What makes you think anybody wants to read about some over-the-hill crook like you?"

"Over the hill, nothing," he said, "I can still kick your ass."

Dwayne wagged his head as if he were hurt, or as if my father just didn't get it.

"You're missing the point, Floyd. This is going to be a text-book, a regular blueprint for every criminology student in the country. They'll have no choice *but* to buy it. *Crime: From the Inside Out*. Every year we hit them with another edition, add a chapter or two, change the page numbers and slap on a new cover. It's a racket," he said, "these textbooks."

Dwayne looked down at me.

"Don't tell me this sorry excuse for a man's your father?"

"In name, maybe."

"Ah, he ain't that bad."

"It depends on who you're asking."

My father gave me a dirty look.

"The kid's a born wiseass," he said.

"Bobby this, Bobby that," Dwayne said. "Your old man wouldn't stop talking about you. I bet I know you better than yourself."

Whether he was telling the truth or not, I couldn't be sure, but I kept a straight face. I didn't want my father getting any ideas that I might've been pleased at the thought. While they carried on, I turned my attention to the books on the shelves, mostly paperbacks, thrillers and Westerns. There were so many they had to be piled sideways on top of each other. The place was cluttered with magazines, too, and thin slices of newsprint from clippings littered the carpet. I thumbed through a copy of *Very Special People* by Frederick Drimmer. It was all about freaks: the Dog-Faced Boy, an elastic-skin man, another with three legs, Siamese twins and dozens more whose lives must've been incredibly distraught.

"How about a drink?" Dwayne said.

My father looked at his watch. It couldn't have been past ten.

"Sounds like a winner," he said. "I don't like drinking before noon, but for you I'll make an exception."

"Don't let me twist your arm now."

"Make it a short one," my father said. "I drank too much coffee and I could use a little something to calm me down."

Famous last words, I thought to myself. One short one generally followed another, and before you knew it he'd be red faced and grinning. He pulled up a seat at the Formica table in the kitchenette, Dwayne set up the drinks, and I sat down on the bed, opened the book and dug in for the long wait. Section eleven was about Annie Jones, "the Bearded Girl," whose face at birth was covered with a heavy down. Section four had to do with the Tocci Brothers, "the Two-Headed Boy," "virtually a single body with two heads," and section eight, my favorite, concerned Eli Bowen, "the Legless Acrobat," who by my age had "entered upon the life of what used to be called an 'exhibitionist.' " Two feet of different sizes grew out of his hip joints. He got around by holding wooden blocks in his hands, and he was managing himself as a child in shows that went from town to town. I couldn't help but admire Mr. Bowen, and though I certainly didn't envy his circumstance, I nonetheless saw him as a model of strength and fortitude. Here was a man who had made a legend of himself. Here was a man who later fathered a "large, healthy family," who rose above and beyond the ridicule of his audience and despite them found his niche in the world. I probably read for about an hour when Dwayne interrupted me.

"You like that book?" he said.

"Yeah," I said.

"It's yours," he said. "You can have it."

I went to the table.

They'd started with a full fifth of Old Crow, and it was already a third gone. My father's eyes were glossy. He leaned back in his chair and took the book out of my hand and glanced at the title. He opened it and thumbed through the pages.

"Freaks," he said. "What do you want a book on freaks for?"

I shrugged.

"Leave the boy alone," Dwayne said. "Just be thankful he likes to read."

"About freaks?"

He glanced at the pink stubs of my father's left hand.

"Don't say it," my father said.

That got a laugh out of Dwayne. He had on his fedora, and he took it off and placed it on my head. It came down to my brows. He looked at my father and wagged his head as if, once again, he just didn't get it.

"Not freaks," he said. "*People*, Floyd. Like you and me. We all make do with what we got, whether we're born into it or lose it along the way."

The hat was too big, but I knew that I'd grow into it. I tipped it back.

I smiled.

seven

MELINDA JOHNSON was now Mrs. Melinda Johnson-Stenovich. They were married in Reno several days after my father was sentenced to prison, and they spent their honeymoon gambling in Harrah's Casino. Why the sudden change of heart on Bo's part remains a mystery. But my guess is that he saw her slip from his grasp that fateful night now years past, and that he realized if he didn't act, and act right away, he'd lose her to another man. How he could've thought that marriage would somehow stabilize what seemed like a shaky relationship from its beginning only served as further evidence of his desperateness. It also didn't say much for Melinda and her choice of suitors, not that my father was any more of a catch. From what I understand she hit a hot streak on their honeymoon, and instead of spending the first night of marital bliss romping in bed, she rode it out at the crap tables until three that morning, up to seven thousand, then blew it all in single roll of the dice. These things, of course, I learned long after the fact.

They were living in a tract house now. My father and I drove past it early one evening in Dwayne's car. He'd loaned it to us, this old Plymouth police cruiser that he bought for a song at a county auction. It was all beat to hell, inside and out, and the Seattle Police insignia on the doors had been painted over, sloppily, as if whoever had done it was in a big hurry. The engine had also been run ragged, it idled rough, and we had to carry a five-gallon can of water in the trunk because the car kept overheating every twenty miles or so, even in the cold weather. Dwayne had warned us about it before he turned over the keys. This was at Fanny's Bowl and Dine, a couple miles from our hotel, and he was riding out the last stretch of his shift.

I sat on one of the red vinyl stools. My father stood, resting his elbows on the counter, leaning forward and tapping his foot against the railing. There was a young cocktail waitress at the service bar in the lounge next door, and my father had his eye on her. She wore a short skirt, she had nice strong legs, and her hair was piled in a bun on top of her head. Every now and then she glanced his way, and once I saw my father give her a smile. But conversation was out of the question, even if my father had wanted to initiate it, as they were a good twenty feet apart. That the diner was separate from the alleys and the lounge did little to buffer the almost deafening noise of bowling balls striking the lanes and sliding down them and crashing, finally, into the pins. Cheers mixed with the din, or rose above it when someone got a strike or a spare, or hit the gutter. There were hoots. There was laughter. I thought to myself that I liked this place with its bright fluorescent lights and the old booths in need of reupholstering. I liked the smell of it even, of the wax that was used to make the lanes smooth and slick, of the grease from the hamburger grill that made my mouth water, and I liked the laughter. I thought to myself that I could hang out here and that this was not a bad spot to lose yourself.

Dwayne served me a Coke and a burger. Then he dug into his pocket for his car keys.

"Whatever you do," he told my father, "don't burn up the engine." He dangled the keys over my father's opened hand,

and I could tell by his eyes that he was seriously having second thoughts.

"Remember," he said, "keep your eye on the temperature gauge."

"No problem."

"I'm trusting you, Floyd."

My father snatched the keys from him.

"All those wonderful nights we shared together, and you still doubt me? Shit, it probably just needs to be run. Driving it like some granny all the time, it gets carbon buildup. You got to blow that crap out now and then."

"It's a bad valve," Dwayne said. "I already had it checked."

Now it was my father's turn to wag his head.

"Mechanics!" he said. "Christ, Dwayne. Who you going to believe? Those guys are out to fleece you." He waved his hand. "I'll check her, and I won't charge you a goddamn cent."

Dwayne looked at me.

"Watch him," he said. "Okay?"

I nodded.

My father slapped me on the back.

"You eat that hamburger any slower," he said, "it'll rot."

"Give 'im a break," Dwayne said. "Instead of bitching you ought to take an hour or two out of your sad old life and teach the boy here how to bowl."

That was an idea, and one I would've liked to pursue. But I knew that my father wouldn't go for it, at least not now. He reached into his pocket and pulled out a pair of dice.

"I'll roll you for the kid's meal," he said.

"C'mon, Floyd, you know I don't gamble."

"Double or nothing on six."

My father tossed the dice on the counter and they came up just as he called it.

"Lady Luck," he said.

"My ass."

Dwayne picked them up, held them to the light and examined each die closely.

"You get these in the joint?"

"Sammy made them," my father said. "A little going-away present."

"You know you could lose a couple more fingers playing with these."

My father smiled, pleased, I think, that he'd gotten a rise out of him.

"The odds have been screwing me too long, Dwayne. Guys like us got to even it up somehow."

Dwayne dropped the dice. They came up six. He looked at me. He looked at my father long and hard. "The hamburger's on the house," he said, then he turned his back to us and walked into the kitchen.

"He's right, you know, about those dice."

"Bobby," my father said, "some things just aren't open for discussion, and this is one of them. Hurry up and eat or I'll leave you."

I finished my burger in about five bites, washed it down with the Coke, and we got on our way. He hadn't told me where we were going that evening, but it was easy enough to figure out. We'd only been in town a few days, and to my knowledge he had made no less than a dozen calls to the Stenovich residence. He used the pay phone down the hall from our room. Most of the time he hung up before he dialed the last number. But other times, I imagine when it was Melinda that answered, he'd cover the mouthpiece with his hand and listen to her. After the third or fourth call, I'm sure she caught on, not necessarily that it was my father, but that it was a crank of some sort. Because I don't think he ever said anything. After three long years I don't think he wanted to start it up again over the phone. It was her voice that my father needed to hear, even if it was only that initial "hello," if only to reassure himself that he and Melinda were both still alive. Afterwards, when he returned to the room, sullen maybe, or with a tender smile, he'd pour himself a shot of whiskey.

The next logical step was to pay her a visit. We drove by their place once, slowly, then parked across the street the second time around, down the block and away from the street-lamps where we couldn't be seen so easily. All the homes looked alike except for the design on the garage door and the layout of the porch, which was reversed every other house. The lawn was neatly manicured and there was a wagon wheel in the flower bed that ran the length of the living room window. Parked at the curb was Bo's stepside with the rollbar in back and yellow fog lights mounted on top of the cab. Outside, a strong wind blew and it was cold, but my father rolled down his window anyway and lit a cigarette. I zipped up my jacket. Down the street a plastic garbage can lid tumbled end over end.

"Can't we ever get a car with a heater that works?" I said.

"Stop your whining."

I nodded at the house.

"I hate to say it, but it looks like she's doing all right without you."

My father gave me this look, as if my words didn't deserve comment, then he blew a stream of smoke out the window.

"At what cost? Ask yourself that. You want to be a cop?"

"No," I said. "It's a dangerous job."

"You been watching too damn much TV if you think they go around having gun battles all the time. Mostly they just drive around looking to give some poor jerk a ticket, and if they shoot anything it's the shit. I tell you," he said. "I tell you true. The guys I knew who became cops, they were the bullies, they were the punks. They were the *dogs*."

A short while later the garage door opened and we saw Bo. He was in his slippers and a terry-cloth bathrobe, and he

had a can of beer in one hand. My father stubbed his cigarette
out in the ashtray and leaned forward for a better look.

"Safe," he said. "He thinks he's so, *so* safe, except there
isn't such a thing. Look at him, Bobby. A sitting duck."

"Knock it off, you're getting weird."

"You don't think I could take him?"

He reached into his coat pocket, and with his bad hand
worked another cigarette from the pack. In the garage Bo took
a drink from his beer then set it down on top of the washer.
He glanced in our direction, but he didn't notice us. From a
rafter above him hung a heavy punching bag with *Everlast*
written across the side, and in the corner stood a bench press
loaded down with weights, the Olympic type, the black iron.
Peg-Boards were mounted on the wall over a workbench, and
from them hung all kinds of tools, claw hammers, screwdriv-
ers and pliers. There was a car, too, an older Dodge Dart, and
Bo slipped behind the wheel, started the engine and carefully
backed out into the gravel driveway.

My father tapped the filter of his cigarette against the
dashboard.

"Well?"

"Well what?"

"You didn't answer me," he said. "You think I could take
him or not?"

"Probably not. But that isn't the point."

"The point is *I* should be in that nice warm house. *I* should
be behind the wheel of that Dodge. That's the goddamn
point, Bobby."

"Forget it, let's just get out of here," I said. "I'm cold."

But he was beside himself now and he wouldn't answer
me. He just stared blankly ahead, even after Bo had shut the
garage door and disappeared inside. Now and then he took a
long drag off his cigarette. When the sun set we saw Bo again
briefly in the living room window, just long enough to shut
the drapes. Then a floodlamp over the garage came on and

cast a wide circle of light across the driveway. It was then, when the door opened a second later, that we saw Melinda for the first time in three years. She had a briefcase. She had on heels and a black dress that fit her tightly, and as she came into the circle of light it was as if she had suddenly reentered our world in one bright and shining moment. With a subtle sweep of her hand, she drew her skirt beneath her and slipped into the Dodge. My father flicked his cigarette out the window. The butt hit the pavement with a shower of sparks.

Just as he'd kept our distance from the house, he again played it safe, and when the opportunity availed itself my father let another car come between us. The Dodge had distinct, square-shaped taillights, and we never let them out of our sight. We followed Melinda from her neighborhood up to a main road and then a short while later onto the freeway. She drove a good ten miles an hour over the limit, and the old Plymouth was running like a dog. The arm on the temperature gauge rose past the middle and into the red. "Better slow down," I said. "Actually, you better pull over." But my father chose to ignore the warning sign and continued on at full barrel—with his foot, on two occasions, pressed firmly to the floor. Steam rose from under the hood, and the odor of hot oil soon worked its way through the floorboard and into the cab.

"I think I smell something," I said.

"It's just your imagination."

"Bullshit, something's burning."

The idiot light on the dash glowed red.

"You better pull over."

"Relax," my father said. "That's just a warning. It doesn't mean you have to stop."

By now I realized that any appeal I might make toward common sense would fall on deaf ears, and so I simply crossed my arms over my chest and sat back for the ride. It wouldn't be long, I thought, before we were stranded on the side of the highway. And I'd do exactly what I imagined Dwayne would, that is, shrug and say "I told you so." Ahead the Dodge's right blinker flashed on, and Melinda took her turnoff.

Downtown Seattle.

At the first red light we hit, two cars behind Melinda, the Plymouth stalled out. Now that we were stationary the steam was more visible; it rose from between the cracks of the hood not in wisps but in a steady stream. My father cursed and tried to start it up again. Nothing. He tried again. And again, nothing. The starter clicked, engaged, clicked, but it wouldn't turn the engine. The only sounds were those of the steam, the tick of the hot metal cooling and the rush of air that the cars behind us made as they pulled ahead and passed.

He slammed the wheel with the butt of his hand.

"A cop car," he shouted, "a stupid cop car. They run it ragged because the tab's on the taxpayer, and then they got the gall to sell it back for garbage." He slammed the wheel harder. "The sons a bitches, there ought to be a law."

He threw open his door, slammed it shut and stomped around to the front of the car. He almost grabbed hold of the hood, but he felt the heat of it a split second before he made contact and saved himself the further embarrassment of burning the hell out of himself. He jerked his hand back and kicked the fender instead.

"Piece of junk," he shouted.

The steam continued to rise and the cars behind continued to pass. I climbed out of the Plymouth and went around to the front, when Melinda pulled up beside us. She rolled down the window on the passenger's side. She leaned over the seat and smiled.

"Welcome to Seattle," she said. "I was hoping to see you guys again, though I can't say I expected it. You're looking good, Floyd. Real good."

We stood there stunned and silent. Neither of us had had even the slightest inkling that she'd spotted us following her. The steam hissed and rose up around my father.

"I'd give you gentlemen a lift but I'm late for class. Torts," she said, "they're a real bitch." She slipped the Dodge into gear. "By the way, if you're trying to piss Bo off, you're doing a great job. You better quit calling me at the house."

Then, quick as she'd come, she was gone again. With her foot to the accelerator, without so much as a good-bye or a simple wave of her hand, she cut off an approaching car in the next lane and merged into the traffic. My father turned to me.

"What the hell's a tort?"

"It has something to do with the law," I said.

"How do you know?"

"I'm smart."

"Too smart for your own good."

Someone honked and swerved out from around us, and my father's thoughts of Melinda, whatever they might've been, however tense or vivid, suddenly faded, suddenly passed, if only long enough to realize our predicament. He tossed me the keys.

"You steer," he said. "I'll push. Let's get this piece of shit outta the road."

eight

M<small>Y</small> FATHER was convinced. "If there was ever two people meant for each other," he said, "it's me and Melinda. It may take some time but you watch, she'll come around. She'll leave that bum. I know it." He patted his chest. "I can *feel* it right here." My father had a great respect for the powers of instinct, and though his own disappointed him as often as not, in this case I suspected that they might well bear him out. But if there's such a thing as fate, and if in fact they were destined to come together again, I wasn't sure to what end it might lead them. *My* instincts, however, told me that it was a hell of a lot more likely to be a complicated and dangerous liaison than a simple affair of two disenchanted lovers meeting under the cover of darkness and eventually going their separate ways, renewed maybe, and no one the wiser.

At the same time, it seemed to me that unlike that pair of loaded dice, where the powers of uncertainty had lost out to my father's more basic, instinctual need to survive, the odds of him winning Melinda's love were not so easily altered. She was married now. She led a new and apparently comfortable life. What could he offer her that Bo couldn't or already hadn't? I mentioned this to him, but he just looked at me and grinned.

"Bobby, there's some things about a woman you don't

know yet," he said. "When you get a little older maybe I'll tell you, but for now you can take my word for it. That punk cop couldn't please a woman if his life depended on it."

This conversation of ours took place at Fanny's Bowl and Dine, a week from our last encounter with Melinda, and to my knowledge my father hadn't called her since. Though I may have been young, though I may not have fully understood the details of their attraction, I knew enough to know that we had more pressing problems at hand than worrying about my father's love life, or lack of it. Our funds were running low and we were now into Dwayne Washington for six hundred dollars: the cost of a remanufactured 327 V-8 on sale at Depp's Auto, including the exchange core, assuming that it was in any condition to rebuild.

The ad ran in the sports section.

"Here's a real deal," he said, as Dwayne served us up lunch.

Again it was on the house. Again it was hamburgers and fries.

My father folded the newspaper and turned it around on the counter, so that Dwayne could see it for himself, this picture of an engine, and beside it a list of the things in it that had been rebuilt.

"Hell of a bargain," he said. "Regularly she goes for six ninety-nine with the core. I'd hate to see us pass it up."

Dwayne looked at the ad, but he did it more out of politeness than with any genuine interest. The gesture was lost on my father.

"Yeah, who's going to pay for it?"

He wiped his hands on his apron and returned to the kitchen. My father sighed. Behind us I heard the crash of bowling pins exploding into the different backboards, and further down the hall the ring and buzz of a pinball machine. Someone had scored a replay.

"You see there?" my father said. "See that? The old

geezer's still pushed out of shape. I'll tell you, Bobby. There's living proof what holding grudges can do to a man. Pass the catsup."

I can't say I blamed Dwayne, though I kept that thought to myself as I handed him the catsup. My father literally covered his fries with it, more out of habit, I believe, than any real love for the stuff. Condiments of all sorts were a staple in his diet whenever we ate out, for they were generally free, and the idea was to load up your stomach, like gas to an engine, just to keep going. We'd skipped breakfast this morning, and our dinner the night before had been lean, a bag of Laura Scudder's potato chips, a quart of milk and a can of cold chicken ravioli between us. By this time of the day I was starved.

When Dwayne first received news of his car he handled it "like a prince," as my father later put it; that is, graciously, with the typical wag of his head accompanied by a long sigh of exasperation. It was as if he'd expected the worst from the beginning and had resigned himself to it long before he ever let the keys pass from his hand into my father's. "It needed a valve job anyway," he'd said, sadly. Of course my father agreed to square up as soon as he got on his feet, and that if Dwayne wanted to go ahead and buy a rebuilt he'd rent a hoist and drop it in himself. "Installation," he'd told him, "that's where they get you, Dwayne." In the end, for all his trouble, my father promised him a car that would run like it had just rolled off the assembly line in Detroit.

The trouble was that neither of them had much money, so that for all practical purposes six hundred dollars may as well have been six thousand. Dwayne lived from week to week, just as my father and I more or less made do. Rent at the Royal Arms was considered cheap at twelve dollars a night, paid daily in advance or by the week, and for the pensioners, the old sailors, other vets and those who had somehow found themselves on relief—what my father called the government dole—the rooms let monthly. We were paid up for the next four days, and the way I figured it, if we handled our money wisely, we might have enough to carry us another week at best. I kept a close tab on our funds and they were going fast, on meals and laundry, on cigarettes, on whiskey and beer for my father.

But Dwayne had a plan that evening. When he came out of the kitchen again he slapped a sheet of paper down on the counter and dropped a pen on top of it.

"Eat up and fill this out," he said.

My father was just about to bite into his hamburger, but he set it down. He looked at the sheet of paper. It was a job application.

"What kind of job?"

"Custodial."

"I'm not picking up after these bums."

"I already talked to the boss about you," Dwayne said. "All you got to do is go in for the interview and act halfway civilized for a change. I'm thinking about the kid, Floyd. You have a responsibility to someone besides yourself."

"He's my problem, not yours. You'll get your goddamn money."

"I don't give a goddamn about the money. How do you plan on feeding the boy? Where you plan on sleeping when you can't come up with the rent?"

I didn't say a word. I didn't want to get involved. I just kept eating.

"I'll figure something out."

"And you'll wind up back in the joint, too," he said. "Or in the hospital, with those dice of yours. You're a real thinker, Floyd."

My father picked up his hamburger and took a big bite out of it. The juices rolled from the bun onto the plate. He reached for his napkin and drew it angrily across his mouth.

"I don't scrub toilets," he said. "I don't sweep anybody's

floors. Those days are behind me. I'm a tradesman, I have skills. You're looking at a man who still has some pride left."

"Square one, that's where you're starting again." Dwayne's voice had risen, and a customer at the end of the counter gave us a sidelong glance. "Skills don't mean shit in your situation. The longer you're out, the harder it is to get back in the game."

My father rose suddenly from the stool. He took one last bite from his hamburger and then threw it back on the plate and pushed it away.

"It's raw anyway," he said. "Talk about pride. Talk about skills. You can't even cook a goddamn hamburger right."

Mine, however, tasted wonderful. I'd wolfed it down in record time, and I'd finished my fries, too, all in anticipation of exactly what had just occurred. And before my father made it to the door I grabbed a handful of fries from his plate.

Dwayne called to me as I left.

"Do us both a favor and try talking some sense into that old man of yours."

But my mouth was full, and for what good it would've done I couldn't answer. I hurried outside and caught up with him as he was walking heatedly through the parking lot.

"Some friend," he said. "Owe him a few lousy bucks and he wants you to scrub toilets the rest of your life. It's not like he lost a Mercedes. The piece of junk was on its last legs anyway."

"That's not it," I said.

"Don't you start on me now."

"We did burn up his engine," I said. "We ought to make good on it."

I emphasized the *we*, hoping to spread the responsibility and lighten his load, but it didn't seem to have any effect on him. He crossed the street and I followed. He wasn't headed for the Royal Arms.

"Where we going?"

"*You're* not going anywhere," he said.

"C'mon, don't be that way."

"Why don't you go back to the hotel? Better yet, why not go sit around with Dwayne and bad-mouth your old man some more?"

"I didn't *say* anything."

"That's right. Because you were too busy getting a big kick out of him putting me down. Go on. Leave me alone."

"It's a free country," I said. "I'll do whatever I want."

"Free country, my ass. Some schoolteacher tell you that?"

I knew full well where he was headed and why he didn't want me around and it didn't have anything to do with Dwayne Washington. It was a week to the day, almost to the hour, since we'd last seen Melinda, and if she had a schedule this was the time to put it to the test. A part of me would've preferred to spend the night alone, for in many ways I still harbored a certain resentment toward her, while another part of me thought it wise to tag along. My father was as angry as he was despondent and I didn't like to leave him in that state.

At the end of the block he stopped and tried to wave me off.

"Go," he said. "Get."

"I'm not a dog. You can't shoo me away."

He walked faster but I stayed right with him. At the corner he stopped and we waited there for the bus. A short while later one pulled to the curb, and when we boarded he pretended like he didn't know me, he made me pay for myself, and when he sat down in the back he threw his leg across the seat so I couldn't sit next to him.

"Don't take it out on me just because you messed up his car," I said. "I warned you, too, you can't tell me I didn't."

"There's nothing worse than some jackass saying "I told you so." I got enough on my mind without you jumping all over me."

"You're acting like a big baby."

He only shrugged.

I took a window seat and looked out on the streets and the broken white line beneath us as it passed under the bus. Soon we came up on the freeway where only the week before we'd broken down in Dwayne's Plymouth, and I could've said something sarcastic, I could've rubbed it in, but I didn't. He rang the bell, and we got off at the next stop and walked a few more blocks until we came to Sander's School of Law, the only one of its kind close to the freeway exit that Melinda had taken the week before. My father found the address in the yellow pages.

It was located in a shopping mall next to the Pacific West Detective Agency and Dianna's House of Beauty. The air outside smelled of chemicals, the kind that hairdressers used, pungent and tart. The lights were out in the detective agency and it looked like it might've been empty inside, maybe out of business. But Sander's was all lit up, and a banner above the door read MAKE THE CHANGE—ENROLL NOW. In the lobby, a group of men dressed neatly in business suits talked and sipped coffee from Styrofoam cups. They had a certain self-conscious sense of poise, and to add to this image, one I considered stodgy, the walls behind them were lined with shelves of law books.

My father looked around the parking lot.

"You see her car?"

It was nowhere in sight.

"Bo could've dropped her off. Why don't you go check inside."

"I can't," he said. "I'm not dressed right."

He had on a decent pair of slacks, his suede shoes and a two-tone shirt with the French cuffs turned back. Over it he wore his green sweater with diamond-shaped leather patches on the breast.

"You look fine," I said.

"I'm not asking you."

"Fuck those guys. Who cares what they think?"

"Don't cuss like that," he said. "You don't hear me using the F word. Maybe I say 'goddamn' now and then, maybe I say 'son of a bitch.' But I don't go around saying 'fuck this, fuck that' all the time. Keep the gutter language to yourself."

I considered leaving. I considered saying the hell with it, catching the bus and heading back to the hotel. Instead, I sat down on one of the concrete parking bumpers while my father lit up a cigarette. We waited. Fifteen, twenty minutes must've passed. The sun went down and the lights in the parking lot came on. One car after another began to pull in and the different students, some of them for Dianna's School of Beauty but mostly for Sander's, hurried to class with their arms loaded with books. Others carried briefcases. Then all the activity ended, and the parking lot was quiet again. Outside Sander's School of Law, a man pulled the door shut behind him.

"She'd be here by now if she was coming. We're wasting our time."

My father checked his watch.

"Give her a few more minutes."

We might've left then, and to my way of thinking it would have been for the better. But my father's notion of fate, that initial gut reaction he'd had, served to keep his hopes alive those few remaining minutes, and with patience and perseverance he proved himself right. She came up the driveway in the Dodge and cut across the parking lot at a considerable speed, turned sharply into a space and killed the engine.

"Fuck," I said, under my breath.

"What'd you say?"

"Nothing, just talking to myself."

"That's what I thought."

My father tucked in his shirt and started toward her car. But this time I didn't follow. Melinda had on a two-piece suit and black pumps. The skirt was short, and as she slipped out from behind the wheel I took note of her legs. I remembered the dime-sized mole on her left thigh where it curved smoothly into her hip, this from our days at poolside back at the River Towers, and I suddenly felt uneasy. Her hair was upswept and the finer strands of it that grew along the back of her neck caught the light from the parking lamp above them.

I don't know what they said. I was too far away to hear. But I could tell by the way that she leaned against the Dodge with one hand resting gently on her hip, and by the way that she smiled, and how, faintly, she laughed, and by the way that she lowered her eyes and then slowly looked up at him, I could tell by all these things that it was starting all over again. The years between them, both in age and those that my father had lost in prison, meant absolutely nothing. He walked her to the door of Sander's School of Law, and when she'd gone inside he headed back across the parking lot to me with this wide silly grin on his face.

"Tell you what," he said, "maybe you should head back. You were up late last night and I don't want you getting worn out and sick on me. It'll be a wait before she's out of class."

"Fine, if that's what you want. Why should I give a shit?"

"Don't be a poor sport."

"Hey," I said. "No big deal. I'm used to being ditched."

I left then, actually less put off than I made out to be. Their night looked to be a long, drawn-out one, and no matter the course it didn't include a third party. I had plans of my own, anyway. I wanted to write Bonnie a letter and I needed the privacy to do it. I wanted to find out how she was getting along. I wanted to tell her that I was okay and that she'd been in my thoughts, and I even wanted to put in a word or two for Todd, as I'd been feeling pretty low lately about robbing him. I realized I'd done wrong. I realized that I was capable of it again and I didn't like that side of myself anymore than when I saw it in my father. The money had come in handy and we'd certainly needed it, that much was for sure, but too much of it was spent carelessly, and it seemed to me that if you had to steal you ought to do it only to feed yourself.

Some nights after my father fell asleep I'd slip out of bed and rifle through his pockets until I found the two things that I wanted: his wallet and his chrome-plated Zippo, worn thin to the brass on one side from continually rubbing up against his leg in his pants pocket. I'd kneel at the foot of the bed. I'd strike the lighter and in the small circle of flame, in its shudder and flicker, silently count what remained of our cash. We'd started out with a little over four hundred—say, fifty or sixty of his own after deducting for gas and the snow chains that he bought in Portland, and three hundred and sixty-two from my end. At last count we were down to a hundred and eighty, and after tonight I figured it would be even less, because he was probably going to take Melinda out for a couple drinks. This, however, didn't include the hundred that I'd brought with me, and which I kept secret. It was my savings, our ace in the hole, and though I was perfectly willing to share it with my father, it would have to be for a good reason. It would have to be for an emergency and an emergency only.

I kept it, two fifty-dollar bills, folded together and hidden under the insole of my left tennis shoe. It put a kind of spunk to my walk when I caught myself thinking about it, and then in the next instant I'd pretend it didn't exist so that I wouldn't be tempted to spend it. But I knew that it *did* exist and that if I ever found myself in real need I had an out, an edge, a backup. Just knowing, it seemed, was enough. I hoped that my father felt similarly about the gun that I found when I returned to our room that night. I was looking for a pen, so that I could write the letter to Bonnie. I had all the words in my head, as I'd been thinking about what to say for days, and I was anxious to get on with it. My father's coat hung in the closet, and I came across the gun as I was going through his pockets. I don't know where he got it, or if he had it before we met up. But I was smart enough to figure out this much:

it was likely stolen, it was old too, though in fine condition, and my guess was that it had once belonged to a German soldier, then a GI who'd smuggled it home. Because this was no fake. This was no replica. It was a genuine nine-millimeter Luger with the Nazi insignia, the black hawk with its wings spread, engraved in the grip. The writing on the barrel was in German, and if there had ever been serial numbers on it they'd been filed off and blued over.

As I held the Luger that night, I worried for my father's safety. He trusted his senses too freely and the odds alone suggested that given his character, given his past and his unwavering faith in the edge, he'd one day find it suddenly dulled and the gambler in him would to have call his own bluff. On the other hand, I had to take into account his fear. Having once found himself staring down the barrel of Bo's .38 and then three years later winding up in the same city as that man must have refreshed his memory, and as a consequence, motivated less by vengeance than precaution, he thought it wise to arm himself.

I admired the gun's heft. I admired its craftsmanship and the fine balance between the barrel and grip. I listened for the return of my father's footsteps, even though I knew that he wouldn't be along for quite a while yet, and when I didn't hear anything I aimed the gun out the window. I took a bead on the cooling unit on top of the warehouse. Then I swung around. I aimed at my reflection in the dresser mirror and let my finger rest on the trigger.

From down the hall I heard a toilet flush, the suck of water, the thump it made in the pipes.

I returned the gun to his pocket.

His secret, I promised, would be mine.

I found a pen and wrote Bonnie Walker that night. It was a letter that started out friendly and routine, but as it went on it got more into my real feelings for her, ones that I didn't even know I had. I finished with "I miss you" and signed it with my love. I don't imagine that my feelings for her were much different than those my father held for Melinda. I don't imagine that he went those years in prison without writing her some strong words of love, loyalty and passion, even if they were never meant to be read.

He came in late that night, long after I'd finished my letter, slipped it into an envelope and put a stamp on it. He undressed, and when he climbed into bed I smelled Melinda's perfume on him, that and the sour odor of whiskey on his breath.

"Bobby," he said, "you awake?"

But I only groaned for effect and turned on my side away from him. For the first time since we'd left Portland, my father slept soundly through the night. I can't say the same for myself.

I slipped out of bed that morning while he was still snoring, dressed and reread the letter. It sickened me, not because it was too sweet, though it was, but because I feared that my words might somehow frighten Bonnie, and I thought if there was ever a chance our paths might cross again I didn't want to tamper with fate and ruin what might never be realized anyway. It was the process, after all, the simple act of writing that mattered most, that brought the pictures of memory and dream more sharply into focus than this other world I saw around me.

I let myself out of the room as quietly as I could, crumpled the letter into a ball and dropped it unceremoniously into the waste can in the hallway. Then I phoned Dwayne Washington.

"Good morning," I said.

"Who's this?"

"Bobby," I said. "I'm calling about that job."

"Your old man come to his senses?"

"Not yet. But I know how we can get your car running again."

nine

*T*HERE WAS a selfish streak in my father that his days in prison had only made worse. I believe that it had everything to do with the pressure of time, and that the lost years had done more to embitter than reform him. The small gains that he'd made as a working stiff had added up to a kind of emptiness, an absence of hope or change, of failed dreams and the realization of his own limitations as a man on the dark side of his thirties. Time was ticking away and the more conscious of it he became, the more anxiety it produced, which in turn led to a kind of moral recklessness best typified in one of his favorite rules for living: "Take what you can get, Bobby, and don't look back. You can bet your sweet ass there's somebody trying to grab it away." It was ruthless advice, steeped in the cynical. Personal gains of any sort came at the expense of another's loss, and the notion of "taking" implied that theft was all right so long as you could get away with it. All this is to say that his interest in Fanny Pringle, owner of Fanny's Bowl and Dine, lacked the sincerity that Dwayne Washington clearly felt for her. I came to understand that my father's rule, or advice for living, included filching less tangible things from others than their money.

Fanny was in a spot when she hired me. Her janitor had suddenly up and quit. No notice, no nothing. In one night alone all the trash cans in the place were brimming over. And all the ashtrays needed dumping. And every urinal and toilet, every sink needed scrubbing, and the floors hadn't been mopped for several days prior to the janitor quitting. In short, my interview proved more of a formality than anything else, for not only was Fanny under pressure to hire someone, and fast, but Dwayne had also given his highest of recommendations. The hitch was that he'd originally spoken on my father's behalf, and given his criminal background I don't suppose that winning her over was an easy chore. She'd already hired one ex-con in Dwayne, and even if he'd proven himself a fine employee, that she had nothing to fear in him, that she had nothing to worry about in terms of his honesty or reliability, the idea of hiring yet another ex-con may well have strained her sense of goodwill. That my father ended up refusing the job could've only reinforced the stereotype that Fanny had ultimately rejected when she brought Dwayne on board: that men of their sort were basically lazy and shiftless. If Dwayne had played on her sympathies before, now he had to do it again for me, big time.

"One of 'em has to get a job." He held his thumb and index finger about an inch apart. "They're that close to being tossed out on the street."

Fanny sat behind her desk. She looked me up and down.

"How old are you?"

"Eighteen," I said.

"If you're eighteen, I'm thirty-five again. How old is he, Dwayne?"

"Sixteen."

"Barely."

"He just looks young," he said.

"I hear your father was up at Salem."

Her words caught me off guard, and for a second there I didn't know what to say.

"It's okay. She knows where I met your dad," he said.

"Fanny's a decent woman. She doesn't hold it against him or me."

"Yes ma'am," I said.

"Yes what?"

"He was at Salem for a while," I said. "But there's a story behind it. It's not like he ever hurt anybody."

"I want you to know I believe people can change if you give them a chance. Dwayne here," she said, "he was pushing for your father. You should have a talk with him. I'd prefer to offer him the job."

"I appreciate the thought, except he's a journeyman," I said, "a regular jack-of-all-trades. He has a hard time settling for anything less."

"Pride doesn't pay the bills," Dwayne said. "The boy has to work, Fanny, whether it's here or someplace else. I'm sure he'll do fine. He just needs the opportunity to prove himself."

"You ought to be in school," she said. "Maybe you'll change your mind and go back once you get a taste of the real working world. The job's five days a week. Nights. A dollar above minimum to start and tips if you bar back."

"Thank you," I said. "I'll do good."

"You're out of here if you don't. Same goes for you, Dwayne."

"I'm your main man," he said. "You'd never do that. What I want to know is when you're going to do something besides work all the time."

"Like what?"

"Dinner, drinks. There's more to life than this bowling alley."

She waved him off.

"Get to work," she said. "If I didn't keep my eye on this place, you'd all be out of a job."

Maybe she was kidding, but Dwayne wasn't. He laughed, though, and so did she. She had a wonderful laugh, too, high pitched at points like the shrill call of a bird, and to hear it made me smile. She was a good, sturdy block of a woman. A former professional bowler, Fanny had retired from the sport a dozen years before our paths crossed, but she kept in fine shape by bowling regularly, a few frames in the afternoon and several before she left at night. Her arms were muscular and her calves were thick and firm and round. Fanny wore her hair short like a man's, and around the alley I never saw her in anything but two-tone suede bowling shoes, a white skirt and a loose-fitting blouse. There was a glass showcase outside the pro shop, and in it were her trophies from all around the country, these figurines perched at the top of each one—a chrome woman rolling a bowling ball, caught in that perfect moment just before it leaves the hand, one leg bent and the other held in an arc behind it, like an ice skater, with her skirt cutting through the air, frozen in a state of motion.

This was my first official job and with it came a sense of independence, pride and responsibility. It didn't matter that I washed toilets, dumped ashtrays and mopped floors, I was making the dollar, paying taxes and reaping the benefits of the working man, which outside of a few extra bucks in my pocket didn't seem all that many. Among my other duties, I picked up beer bottles from all the bowling stations every hour on the hour, I bused glasses for the lounge and lugged in cases of beer from the coolers in the kitchen. I had a set of keys that I wore on a ring attached to my belt loop. They jingled when I walked and they allowed me access to the storage rooms, the utility closet, the pro shop and Fanny's office, which I cleaned every night before I left. I was also on call as a porter for bowlers who spilled drinks or dropped their beer bottles. It happened, without fail, no less than twice a night.

There were fifty lanes at Fanny's Bowl and Dine, twenty-five on one side of the building, twenty-five on the other, and on Friday and Saturday nights every lane was packed with teams from the local Moose lodge, Spivey Electric, Carl's Machine Shop and a host of others whose names I can no longer recall. All of them, however, sported polyester shirts with company logos embroidered on the back in slick, shiny thread. I had a uniform of sorts myself, a baggy pair of khaki pants and a shirt several sizes too large, so that when I tucked it in it wadded up, and I had to pull it out whenever I sat down. During the course of my employment I saw hundreds of custom bowling balls, with peppermint swirls in them, and gold flecks, and solids bright enough to make you wince as they whizzed down the lanes. If I worked fast, as I made it a point to do, I could finish my routine in the first few hours and spend the remainder of my shift helping the bartender. That's where the real money was at. The cocktail waitresses and the bartenders pooled and split a portion of their tips with me at the end of their shifts, and the cut was often better than my regular wages, minus the long list of deductions. Some nights I came home with twenty extra in my pocket. Tax free. My father was pleased.

"You remind me of myself when I was your age. My old man put me and my brother to work on our ranch feeding and looking after the turkeys. Now there's the dumbest animal that ever lived. A wolf spook 'em and they'll all scramble to one end of the pen and literally *smother* each other to death. I'm talking the whole damn flock. Two thousand plus. That's a lot of dead turkey.

"And the rain," he'd add, shaking his head. "I already told you about that. They'll drown just looking up at it. Me and Luke worked night and day to keep those fool birds alive, we actually had to *sleep* out there with them, and we never saw a cent in wages. The old man used to say 'your turn's a comin', boys,' but of course it never did." There was bitterness in his voice as he came to a finish. "If I had half of what that old bastard spent on booze, I tell you, Bobby, we'd be rolling in it now."

This was his way of suggesting that as the grandson of a drunken turkey farmer I didn't have it so bad, and even if my father rarely came out and asked me for a loan, I felt a responsibility to turn over my checks for rent, other bills and food until he got on his feet again.

"One of these days I'll make it up to you," he'd say. "We'll hit it big, Bobby. We'll hit it big and look back and laugh about it all."

That I didn't know about, but I figured that if he had a few dollars to blow he was less likely to find himself in trouble again with the law. Half my tips I gave to Dwayne, which amounted to about forty dollars a week, and the other half I kept for myself. Unlike my father, however, I preferred to squirrel away what I could rather than spend it. We'd known too many lean times, and if I had the means to guard against them in the future I most certainly would. I kept a daily account of my earnings in a pocket-sized notepad that I'd bought expressly for the purpose, and within a few weeks I'd reimbursed Dwayne a hundred and seventy-two dollars. In a few months, if all had gone well, I would've had him paid off.

My father had been in fine spirits since he'd met up with Melinda at Sander's School of Law, the finest that I'd ever seen him. He was back on schedule, rising early each morning and doing a hundred push-ups and two hundred sit-ups.

"Got to flatten this stomach," he'd say, lifting his T-shirt and patting his belly. "Got to harden this body. It's time to get back into shape."

He'd take a boxer's stance in front of the dresser mirror and finish up the workout by throwing punches at his reflection.

"Jab. Jab, jab, hook." He'd snap them out hard and fast, feinting and weaving. "Overhand right. Uppercut. Jab, jab, hook."

In a few minutes he'd break a terrific sweat, all the whiskey and beer from the night before pouring down his face, and then inevitably he'd turn to me.

"C'mon," he'd say. "Drag that sorry ass out of bed and I'll show you some moves. Every boy ought to know the art of self-defense."

I hated it.

But he'd keep after me, prodding and poking under the blankets until I came up for air and took a stance before him in my underwear.

"Keep your hands up. Elbows tight."

He'd wing punches frighteningly fast. I could hear the wind from them slip past my ears.

He'd holler.

"Don't flinch now. Don't look at my fists. Keep your eyes on my mine and trust your hands. They'll do the work."

And if I so much as took a step back, he'd holler even more.

"You afraid?"

"No."

"You afraid?"

"No."

"I can't hear you."

So I'd shout it.

"I'm not *afraid*."

"Prove it."

He'd stick his chin out, begging for it.

But when I reared back and stepped into my punch, as he'd instructed me countless times before, and took a tremendous swing at him, he'd duck it and pop me on the side of the head. Though it was always a light blow, meant to instruct, never to hurt, it nonetheless embarrassed and frustrated me.

"Got to be quick to catch your old man. I was Golden Gloves champ two years running. Middleweight," he said. "Not one of those big dumb hulking heavies. Now show me the jab. Snap 'em out. Keep your chin tucked and your face covered or I'll pop you a good one."

That's the way our mornings often started out, sparring around the bed, backing me into the corner with his arms and fists and then goading me to fight my way out.

"Don't let me back you up," he'd say. "Punch *through* me, not at me. *Make* your opening. Nobody'll give it to you."

And on it went until my arms felt so heavy I could hardly hold them up. Afterwards we took a shower together, and I remember admiring and envying his muscles and the thick patch of dark hair on his chest. I'd only just begun to sprout a sparse, blond trail of it from my groin to my stomach, and you had to be in the right light to see it at all. His penis seemed enormous in comparison and the hood of skin over its tip remained, while mine had been removed at birth, which according to my father had been a horrible mistake. "Your mother wanted it done. If I'd had my say I would've spared you the pain. Circumcision," he said, "it's mutilation. A conspiracy, Bobby, on the part of the American Medical Association in the name of public hygiene. A crock of shit is what it is. All they care about is making that first quick buck off every little pecker in the world. Ain't no reason in hell for it except simple greed at your expense." His theory struck me as eccentric, and yet for the longest time I harbored this absurd vision of doctors, an entire roomful, gathered in secrecy for the express purpose of deciding the fate of my precious foreskin and those of our nation's male population. I pictured the scalpel, the blood, and though I couldn't recall the pain I knew how sensitive I was down there and could imagine it intensely enough. My father further contended that my loss, in terms of future sexual pleasure, was of greater consequence than I'd unfortunately ever know.

"The head gets numb without that skin and after a while you can't feel as much, like a callus," he said, "on your hand. It gets toughened up from use."

I could not, of course, ever make the comparison, and I didn't see how he could, either, given that he hadn't suffered my fate, but I hoped, regardless of the contradiction, that someday soon I'd have the opportunity to put his theory to the test. It was my prediction that the pleasures of the process would far outweigh the risk of discovery.

Later over breakfast or maybe just coffee, he'd scan the classifieds for work. But nothing seemed to suit him. The mills weren't hiring and they hadn't been for quite some time. And as far as carpentry and electrical jobs went, most of the contractors required that you have your own tools and truck, and the few that didn't weren't paying much more than I made.

The best times of day for him came in the evening, particularly Thursday nights, when Melinda cut class and met him, fairly regularly, at the lounge at Fanny's Bowl and Dine. What I didn't observe of their evenings together my father often later described for me in minute detail. He usually arrived first, fresh out of the shower, dressed in his best clothes, clean shaven and smelling of cologne. He took a seat at their regular table at the back of the lounge under the dim glow of the Olympia waterfall sign hanging on the wall. There he ordered the usual, a shot of whiskey and a beer chaser for himself, and when Melinda arrived, a double Kahlúa and coffee with extra whipped cream on the side. She detested the canned stuff, and if the cocktail waitresses were busy the bartender had me run back to the kitchen and get her the real thing. Occasionally, either as I approached or left their table, I picked up bits of conversation, and over the course of the next few weeks I came to learn more about her relationship with Bo. He was the focal point of much discussion, at one moment seemingly deserving of her praise, and in the next her contempt.

"You might not think so," she said, "but Bo can be a pretty decent guy when he wants. He's trying to help me become a better person and I could use all the help I can get in that department."

Then, say, by the time I left and returned with the whipped cream, she could've taken a completely different tact.

"One of his stupid buddies pinched my ass last night, and I swear to God all he did was laugh. They're like a bunch of overgrown high school jocks."

I believed that their first few meetings were platonic in nature, for she generally left alone after an hour or so. My father, however, either remained at the table or moved up to the bar for one more nightcap. There he mulled over her parting words, measured his success for the evening, planned his strategy for their next encounter, and if the opportunity presented itself, as it did on at least one occasion that I witnessed, turn a few dollars into a fistful, relying on his skills as a manipulator more so than chance or outright cheating. And I'm confident that he could've made a lot more pocket money if Fanny hadn't eventually stepped in when she did and put a stop to it. I never had any idea that my father knew the first thing about bowling; he certainly never took the time to show me anything about it. But I do know that actual bowling skill played less of a role in his talent to turn a dollar than did his eye for scoping and psyching out the chosen mark. He was adept enough, anyway, to roll a strike when the heat was on, to gutter early in the match, build confidence, raise the ante and make it worth his while. My father could've invited himself into a perfectly friendly game of Sunday croquet and an hour later have everybody reaching for their wallets.

Once, while I was bar backing, a young marine in uniform and his buddy strolled into the lounge and ordered a beer. It was a slow night and that worked against them. Normally the bartender was in such a hurry that unless a customer looked obviously underage he stood a fair to middling chance of being served. In fact, I'd seen these two same guys buy here before and never cause anyone trouble. But tonight it was a different story. The marine, I'd say he was close to twenty, slapped a twenty-dollar bill on the bar and held up two fingers. My father watched it all from his stool, now and again taking a sip of his beer. On the TV above the bar, the young up-and-coming Roberto Duran, fighting as a lightweight, charged out of his corner for the seventh round.

"Two Coors."

"Glasses?"

"No thanks."

The bartender brought out the bottles. He almost popped the caps, but then he paused. He looked at them more closely, first one then the other.

"You boys got IDs?"

"You know me. I used to come in here all the time."

"So did my nephews," he said. "That doesn't mean I served them."

"Ah, man."

"No ID, no beer."

The marine grabbed his twenty off the bar. The other guy looked even younger and he didn't seem too interested in pushing the matter. He wore a Caterpillar cap turned backwards on his head, and his hands were dark with grease, the kind you can't wash off completely no matter how hard you scrub, like he worked on cars for a living or in some kind of machine shop.

They both left.

On TV Roberto Duran had his man against the ropes, exactly where he liked them, and he was hitting him at will with hard rights and uppercuts. It was only seconds before the poor guy went down.

"Now there's a real fighter," my father said. "You know his eyes turn red before a fight? *Red.* I kid you not. You can bet your bottom dollar he'll be a champion soon." He rose from his stool. "Give me another beer. For that matter, let me have two."

"For you and who else?"

"Me and myself."

"If you're thinking about bringing them out to those boys, you better think again."

Of late, my father had begun carrying his cash with a money clip, with a thick wad of one-dollar bills folded inside a twenty, two tens and a five. At a glance it looked like he was a wealthy man. He peeled a few ones from the middle and tossed them on the bar.

"I'm thirsty," he said. "You got a problem with that, I can take my business down the street."

"Don't go getting hot under the collar. It's your ass if there's trouble."

My father gave him a glare to match Roberto Duran's.

"Bobby," the bartender said. "Get me some ice."

There were no customers to speak of, no real need for more ice, but the bartender didn't like to see me standing around, particularly when my father was intimidating him. He'd once given me a bit of advice: "Even if you have nothing to do, you want to look busy." But, by his own words, he was more worried about *his* ass than my father's for giving beer to minors, or my own for not looking busy, which for the most part was well protected by my lowly rank as bar back, my youth and literally by the thick padding of my over-sized shirt.

The ice machine was in the kitchen back of the diner, and by the time I returned with a bucket of crushed ice my father had left his stool. I went about my rounds several minutes later, carrying with me another smaller bucket into which I dumped the ashtrays, and sure enough I found him with the two young men. They were bowling on lane twenty-four, one lane shy of the farthest from the lounge, and several away from the next nearest group of bowlers—a quiet, serious bunch with custom bowling balls, custom leather cases, with all but one wearing wrist braces. They were, in my estimation, either professionals or those who badly wanted to be.

What I witnessed came in glimpses and snatches of conversation, for I couldn't very well just stand around and watch them all night. My father's plan, however, was apparent enough; that is, I didn't have to hang around long to know what he was up to. After he'd endeared himself by bringing them the beer, he asked if he could join them for a few frames.

"It's better than sitting around with that bartender," he said. "I can see with one eye closed that you're both men enough to handle a couple beers, especially you." He nodded at the marine. "You can vote, you can go to war and die for your country and then when it comes to having a cold one they treat you like a punk kid." My father held up his hand with the missing fingers. "Lost them in 'Nam on my second tour. Machine-gun fire. I'm not much of a bowler anymore, but it's the fun that counts."

I went about my chores then, and when I passed by again I saw that he had on a pair of bowling shoes and that he'd also bought them another round. The score on the overhead projector showed that he was a solid thirty points behind. Lots of gutters. I picked up their empty bottles, but my father made no attempt to introduce me, and I sensed that he'd rather I made myself scarce. It was his turn to bowl. He stepped up to the line, took his sweet time aiming and let it go. The ball veered to the left at the last moment, so only a few pins went down. He made out like he was disgusted with himself. Like he'd really had it.

"That's it for me. I better stick to what I do best and that's drinking."

But they'd already had a couple by now, maybe a few before they even got here.

"We'll get the next round."

My father sat down on the bench and began unlacing his bowling shoes.

"I couldn't do that."

"Why not?"

"You boys work too hard for your money."

"Hell, you bought us."

"Tell you what," he said, "seeing as how you both aim to please, let's roll for it. One time and I'll be on my way."

They took the bait, and though my father was no bowler his skills improved remarkably after he lost for the first and second beers and switched the bets to money. I came back around an hour later toward the end of my shift, and he had both of them so tense that they couldn't have rolled a strike if the pins were twenty feet away. He won something like eighty dollars that night, all the while clucking his tongue and wagging his head like he just couldn't believe his own good fortune.

"Beginner's luck," he kept saying as the two young men found themselves deeper and deeper in the hole. And the deeper they got, of course, the more desperately they tried to pull themselves out.

Where they became reckless, my father found control. I remember, sadly, seeing the guy with the grease-stained hands opening his wallet and finding it empty. The finger on one was black where he'd lost a nail.

If my father had been a professional ringer none of it might've worked. Because these guys, though drunk, weren't complete pushovers. Because my father really didn't know the first thing about bowling, his act was no act, the performance nothing less than authentic, nothing less than a cool head and the need to make some money.

At least he had the courtesy to buy them another round before I clocked out.

"Hey," he said, as we were walking back to the hotel. "How about some breakfast? Steak and eggs. On me. I put in a few hours myself tonight."

"That wasn't work."

"I won it fair and square. Those boys were egging me on."

"Sure," I said.

That last image of the one guy looking into his empty wallet bugged me, and I told him so.

"It was his choice," he said. "It's yours, too, if you want to buy your own breakfast."

I'd put a damper on his mood, but I didn't like seeing him so full of himself. After a while, however, as we continued down the street with our shoulders hunched against the cold and our breath visible in the air, I looked at it from his point of view and decided to let him foot the bill for a change. We stopped at Denny's and had the Early Bird Special.

That morning we went to the florist, where he dropped thirty dollars of his winnings on a dozen long-stemmed roses. The card he left blank but the message, as sentiment, was clear enough. It was all part of a larger plan: working from the inside out.

You don't send flowers to a married woman without causing just a slight touch of commotion.

He wagered and lost as much as he won at Fanny's Bowl and Dine. But somehow or another his money clip, silver plated and inlaid with a large fake diamond, always seemed loaded with cash. And he had no reservations about flashing it around, either. It was a ritual of sorts, the easy way he sidled up to the bar and slipped it out of his pocket, licked his thumb and proceeded to count off the bills. On occasion, if he'd had a particularly good night, he bought the whole bar a round, and in a moment of glory raised his glass of whiskey and saluted them all. For a man without a regular nine-to-five job, he seemed to do fairly well for himself, or at least he gave the appearance of it. I rarely questioned his affairs, because I knew he'd snap at me if I did, and also because I really didn't *want* to know who he'd taken and for how much, or if it was the other way around. Money came too hard for me to encourage or condone his gambling.

He played pool, and though he wasn't what you'd call a shark, it never stopped him from trying. He bet on hockey. He bet on football. He bet on baseball and basketball and the fights, for which he generally lost his shirt by picking the white guy. It was an act of foolish bigotry—a throwback to his Irish and English heritage—suffused with stubborn wishful thinking. Dwayne Washington struggled to educate him.

"When are you going to learn, Floyd? White guys can't fight."

"Tell that to Marciano."

"Marciano's dead."

"Benny Leonard."

"That was back in the Stone Age."

"LaMotta then," my father said. "Carmen Basilio."

Dwayne waved his hand, dismissing him.

"The Sugar gave those guys boxing lessons. Besides," Dwayne said, "you're talking old Italians and dead men. Who's out there now? Nobody. If you have to bet, bet with your *mind*, go with the odds. I'm tired of seeing people taking money you owe me."

That just irritated my father more, and made him bet more heavily on the fair-skinned underdogs, as if the more he wagered the better the chance of their winning.

My father set up office at his favorite table at the back of the lounge under the Olympia waterfall sign, where he and Melinda normally drank on Tuesday or Thursday nights when she was supposed to be at Sander's School of Law. The public phone and the cigarette machine were both within arm's reach, and he could, if he chose, either make a call to his bookie or take one. If he wasn't at his table he was perched on a stool at the bar, staring at the TV and trying to coax some poor soul to bet on whatever game happened to be playing. And if he wasn't around when I came on my shift, or by the time I left it at the end of the night, I could reasonably assume that he'd been there sometime during the day, and if I wanted to confirm it all I had to do was ask one of the bartenders. It's my opinion that if I hadn't taken the job at Fanny's Bowl and Dine that my father might not have spent so much time there, for typically when he owed someone money, as in the case of Dwayne Washington, he preferred to make himself scarce.

My presence, if only in spirit on my days off, justified his own. If one of the cocktail waitresses took it upon herself to ask him why he hung around so much, he'd say that he was "supervising" his son. Keeping the boy on his toes. It was a weak excuse at best, but then my father was a particularly handsome and well-groomed man; he always left generous tips, he had a bright smile, a fair sense of humor, and if any of the employees outside of Rick, the bartender, considered him a nuisance, he was a tolerable one. But Fanny Pringle had more at stake. Having my father underfoot all day and often into the night didn't exactly further the image of bowling as good, clean family fun, especially when he hit on one of her more sensitive customers.

I also think that she felt sorry for him and myself, seeing as how he was an ex-con without a job, and seeing as how the ex-con's son had taken up the slack of his father's laziness, or lack of opportunity. Or maybe it's not that complicated. Maybe a few customers complained about him, and rather than start a small war by showing my father permanently out the door, she thought it wiser to make use of his varied talents. It's also possible that her intentions weren't altogether altruistic, and that, like my father sending a dozen red roses to Melinda, she too had a plan with ulterior motives. She seemed to have taken extra time with herself in the dresser mirror, with a little extra makeup and perfume, the evening that she paid my father a visit at his office under the Olympia waterfall. Her timing was poor, or good, depending on how you looked at it. It was fight night, and Muhammad Ali, or Cassius Clay as my father called him, for he considered this fairly recent name change unpatriotic and adamantly refused to acknowledge it, was hot on the comeback trail. He'd been stripped of his title a few years earlier for not submitting to the draft, or to use my father's words, "ducking it." Tonight he was fighting hard-punching Jerry Quarry, another great white hope, and a strong one.

The office phone rang before Fanny could take her seat. She picked it up, since she was the closest. The expression on her face was stolid.

"It's for you," she said.

My father feigned surprise. He tapped a finger on his chest.

"Me?"

"If you're Floyd," she said. "It's some guy named Roy. I believe he works out of his newsstand."

My father turned his back to her when he answered it, shielded the receiver with his shoulder and spoke in a low voice. I was hauling a case of beer in from the coolers at the time, helping stock the bar for the big fight, and even if I couldn't hear what he said any better than Fanny, it was obviously shady business. The conversation lasted only a few seconds.

"So what're the odds?" she said.

"On what?"

"The fight. I hope you put your money on Ali," she said. "That boy's fast and I'd hate to see you lose your last bet here."

The cocktail waitress arrived then, with drinks for the both of them, and for my father's part it must have been a welcome distraction. The moment was an embarrassing one, and there was nothing he could do but smile awkwardly and fumble for his cigarettes. Fanny reached for his Zippo lighter and lit it for him.

"It's just a warning," she said. "Don't take it personally. I know you're going through some rough times adjusting, a man on the rebound. I understand you're a jack-of-all-trades."

I left then, so what was said thereafter I know nothing about. But when I came back Fanny was gone and Melinda had taken her place. I don't know if their paths had crossed, but I suspect that they had. I overheard her use the term "old bitch," and if my guess is correct, and I'm confident that it was, it was in reference to Fanny. Melinda looked up about that same time and caught me staring at her from across the bar, at her stocking legs under the table, those wonderfully long, beautifully shaped legs. She smiled and waved to me. But I made out like I was busy, like I didn't notice.

They stayed for two drinks, and before the fight crowd wandered in and it got too noisy, I heard her express some doubt about Sander's School of Law. "You wouldn't believe the pompous jerks I have to deal with," she said. "Bo wants me to stick it out though. He's got this thing about quitters and losers and finishing what you start." Although my father more than shared her disillusionment, to the point where I think, he would have liked to shoot Bo, I seldom heard him speak poorly of the man—to Melinda, that is. By leaning over the table and gently taking her hand in his, he showed compassion, sympathy and affection for her plight without making himself look like the bad guy. It was one thing to criticize your own spouse but an altogether different matter when someone else did. My father had courted many married women before Melinda ever came along, and he knew from experience that it was best to keep your mouth shut in matters such as these. Progress was coming along fast enough without him forcing it.

Until now their Tuesday or Thursday night rendezvous ended at the same time that Melinda would've gotten out of class. My father had advanced from simply going up to the bar after she left to walking her out to the parking lot, where if I wanted I could spy them kissing, long and passionately, before she broke away, slipped into her car and drove home with her schoolbooks resting neatly, and unopened, on the seat beside her. But tonight, when my father accompanied her to the parking lot, he didn't return to the bar. That in itself wouldn't have been unusual, except that Ali was fighting Quarry, the preliminary bout had just ended, and he had money riding on the big one. Also, and just as importantly in this instance, he wanted what ninety percent of the others at Fanny's wanted, if not most of the state of Washington: to see young Ali get his comeuppance, to watch Jerry Quarry beat some humility into the man that my father referred to, without the least bit of compunction, as a "loud-mouth nigger who believed the world owed him."

I clocked out at twelve.

It was a short, cold walk back to the hotel. The sidewalk was icy, but the days were growing warmer and longer now, a thaw was in the air and I welcomed it. My night had been a busy one, and I looked forward to getting home, climbing under the blankets and sleeping. But at the door, as I stood in the hallway and felt through my pocket for my key, I heard Melinda and my father making love.

If she'd held off until now, if seeing my father with Fanny had made her just jealous enough to ignore the risks involved, she finally gave herself over to him that night. To my knowledge, it was the first time since their encounter on the Willamette River. I don't know if my father was any great lover—I'm sure he liked to see himself that way, but he knew how to please Melinda. There was no argument about that. She was moaning like I've never since heard a woman moan. Deep and consistent, no holding back. The Murphy bed bumped steadily against the wall, the rhythm at times fast, then slow, very slow, the long, even pace of lovers working in tandem. From there it progressed, from moaning to words, with the language becoming increasingly more bold. It was only a word or two at first, then it grew into full pornographic sentences, whispers hardly audible unless you had your ear pressed to the door, as I did.

Melinda had a genuine talent for describing the act of love with lurid and sensual precision, and I found myself highly aroused. I listened until I didn't think I could take any more, then I left and bought a hamburger, just to kill some time and collect myself. I gave them well over an hour, but when I returned they were still at it, stronger than ever. If there was anything remarkable about their lovemaking, it was their endurance and appetite. I didn't get to sleep until early that morning, when Melinda finally left.

She passed me in the hall on her way to the elevator as she was fumbling through her purse for a brush. Her lips looked swollen, around her mouth the skin was slightly chafed, pink, and she hadn't done a great job of tucking in her blouse. If she was embarrassed, she didn't let on, but nonetheless it was an awkward moment for both of us.

"Just get off work?" she said.

"Yeah, a few hours ago."

She jabbed the call button, then pulled the brush through her hair.

"What time is it?"

"A little after two," I said.

At this hour the elevator was not in great demand, and soon enough it came clamoring up the shaft. Melinda stepped inside, and just before the doors closed between us I called out to her.

"Don't forget to tuck in your blouse. It's not in on the side."

The doors clanged shut.

When I returned to the room, my father was quick to apologize. He knew I'd been waiting on them.

"If I'd known what was going to happen," he said, "I would've warned you."

What good that would've done, I hadn't the slightest, for it wasn't as if I had another place to go. But I was too tired to question his logic, let alone argue, so I let the matter slide.

"Forget it."

"Don't be mad."

"I'm not mad," I said. "Just turn off the lights."

I undressed and slipped into bed. The sheets smelled faintly of Melinda's sex and her perfume, and I thought of myself in my father's place. I thought of Melinda and how it would be.

"Who won the fight?"

I answered him with spite in my voice, hoping to irritate him.

"Ali."

"Is that so?"

"He sliced him all up," I said.

"What round?"

"The third."

My father turned off the light and climbed into bed. He fluffed his pillow up and crossed his hands behind his head.

"You ought to be proud of your old man. I bet it on the nigger this time. KO by the fifth, with a two-round spread. We're a hundred bucks up. What do you think of that?"

But for once I didn't think of the money. I thought instead of the roses and the commotion they must've caused if she hadn't gotten rid of them fast enough, or if Bo was the one who had happened to answer the door. I thought of Melinda, arriving home soon, and wondered if she had a decent alibi. I wondered if he'd believe it. I wondered if she even cared.

I rolled over onto my back.

"What's going to happen?"

"With what?"

"Melinda and Bo."

"That's their business," he said.

"Ever wonder if maybe they're better off together?" I said. "Ever think maybe you ought to just leave them alone?"

"Bobby, you don't know the first thing about it. Now hush, I need my rest. Your boss wants me to bid on a job tomorrow. A real job. No pushing a broom. I don't mean to slight you by that," he said, "because I'm proud of you working. Working hard." He turned over and kissed me on the cheek, and I remembered that kiss as a sign of hope, as one of change for the better, and a brief sense of comfort came over me.

Outside, while I lay there with my eyes open, I heard the distant sound of a foghorn as a steamer arrived into port. The old man in the room next to ours began to cough, a raspy cough full of phlegm, congestion and abuse. None of it bothered my father though. He was snoring already, steadily and deeply.

I pressed my face to the pillow and inhaled the scent of Melinda's glorious sex.

Ten

ONCE I SAW my father break down and cry, right at the kitchen table over pepperoni pizza, on the anniversary of his brother's death. "Beautiful, beautiful Luke," he called him. "I wish you two could've met. He was something, Bobby. Something special. Something dear." Luke had passed from this world by way of a car wreck the summer he graduated from high school, with my father, two years his junior, seated behind the wheel. "I didn't get a scratch," he said, "not a goddamn scratch. Why's the Lord take one and leave another? I don't understand. I never will, long as I live." The memory of Luke persisted over the years—"not a day passes," my father told me, "when I don't think about him"—and for me he existed as a kind of ghost in the form of dimly lighted pictures from tales of their past, secondhand impressions of fortune and misfortune, of place, of sight, smell and sound.

As for my father's sister, Mary Ann, he hardly spoke of her, and as for their parents, I knew little about them other than that old man Barlow was a big drinker who at one point in his career had raised and slaughtered turkeys for a living. They had a ranch in Shasta County just above Redding, California, where the land was flat, and where in the summer it could get as hot as a hundred and ten. I understand that old man Barlow beat my father for the smallest mistakes, say, spilling a glass of milk at the dinner table, or not addressing him as sir, or not addressing him with it quickly enough, but that he never laid a hand on Luke Junior or Mary Ann. And Mrs. Barlow, a firm believer in the rod herself, must've also felt threatened by this turkey farmer and never interfered with his harsh, bogus methods of discipline.

With Luke as the eldest and Mary Ann eleven months his junior, my father was the runt, as he put it, "and the runt, he's got to be the toughest to survive." Mr. Barlow favored Luke, and I'm guessing that it had something to do with him being the first, and because he excelled at just about everything he did. I'm guessing, too, that the old man liked to imagine himself as his eldest: a top quarterback in high school, a regular honor student and popular around town with the girls. And I'm guessing that he liked to take credit for Luke's accomplishments, when in fact, in terms of character and temperament, he had more in common with his youngest, who did not do so good at school, who was not any kind of athlete outside of fighting and who, like himself, enjoyed drinking at an early age. But it's no guess that he held my father responsible for the death of Luke Barlow, accident though it was. "We're driving back from a dance," my father told me, "and this pickup, no headlights, nothing, comes out of nowhere. I swerve and there's this telephone pole. That's all, that's it. The other guy just keeps going." And in a sense, I thought, he was still going, only that other guy was partly inside my father now, him and the ghost of his brother. For his own father, from what he'd told me, had made his life so miserable after Luke's death that he had no choice but to pack up and go his own way at the tender age of seventeen—an event as sudden and blind as the accident itself.

My father talked most about Luke and their days on the ranch when he drank whiskey. Beer didn't seem to have quite the same effect. After a few shots, or highballs as he called them, he'd lean back in his chair, smile and say, "Bobby, did

I ever tell you about the time . . ." Usually he had, but unless I was mad at him about something I'd play along. It seemed the least I could do, and after so many tellings his stories became mine. I imagined them in my own way, supplying details where the details were thin, twisting what I thought was fact with what I suspected was fiction, and in the end recreating something of a world apart from my father's.

His favorite always began several weeks before the annual slaughter. He and Luke had to camp out on opposite sides of the turkey pen, on pallets of canvas and blankets. "The smell was so damn bad you couldn't hardly hold down dinner. Sleep," he said, "hell, that was for our old man and the turkeys. Luke and I took walks to get away from it." I pictured them, my father at around my age, walking together along a dirt road lit by the moon. In the background, beyond the turkey pen, was the place they called their home—a shack of a house with no windows, no foundation, running water or electricity. These details came from an earlier rendering, and they suggested to me that unless it was raining, camping out with the turkeys wasn't much rougher than sleeping in the house. I suspect, too, that if Luke and my father were as close as he made them out to be, that it was because of occasions like these—two young men alone in the darkness, with the stars above and the stink of the turkeys downwind.

"There was a creek," he told me, "at the edge of our property and we'd sit there and talk and when we ran out of things to say we'd just listen to the water. I looked up to my brother. I looked up to him in a big, big way. He was more my father than the son of a bitch who went by that name."

They talked about the old man and shared their anger. They talked about their mother and her silence in matters where she should've had a voice. They talked about their sister, their futures, everything about sports, and they talked in greatest detail about girls and the mysteries of sex. "Luke knew it all," my father said. "I had the general idea, but I didn't know exactly how you went about it. I worried myself silly thinking there was something wrong with me, because it stuck up in the air when I thought it was supposed to go straight. For the life of me, I didn't know how you got in from that angle. Luke enlightened me, but not before he had himself a good long laugh."

Eventually they had to return to their pallets and try and get some sleep, for they both had school the next day, or more work around the ranch. "It was worst in the summer," my father said. "The stink of the birds, the dust off the ground, the dust off the feathers. It caught in your nose, it caught in your throat, it got in your eyes, it *burned*."

Despite the constant gobbling, the stench of dung and my father's general sense of derision for turkeys as a species beyond stupidity, he found solace in those evenings with his brother. I'd venture that they came to think of the turkeys as if they were their own, protecting them from harm, from coyotes and foxes, harsh weather and themselves. The turkeys, for all their ridiculousness, became a source of love and hate for my father and Luke.

As for myself, I had no real sense of family history, including the whereabouts of my mother or if she was even alive. Whenever I mentioned her, he'd say that he didn't know, though he had no reason to believe otherwise. He'd also add that "She was a good woman, the best. We were just too young and she just didn't know what she wanted. Wherever she is, I hope she's doing well."

I believe that the past informs the future. But without one it's all speculation. It seems as foolish now as it did back then, when the thought first occurred to me. To expect form without history, character without future.

To hope, that is, that there's any legacy beyond the self.

My father bought a dead man's tools in a garage sale advertised in the local *Penny Saver*. It was one of those green

colored tabloids that listed all kinds of ads, from used refriger-
ators to pet alligators, and in no particular order. He picked it
up in the lobby of the Royal Arms, where you could also find
copies of yesterday's newspaper, or last month's edition of
Life, its glossy cover dulled from handling, the pages crimped
at the corners. We took the bus to the garage sale the following Saturday morning, but we got off too soon. My father mis-
read the map and we had to walk the last couple miles.

The tools were old and rusty, but the price was right. As
we got closer to the house, paper plates with arrows drawn
on them, arrows pointing us in the right direction, began ap-
pearing on the telephone poles. Cardboard signs stapled to
wooden stakes and driven into the ground were posted up
and down the block. ESTATE SALE, they read. ABSOLUTELY EV-
ERYTHING GOES. Cars were parked all along the street and
there were people swarming over the front lawn, which was
yellowed and close to dead.

Until that morning the word *estate* had, for me, conjured
up pictures of mansions situated on green rolling hills and
surrounded by tall fences and trees. I think that my father
held a similar notion, for as we approached from down the
block I sensed disappointment in his voice and a slight hesitation in his step.

"This isn't exactly what I expected," he said, "but let's
check it out anyway. You never know."

The dead man's house was small and in disrepair, and it
was located in a neighborhood that had seen better days.
Some of the wares were on display in the driveway. Some
things, like the dinette set for four, a perfectly made double
bed with the frame and a Laz-E-Boy chair, had been carried
out and set on the front lawn. An extension cord ran from the
living room window out to the table lamps, so you could
check them for yourself. One lady sat herself down in the Laz-
E-Boy and leaned back to make sure the footrest came up. It
took some effort. It made a harsh whine before it worked.

The dead man's son took notice and stepped forward.

"Just needs a little oil. I bought it for my father last year." He paused, as if the memory hurt. "By then he couldn't use it much, the cancer had taken its toll. That chair's good as new."

You could see that wasn't true. There was a tear in the vinyl armrest, a spot of rust on the inside of one of the hinges, and the seat looked pretty well broken in.

"What do you want for it?" the woman said.

"It cost me two hundred," he said. "But I'll let it go for one."

"I'll give you fifty," she said.

"It was my father's chair, ma'am. Out of respect I'd rather *give* it to some poor person than throw it away for fifty bucks."

"Seventy-five."

He took her aside in confidence.

"I'll let you have it for eighty-five if you don't tell my wife." He glanced at a tired-looking woman sitting on the porch. "I promised I wouldn't part with it for less than a hundred. We'd keep it ourselves if we had the room."

They made the deal, and it about sickened me, the way this man carried on with his line of bullshit. About that time he saw my father eyeing the tools all spread out on a drop cloth in the driveway. He wandered over to us. There were old dull handsaws, a couple twenty-ounce framing hammers, one sixteen-ounce, a beat-up chalkbox, an antique door level made of wood. A plumb bob. A cat's paw. A pair of tin snips, a bunch of other tools and a T square, too, but so rusted you could hardly read the numbers. The man sidled up to my father.

"That's American steel in those tools," he said, "not that Jap tin they send over now."

"How much you asking?"

"A hundred for the lot."

Seemed to me a hundred was this guy's favorite number. "That's steep."

"Clean 'em up a touch. Some steel wool, some elbow grease, and you could turn around and sell 'em for double your money."

"I'm not interested in selling them. I plan on using them, and if I was made of money I wouldn't be looking to buy a bunch of rusty old tools. I'm trying to get on my feet and make an honest dollar."

"I don't care how you get by," he said. "You want the tools or not?"

We ended up buying the lot for ninety dollars. To sweeten the deal, the man threw in a toolbox that resembled a small coffin. The perfect size, say, for a young child. It was made of pine, it had a hasp and lock in the middle, handles on both ends, and all the tools fit neatly inside the different compartments. Without it I don't know how we would've carried them home. They had to weigh well over a hundred pounds, and with my father lugging one end, myself the other, walking was awkward. The handles were made of canvas and they cut into my fingers. Every block I had to stop and switch hands.

"For Christ's sake," he said, "can't you hang on to it? I thought working would've toughened you up by now. We'll see that changes pretty quick."

It was his intent to teach me the trade of carpentry, and in so doing broaden my prospects for future employment. "You have to think ahead, Bobby," he said. "Or you might find yourself scrubbing toilets the rest of your life." There was more to my job than that, and I happened to like it except for the part he'd mentioned, but I didn't protest. Once you learned a trade, according to my father, you could go most anywhere in the country and find work that paid a decent wage. My training began at Fanny Pringle's house in the posh suburbs of Seattle shortly after we acquired the necessary tools.

She lived, as my father put it, in the neighborhood of "the money people." The homes were all large, the lawns and bushes well-manicured. They were custom-built houses, each one different, some with circular driveways, all with thick shake roofs. A few had miniature, cast-iron jockeys posted at their curbs, the arm extended, holding a brass plate with the house numbers inscribed on it. I felt odd walking down these streets, self-conscious and stiff, as if a cop might pull up behind us at any second and ask us our business. It was plain enough that we didn't fit in, and I found myself thinking that here was where the term *estate* seemed apt. "I believe I could get used to living here," my father said on one of our first trips to Fanny's house. But I doubted if the neighbors would've welcomed us into their community as anything other than its gardeners, carpenters or trashmen.

The days were growing longer and warmer; it was spring now and the trees were in bloom, and when we stepped into Fanny's house there was a certain coolness about it, with the high ceilings and the Mexican tile floor in the foyer. It didn't have any distinct smell that homes with families often do, except one of cleanliness, which was really an absence of smell. The furniture all looked brand-new, too. My father warned her that once we started working there would be plaster dust in the air, and she might want to put some drop cloths around. But Fanny wasn't concerned.

"Do what you have to," she said. "I'll take care of the rest."

She wanted her master bedroom enlarged. She wanted walnut paneling put up, a walk-in closet built and a new window looking out on her backyard. That was only the beginning. There were a host of minor improvements to add to her list—new fixtures, switches and outlets—none of which I saw any real need for, outside of change for the sake of change. Her bedroom alone was bigger than the hotel room that my father and I shared, and the house, with four bedrooms and three baths, could easily accommodate a family of eight or more. She was the only one living in the place, and since she spent so little time there the idea of knocking out walls and making a big house still bigger seemed to me eccentric. But I wasn't being paid to judge her. My role, as gofer and apprentice, was to do exactly as my father told me, and he didn't like to tell me twice. He was from the old school of watch and learn, and if my attention strayed in the least I could expect a swift cuff on the side of my head.

I think that Fanny would've given him the job whether he'd come in low on his bid or not, for over the course of the next few weeks I sensed that she was more interested in having my father underfoot than remodeling her bedroom. We kept running into unforeseen complications, which led to more labor and material costs. Anyone else might have fired us after the first few oversights—me, an apprentice who couldn't drive a nail straight, and my father, a self-proclaimed class A journeyman who hadn't planned for the unexpected, and occasionally the obvious. On our second day on the job, with the first wall that we tore into, we encountered a nest of colored wires. My father took it personally, as if his fellow tradesman had intentionally conspired against him.

"Of all the places to run his lines," he said as we stood there before the opened wall with chunks of plaster and sharp steel laths at our feet, "he had to run it here, the damn fool. Go get Fanny. This'll throw a kink in our schedule."

I went to the kitchen where she was busy making herself breakfast and brought her back. Fanny took the problem in stride, as she would others time and again. My father, with a serious look of concern on his face, explained the situation in agonizing detail, all the while gesturing with his hands as he pointed out the magnitude of the complications. There, in the ceiling, we'd have to put in a four-o junction box. Here, at the base of the floor, was where we'd have to cut and splice. This light would have to come out, this switch would have to go here. And there we'd need a fire block.

"Just do what you have to."

"I'm sorry," he said. "There's just no telling what you're up against until you get into it. It's the nature of remodeling."

But there was still more involved. Before we could continue we needed to rerun the wires, at least temporarily, so she'd have power until the job was done. My father put his hands on his waist, sighed and looked at the nest of wires.

"Trouble is, we'll need some Romex if we're going to keep going today, and I didn't figure that in my original bid."

That's all the urging it took. Fanny left the bedroom and returned a few moments later with her purse. She'd already advanced us the first week's wages, as well as money for the material, the bulk of which had been delivered by truck, and now she had to dip into the kitty again.

"How much do you need?"

"Twenty should cover it."

She gave him forty.

"Just in case," she said.

Then she dug deeper into her purse and pulled out a set of keys.

"Take the Chevy," she said. "It's in the garage. You may have to stop for gas on the way. It hasn't been run in a while."

Giving my father the keys to your car was tantamount to saying that you didn't care what happened to it. The likelihood of it coming back with a smashed fender or the engine burned up was considerable. Either she hadn't heard about Dwayne's Plymouth or she was taking a leap of faith, fully aware of the odds and still willing to gamble.

"We shouldn't be more than an hour," he said, closing his

hand around the keys. "I'll check the oil for you and gas it up on the way back."

It was a Chevy Impala in perfect condition, canary yellow with chrome piping on the sides, a really good-looking car, and a convertible no less. My father stopped and lowered the top as soon as we were out of sight of Fanny's house. "To make sure it works," he said. "You have to use these things or they get stiff." The fact was that he liked it with the top down, and so did I, for it was a wonderful spring morning, and the warm sun and the wind felt good on our faces. He stepped on the gas and we blew down an open stretch of road with the trees all in bloom and color whirling past us. The force of acceleration pulled me against the seat. He glanced in the rearview mirror to make sure that there weren't any police behind us, then he drew his fingers through his hair, rested his arm across the top of the seat and grinned. I didn't approve of the way he drove with one hand, his elbow perched on the window frame, and occasionally drifting over the line and jerking the wheel back.

"Talk about fringe benefits," he said. "A minute ago we were ripping out a wall and now we're cruising in a convertible. Hell, it's too nice a day to rush back and work."

The way he figured, by the time we picked up the Romex and returned to the house, it'd be too late to pull out the old wire and put in the new without Fanny losing her power for the night. "And you know she wouldn't want that," he said. "Check the glove compartment and see if there's some sunglasses." I did as he asked, and I found a pair of aviator style with a crack in one lens. Beside it was an old registration card made out to Maurice Pringle, who I assumed was Fanny's ex-husband.

I showed it to my father. He took one look, held it up to the wind and let it fly.

"It's five years old," he said. "No good to old Maury now."

Then he put on the sunglasses and turned onto the high-way. In town we found a self-service car wash and gave the Chevy a thorough scrubbing. Next we stopped at the Shell station and filled up the tank. By now, of course, it was al-most time for lunch, and seeing as how we had an hour or so to kill my father decided to take a spin past Melinda's place. I didn't think it was such a great idea, but as usual my opinion didn't count for a whole lot. I slouched in my seat and sighed, fully resigned to the fact that he'd have his way.

We cruised her neighborhood in the freshly washed and shining Chevy convertible, and as we drew closer to Me-linda's house my father eased his foot off the gas. Her Dodge was parked in the gravel driveway, and the living room drapes were open. Further up the block an old woman was watering her lawn.

"You see Bo's truck anywhere?"

"It could be in the garage. I say we just get back to work."

"Quit your bellyaching."

"You're asking for trouble," I said.

"There some law against driving? This some kind of pri-vate road?" He glanced from left to right just to irritate me and he succeeded. "I don't see any trespassing signs."

They were visible enough to me, though.

We went by Melinda's house and circled the block. The second time around we saw her pass through the living room in a pair of Levi cutoffs and T-shirt. She had a bottle of sham-poo in her hand, and her hair was wrapped in a towel like a turban. My father slowed to a crawl and tapped on the horn. Melinda came to the window, looking hesitant at first, looking cautious, but when she recognized us she smiled and shook her head in mock disapproval. We pulled into the drive-way, with the gravel snapping and ticking against the fend-ers of the car. A moment later the screen door swung open and she came outside, without the towel on her head. She drew a big pink comb through her hair and took her sweet time walking over to us. The comb caught on a snag and she winced.

"Let me guess," she said. "You finally settled up with Quality Life and you want to go for a little ride and celebrate again."

My father leaned back in his seat. He lifted his sunglasses up and peered out from under them.

"The way I remember it," he said, "it didn't take much coaxing."

"Is that so?"

"That's so."

He drummed his fingers on the steering wheel.

"Want to go for a quick spin or stay home and vacuum, do the dishes and mop the floors? I'll have you back in ten minutes."

"I heard that line before."

He slapped the side of his door. It made a hollow sound.

"This one's a loaner," he said, "compliments of Mrs. Fanny Pringle."

Briefly he explained the situation about his new job, the bedroom we were remodeling, about the wires. Melinda didn't take to it kindly.

"I'm sure she wants more than her bedroom worked on. You just keep your pants buckled, Floyd. I know how fast they come down."

"Baby," he said, "she's an old woman."

Until now I hadn't said a word, and except for tossing an occasional glance my way Melinda had yet to acknowledge me.

"We're supposed to be working," I said.

My father elbowed me in the ribs.

"Mr. Responsible here is getting crotchety in his old age. Be a gentleman," he told me. "Open the door for the lady and get in back."

I opened my door with a certain amount of reluctance, but

before I could get out Melinda hopped over my lap and slipped between us. She bumped her knee against mine and laughed.

"God, you've grown. Last time around you were just a squirt and now you take up half the seat. What're you feeding this boy, Floyd?"

"Whatever it is, it ain't enough. The kid eats like a damn horse."

As we headed down the street, the wind blew at our faces and lifted the scent of Melinda up and around us. It was the scent of Ivory soap, of the cream rinse in her hair, and the Juicy Fruit gum that she was chewing, now and then snapping it as she talked. She put her hand on my knee and squeezed it.

"So how you been?" she said. "We haven't had much of a chance to talk."

I don't remember ever feeling this tense around her before, and I don't know what happened. But I suddenly felt my face burning with embarrassment, and when I attempted to answer her, to say something as simple and brief as "Fine," I found myself at a complete loss. What came out was more like a squeak than anything vaguely resembling a one-syllable word. It never occurred to me that I was capable of making such a strange noise, and I was as much flustered as surprised by it. I immediately coughed into my hands, hoping to retrieve the sound in midair, or at least mask it as something remotely human. But it was too late. Melinda, whether she believed my act or not, played along with it by slapping me on the back.

I cleared my throat.

"I swallowed wrong," I said, proud that I'd managed to form three intelligible words. I coughed a few more times for general effect. Melinda drew the big pink comb through her hair again.

"We better get you something to drink before you go and

choke to death." To Melinda he added, "How you running for time?"

"Don't worry about it."

"When's he get home?"

"Not till three, and that's if he doesn't stop and get drunk with his buddies. I'm sick of trying to plan dinner. He's on his own, far as I'm concerned."

I estimated that we had three hours *maximum*, and that didn't seem like much of a cushion. By now, however, judging by the development of their relationship over the last several weeks, and how Melinda had jumped into the car with us today, I don't think she cared much one way or the other if he found out. For all involved, if it had been anyone other than Bo, it might've come as a relief. But I, for one, didn't trust the man and thought it best that my father maintain a low profile. Violence wasn't beyond either of them, and even if I respected my father's strength and boxing acumen, I feared that any confrontation might well escalate into, say, the use of guns, where considering Bo's line of work he'd have the obvious advantage, or ought to, and I didn't want to run any unnecessary risks when it concerned our safety, including Melinda's, whose role in this whole thing struck me as hardly worth dying over. I soon recovered full control of my voice, though I didn't use it to air my grievances, and nothing of any greater consequence occurred that afternoon.

We stopped at the A&W drive-in for burgers, fries and Cokes, and where, for the practical reason that there simply wasn't enough elbowroom to comfortably eat our lunch, I relegated myself to the backseat. From this vantage point, I could watch Melinda more or less undetected, and it struck me, as she was biting into her cheeseburger, how young she really looked. Her skin was extraordinarily smooth. Her eyes were large, the lashes long, and her lips were a soft shade of pink. Her hair, which now and then she ran her hand beneath and gently lifted from her shoulders, was long and fine and thick. The smallest of them, a swirl of soft blond, formed a faint widow's peak at the base of her forehead, under the line of darker hair, and except for a small pimple on the left side of her jaw her complexion was flawless. If I had to guess how old she was, I would've said twenty, or twenty-two at the most, and it occurred to me then how much closer she and I were in age than she was to my father. Melinda dabbed her napkin at a speck of mustard on the corner of her mouth.

After lunch we took a short drive through the country, and then we dropped her off at home, where she confirmed my earlier suspicions regarding her concern for secrecy by recklessly and passionately kissing my father in full view of the entire neighborhood, had anyone cared to watch. I acted as their self-appointed lookout, silently counting off the seconds while I checked up and down the block, half expecting Bo to come whipping around the corner at any moment in a police cruiser with his gun drawn. I made it up to twenty-eight, and that was counting slowly, before they parted and she climbed out of the convertible. My father remained still in his seat, watching the swing of her hips as she walked to the door, turned at the porch and waved good-bye to us. Then she disappeared inside.

"There," I said, "you happy? Now can we get back to work?"

He slammed the car into reverse.

"You know, Bobby, you're a real sensitive kid sometimes. We'd both be a whole lot better off if you kept that trap shut."

We bought the wire and returned to Fanny's in time to finish tearing out the inside portion of her bedroom wall, the one facing her backyard. She didn't ask why we were late, only if we'd had lunch, and when my father mentioned that he'd filled the tank and washed the car she told him that he could borrow it for the duration of the job. "To save time," she said, "to run your errands and stuff. It just sits there anyway. Someone may as well get some use out of it." Knowing my father, and if the first three days were any indication of our future progress, I expected that the job might now run far longer than she ever anticipated. Loaning him the Chevy, I thought, would serve less to save time than consume it, for it would provide him the means to take off when the urge struck. I considered warning Fanny about the wisdom of her generosity, but I kept my trap shut, as my father had advised earlier.

He drove me to the bowling alley late that afternoon, and on the way there he took stock of our recent good fortune.

"Hell of a nice woman, isn't she?"

"Yeah."

"Not so bad looking, either. How old you suppose she is?"

I shrugged, for it made little difference to me. Beyond thirty all adults seemed ancient.

"Late forties I'd say, even fifty. For some women," he added, "that's the prime of life." He reached over and slapped me on the knee. "I told you our luck was bound to change."

At the bowling alley, my father accompanied me inside. The time clock was located in back of the diner in the kitchen, and after I'd punched in, on my way out, I passed him sitting up at the counter. Dwayne was wiping it down with a dishrag. My father had ordered a beer and brought it into the diner.

"You'll be glad to know I'm an employed man now."

"Since when?"

"Since three, four days ago."

"They got you running numbers? Busting legs for the mob?"

"Between you and the boy here I'm knee high in smart asses. This is a real job," he said, "remodeling Fanny's bedroom."

"Who?"

"Fanny, your boss."

"You're doing what in her bedroom?"

"*Remodeling* it. You deaf or what?"

My father took the car keys from his pocket and tapped them against one of the glass sugar dispensers on the counter.

"She loaned me one of her cars, too, a sweet Chevy convertible," he said. "You ever need a lift, just give a holler."

Dwayne tossed the rag under the counter.

"I'd walk to hell and back before I'd catch a ride with you."

"I told you I'd fix that piece of junk when I got a few dollars ahead, and I meant it." To prove his earnestness, my father reached for his money clip, peeled off a twenty-dollar bill and tossed it on the counter. "Starting now you got no reason to be sore."

"You just don't get it, do you, Floyd? I don't give a shit about the money."

He stormed off into the kitchen.

"What's the hell's eating him?" my father said as I passed by. "My money not good enough for him?"

"You figure it."

It wasn't hard, I thought, and I had little sympathy. For I, too, felt that Fanny would be better off without the likes of my father.

I continued on my way.

The night was bound to be a big one, with teams coming in soon. The pro shop was already doing a lively business, and I had my first service call: "Porter to lane fourteen," the clerk at the main desk called through the P.A. system. "Bring a mop."

It was a real mess, all right. Of glass and beer. Two bottles' worth. But I was fast, I was thorough. That's what I was paid to be. I rose to my calling, as I had before and would again— as passionately as my father had risen to his.

eleven

I USED TO VISIT with Dwayne before his shift ended and before I came onto mine, but now that I was working with my father I rarely made it to the bowling alley with more than a couple minutes to spare, and half the time I was an hour or two late. Something was always delaying us, whether it was job related or just small talk between my father and Fanny while I was picking up our tools, wiping them down and putting them away for the day into the coffin-shaped box. Though he never came out and said it, my father felt that our work on Fanny's house was more important than my other job. He assumed that whatever time I lost I could make up by working faster, or a little later, and seeing as how we both shared the same boss and how Fanny was often responsible for my tardiness, being fired wasn't a concern.

The thing was, I didn't like rushing from one job to the next. I didn't like everybody knowing that I could punch in an hour late without the slightest fear of reprisal, where they'd catch hell for the same, regardless of the excuse. I also missed the time I used to spend with Dwayne. I missed the big double-patty cheeseburgers he made for me, the fresh fries heaped on the side and the tall glasses of Coke slick with beads of condensation. But most of all I missed our conversations, for when I had no one to talk to, or a gripe to air,

Dwayne was there to lend a sympathetic ear. Whatever the problem, he had a way of putting it into perspective, so that in the larger scheme of things my worries seemed a minor affair.

"You're still a kid," he'd say. "Don't take everything so seriously or you'll wind up with a heart attack. Then again, one of you has to look out for the other, and since your old man won't do the job I guess that leaves you."

Sometimes my father didn't come home at night, or he came home so late in the morning that it counted for the same thing. I figured he was out gambling, drinking, sleeping with Melinda or all three at various points in the night, and I knew better than to ask when he finally came back, dragging his ass, with his eyes beet red and complaining of a splitting headache. Until then I'd lay awake worrying, or else I'd turn on the light and whittle away the hours belaboring a crossword puzzle, which had become an obsession with me lately. I saved the ones from the paper. I bought crossword puzzle magazines, a good Webster's with over a hundred thousand entries, a dozen number two pencils and a sharpener. I was good at the puzzles and getting better fast with all the time I had to kill at night waiting up for my father. They took my mind off my worries, if only temporarily, but it was Dwayne who made the larger difference, and who when I expressed my concern the next day told me everything would be all right and I believed him. He had a certain distance on the situation, one that only age and experience could've provided, and then only in the event that you lived your life with your eyes at least half opened.

"I don't know about your father before Salem, but after three years in the joint he's got some catching up to do. It'll pass though, you watch," he'd say. "I know what he's going through and sooner or later we all wise up."

Or die, I thought. And I worried that the latter might come first.

Though they shared a criminal past, they seemed like opposites, and despite my bleak outlook for the future I relied on Dwayne's words for comfort and support. Unfortunately their last encounter at the diner had affected my relationship with them both, particularly Dwayne, as I felt, perhaps unjustly, that I had to choose sides. It wasn't so much what they'd said to each other as what they hadn't said—no truce was declared, no apologies spoken, no middle ground met—and I found it hard now, on the few occasions where I had the time to spare, to sit up at the counter and pretend like nothing had ever happened. Like nothing was wrong. I was embarrassed for my father, and in complete agreement with Dwayne—if anyone deserved the loan of a car it was him. But that was nothing more than a quibble compared to the real issues at hand, which had everything to do with how he felt about Fanny Pringle. I learned from one of the bartenders that he'd asked her out a half dozen times before my father ever happened along, and that she'd politely but firmly refused each and every overture. Dwayne, again according to the bartender, figured it was because he was mulatto, and he may well have been right, though I think it also had to do with his age. He had to be ten or twelve years older than Fanny, and if she planned to date again she may have preferred a younger man, or at least one her own age.

I don't know when he finally stopped asking her out, but I felt sorry for him. I thought they might've made a fine pair and I wished that Fanny would've accepted just once, if only to build his confidence, if only to give him the sense that it could still happen, if not with her then some other woman, that he still had it. He was getting up there in the years and could've used the companionship. My father had more than his share already in Melinda, and with Fanny it seemed like a theft of sorts, especially because I didn't trust that his interest in her was anything other than fleeting, while hers continued to grow. I still made my weekly installments to Dwayne, and he still took them, thanking me every time. But it wasn't the same between us. Not after they'd argued. Not after I knew that he was jealous of my father, or if not jealous, he was at least made more aware of his own powerlessness in terms of color, age and the status of ex-con. He had left the twenty dollars on the counter.

"Hell with you then," my father had said, and the cash found its way back into his pocket.

Although he boasted of being a regular jack-of-all-trades, a real first-class journeyman, his skills as a carpenter were questionable, and there were days on the job when I wondered if he knew what the hell he was doing. But I kept my observations to myself, seeing as how he wasn't likely to take kindly to them, and I helped him pull nails and pound them, tear out flooring and plaster walls, dig a narrow ditch for the foundation and set the forms in place to pour the concrete. Meanwhile Fanny began preparing us elaborate lunches, sandwiches, mostly, from a variety of breads cut into small triangles filled with generous portions of the finest cuts of meats and held together with decorative toothpicks. She put out cans of olives, sardines and smoked oysters, fresh fruit, boiled shrimp and odd-tasting imported cheeses. The list went on.

Lunches like these took quite a while to eat, and she wouldn't hear of us rushing. She had a habit of refilling my father's coffee cup whenever it dropped below the halfway mark, and loading up our plates with the small triangular sandwiches before we had a chance to polish off the first batch.

"I don't want it going to waste," she'd say.

Willingly, I obliged.

"The boy can still put it away," he said. "He's growing up, I'm just growing fat."

Fanny laughed.

"You could use a few pounds yourself. I know how it is with bachelors. Eating on the run."

After an hour or more, when it seemed high time for us to get back to work, and my father made a motion to stand, she often put her hand on his shoulder and held him to his seat.

"Sit down," she said. "There's dessert coming."

There was always dessert, and Fanny prepared them as elaborately as she did her lunches, and when we'd finished neither of us wanted to do anything but sit there like lumps. So more coffee was in order. But first she had to brew another pot. Then it was time for my father's after meal cigarette. I learned more about fine food and the art of procrastination while we worked for Fanny Pringle than I ever did about carpentry. And none of this included the snacks on our breaks, which at her prodding we took at ten in the morning and again at three. I must've put on five pounds in half as many weeks. My father said I looked beefier, stronger, and attributed it to my swinging a hammer, wielding a wrecking bar and digging ditch.

"Keep working with me," he said, "and nobody'll pick on you."

Another time she went all out and served us drinks in pineapples hollowed out in the middle, with small umbrella toothpicks stuck in the top, the kind they serve in restaurants. My father had rum in his. Two of those and not much work got done that day, either.

She also gave him clothes, silk shirts and expensive slacks, and a pair of Florsheims that had never been worn. They belonged to her ex-husband, Maurice, or Maury the Weasel, as she called him. He'd run off with a younger woman, and in his haste for freedom left behind the larger part of his wardrobe.

Like the Chevy, Fanny felt that somebody ought to get some use out of it.

"What size shoe do you wear?"

"Why's that?"

"I might have something for you here."

"Nines," he told her.

She rummaged through some boxes, for all the things in her closet had to be taken out in order for us to widen it, and came up with the Florsheims. My father sat on the edge of her bed, this huge king-sized thing, and tried them on.

They fit perfectly.

"I don't know if they're your style, though."

"They're terrific," he said. "You sure he doesn't want them?"

"I wouldn't care if he did."

"I'd hate to cause any trouble."

"He doesn't have the guts to show his face around here anymore."

My father tested them out by walking around the room, rising to his tiptoes once, looking down at the shoes and smiling at what he saw. They really were a good pair, and to my knowledge the finest he'd ever owned. It progressed from there to the slacks, which were a couple inches too long. But they could be hemmed. Then it was the shirts, which fit a little tight across the chest but still looked sharp on him, and he was grateful to get them.

Between trying on clothes, the long lunches and conversations and the unforeseen trips to the hardware store, we were still able to get some work done. We poured the foundation one day and framed it up the next. Ideally, when we tore out the back wall we should've worked until we had the room enclosed again, so that Fanny didn't have to worry about someone just letting himself into her backyard and waltzing into the house, robbing her or worse. But it was a Thursday when we tore it out, the night that my father normally met with Melinda, and by five o'clock he was anxious to put away the tools and get on the road. Fanny was out somewhere, but she'd be coming home shortly, and no matter how understanding she may have been I had a feeling that she wouldn't appreciate us leaving the house unattended. It would've only taken another couple hours to get the plywood up.

I told my father that we should just do it and get it over with. He didn't think it was necessary.

"It's a safe neighborhood," he said. "There's no reason to sweat it."

I wasn't against the idea of leaving. I'd been ready for it since morning. The possibility of rain, however, was always an issue in Seattle, for it came and went on a moment's notice, and in a case like this it was only wise to be prepared. I'd seen some plastic tarps in the garage, and I suggested that we put them to use, as a kind of compromise.

He looked up at the sky.

"There's not a cloud in sight."

"You never can tell," I said. "We should tack them up anyway."

"How come you always expect the worst?"

"Maybe I'm used to it."

"So now you're feeling sorry for yourself?"

"I'm just stating a fact," I said.

He had no reply for that, but I did tack up the tarps, so that even if it didn't rain they'd at least act to break the wind. Though the days were sunny, it was still cold at night.

We were running late by then, and my father had to drop me off at the bowling alley first, which didn't settle well with him.

"If you see Melinda, you tell her why I'm late. It isn't my fault."

I'm sure Fanny knew about Melinda from having seen her and my father at the bowling alley, but if she was jealous or resentful she never let on. Maybe she thought that my father would, in the end, come to realize how much more she had to offer, at least by way of material things and financial security, and for a man his age, particularly in his situation, being an ex-con with a boy to raise up, that was certainly of some consideration. What she didn't realize, assuming my take on the matter was even partially accurate, was that he'd traveled a long way, in both miles and time, just to find Melinda, and now that he had he wasn't about to get serious with another woman.

While he headed back to the hotel that evening to shower and shave and put on some of the nice clothes that Fanny had given him, I began my shift. I made my rounds. It was a slow night, the slowest I'd seen. But that would change on Saturday, when Fanny's Bowl and Dine sponsored the Pacific West Brunswick Tournament Division Title III Eliminations, and from what Dwayne had told me it was an event to dread, with plenty of spilled beers, noise and chaos. Tonight, though, most of the lanes were empty and there were only a few diehards lingering in the bar, Dwayne among them, off shift, wearing his fedora and sipping a bourbon and seven.

"Where's your old man?" he called when he spotted me. I was bringing in a bucket of ice.

"He'll be around."

"I just want to know, so I can leave before he gets here. How you holding up?" he said. "I haven't seen you around lately."

"I've been busy. Working two jobs."

"Then I won't take it personally."

"Don't," I said.

"He paying you?"

"Yeah," I lied.

"Get it up front. Cash. No checks and hide it, too. Hide it good."

My father showed up about an hour later, wearing the Florsheims and a tailored white shirt, with a sport coat draped over his arm. In his free hand he held the daily racing form rolled into a tube, and from time to time, as he stood at the bar ordering drinks, he struck it against the palm of his other.

Melinda had arrived as well and taken a seat at his former place of business, the table under the Olympia waterfall. A Hank Williams song played on the jukebox. My father motioned to me with his chin, and when I walked over to him he tapped me on the shoulder with the racing form.

"Want to go to dinner?"

"I'm working."

"Take the night off. Fanny won't care. There's nobody here anyway."

Dwayne was still at the bar, sipping on another bourbon and seven. Up to this point he'd ignored my father, but now he leaned our way.

"For once in his life, your old man's right. You deserve a break," he said, "though I can't say the same for the playboy here."

"Playboy?"

"You heard me."

"I'll ignore it for the boy's sake."

"Ignore it for your own. He's nobody's fool."

"You're drunk," my father said. "There's no talking to a drunk."

"You ought to know."

"Don't push me, Dwayne. I don't want to have to get my nice new clothes all dirty on account of some lowlife like you."

Dwayne winked at me.

"Go on," he said. "Clock out before I have to teach your old man a lesson."

My father put his arm around me and walked me out of earshot. At the end of the bar he stopped and looked down at the floor as if he were thinking hard, and then, slowly, he looked back up at me. I stared at Melinda's legs from across the bar. They were crossed, and she was working her ankle around. She caught my eye and smiled. My father lowered his voice.

"I could use a loan," he said. "I'm a touch short on cash tonight."

"How much you need?"

"How much you got?"

"Twenty."

"Make it forty. I don't see how we can manage dinner on any less."

I reached for my wallet.

"Not *now*," he said. "That son of a bitch would never let me hear the end of it."

But it was too late. Dwayne was already wagging his head. There were a few crumpled bills and some change on the counter in front of him, and he scooped it up, slipped it into his pocket and with a tip of his hat to me he got on his way.

My father called to him before he passed through the door.

"Need a ride?"

It was less an offer than a last dig. Dwayne didn't miss a step.

We ate at the Red Onion off Interstate 5 that night, at a table overlooking the Puget Sound. My father and Melinda had a couple drinks before they ordered—steak, it was—cooked rare, or as my father told the waiter, "Just walk it through a warm kitchen." I had my usual, a cheeseburger and fries. The dinner conversation consisted mostly of small talk, not worthy of mention, but afterwards, when I was coming back from the bathroom, I overheard Melinda discussing Bo's sexual prowess, or rather his lack of it. In such matters, my ears picked up the least audible of voices. Whispering was useless when it involved sex, for it was a subject that fascinated me, and which even today, at the age of thirty, is only slightly less intriguing than it was back then. I was and still am an avid listener.

"The last time we made love," she said, "was about a month ago and then he lasted like a whole three minutes. And *that's* being generous. All he wants to do on weekends is sit around with his cop buddies and drink beer, watch football and goof off with their guns."

I would've like to remain at a distance and listened to more, but I couldn't very well just stop there in the middle of the restaurant, and besides, my father had spotted me. He rose from the table and paid the bill with the money I'd slipped to him earlier and that I didn't anticipate ever seeing again, whether he intended to pay it back or not.

In the parking lot, Melinda decided that we ought to go down to the beach, and as far as I was concerned it was a rotten idea. It was cold out, the wind off the water cut to the bone, but she slipped out of her high heels and insisted that my father and I remove our shoes, too.

"It's the only way to walk on the beach. You have to feel the sand squishing between your toes," she said. "I lived in Hawaii for eight months once and I almost never wore shoes."

Melinda dug the balls of her stocking feet into the sand as she walked, giving an exaggerated twist to her hips. She carried her shoes in one hand, and now and then she swung them in a big arc over her head. She was pretty drunk by this time.

"Take 'em off. Both of you."

"This isn't Hawaii," I said. "The weather's a tad cooler."

"It's all in your mind."

No, it was in my aching ears, my runny nose, my numb lips.

"The power of positive thinking," she said. "It could change your life."

My father slipped his arm around her waist.

"My life's fine."

"It can always get better. All you need is a little push."

And that's what she did, she pushed him, and then in one swift motion she dropped to her knees, grabbed his leg, tucked her shoulder into his hip and took him to the sand like a champion wrestler.

My father went down laughing.

She set to work on him. He put up half a fight.

"Careful," he said. "They're expensive. Real Florsheims."

But Melinda was quick, and despite my father's efforts she had them both off in no time. She laughed and tossed one to me.

I caught it.

"Run," she hollered.

"Where?"

"Just *go.*"

I turned then, and with the shoe tucked under my arm I took off down the beach. I expected him to give chase, but that wasn't the case, and after I'd run fifty or so yards I realized that the joke was on me. I was as much in the dark as they were now, and if only briefly I suddenly felt all turned around and more alone than I'd ever thought possible. It was all blackness except for the sliver of moon suspended high above the ocean, and my heart quickened. Somewhere down along the beach, I heard them—their laughter over the slap and rush of the waves. It gave me my bearings, it gave me a sense of direction.

I thought of the word *power*. I thought of a storm and how one might be brewing out to sea.

I thought of dark clouds.

Lightning. The works.

In the distance, I fixed on the lights in the windows of the Red Onion. A truck with a pair of yellow foglamps moved slowly through the parking lot.

Twelve

I FINALLY GOT an answer to the question I'd been wanting to ask Melinda since she ditched us that night three years before on the Willamette River. Whether I believed it or not is another matter. But there's no question that the ensuing events permanently altered all of our lives, both swiftly and radically, and that Bo, who for the last several months had hardly figured into the picture, suddenly stepped out of the shadows and announced his presence, his anger and frustration in what seemed the only way he knew how, that is, violently. Only this time around it was Melinda, not my father, who suffered the brunt of his rage. She showed up at our hotel room early the next morning wearing dark sunglasses and looking scared. I'd just rolled out of bed and hadn't had time yet to shake the sleep from my head. It was a hell of thing to wake up to, for her fear became mine the second I opened the door.

"Your dad here?"

"He's down the hall," I said. "Taking a shower."

"Mind if I come in?"

I stepped back and let her by, and she went to the window and looked out at the tar and gravel roof of the warehouse across the way, so that her back was to me. She had on a long wool coat, and she kept her arms wrapped around herself as if she were cold. I didn't know what to say or if there was anything to say. I wished that my father was there.

"You want me to go get him?"

"That's okay."

But a big part of me didn't want to be in that room with her.

"I'll be right back."

"Stay," she said.

The cooling unit on the warehouse kicked in and the even hum of the motor filled the room. Other than that, it seemed uncommonly still, uncommonly quiet. For a long while neither of us said anything. Then Melinda let out a kind of sad laugh.

"How do you guys sleep with that noise?"

"You get used to it," I said. "Pretty soon you don't even notice." I paused. "Does Bo know you're here?"

"No."

"You sure?"

"I'm sure."

I took a deep breath.

"Can I ask you something?"

"Depends."

"Where did you go that night on the Willamette?"

She drew her hand along the windowsill, as if she was debating whether or not she wanted to answer. She shifted her weight from one leg to the other.

"I didn't tell on your dad, if that's what you're getting at."

"It crossed my mind."

"Bo's a cop. Those guys stick together. They figured it out themselves."

"I'm sure you can come up with something better than that."

"Believe what you want. It's not like he didn't know about that spot. It's not like I hadn't been down that road before."

At that she turned around, and though I couldn't see her

eyes behind the sunglasses, I knew that she was trying to stare me down. I didn't look away, I didn't so much as flinch.

"It doesn't matter what I believe," I said, "I'm thinking about my father. I'm thinking how he doesn't need any more trouble."

"Maybe it's time you started thinking for yourself. If I remember correctly, it was a full moon. I bet you saw plenty."

I heard the key in the lock then, and my father came into the room with his hair slicked back wet and a towel over his shoulder, a razor and a tube of Crest in his hand. One look and he knew.

"Oh Jesus," he said.

He threw the stuff on the bed and went and put his arms around her. She rested her head on his shoulder and began to weep, but not loudly, no sobbing. No big dramatics. My father kept patting her gently on the back and saying, "Now, now. Now, now," over and over. Then he leaned away from her and reached for the sunglasses. She grabbed his wrist, but he made a cooing noise. "It's all right," he said. "It's all right." And she let him ease the sunglasses off. One eye was swollen, the skin around it a pale shade of purple. My father winced.

"I'll kill the bastard," he said. "I'll fuck that punk up good."

Then he turned on me.

"Get *out.*"

I couldn't remember the last time my father shouted at me like that, maybe never, and I think it was because he'd done it with such fury that it had the immediate effect on me that it did. I grabbed my jacket and made for the door with no intentions of arguing or coming back any time soon. I spent the morning hours walking the streets and wondering what he'd gotten us into and how he planned to get us out. I thought of the Luger. I thought of Bo Stenovich. I thought that my father might do something we'd all later regret, but I

didn't have any idea how to stop it. It's not like I could've
gone to the police. It's not like I could've gone to Bo, sat down
and had a heart-to-heart. Seemed there wasn't a whole lot I
could do, except hold tight and hope.

Two Mules for Sister Sarah was playing at the Bellevue, and
I bought a ticket when the box office opened and took a seat
in the back row. It wasn't so much that I wanted to see a
movie, though I idolized Clint Eastwood and enjoyed westerns in general, but I was beat from all my walking and worrying. The theater was dark and warm and I pulled my legs
up to my chest and locked my arms around them. I pretty
much had the place to myself, which was the way I preferred
it, particularly in my state of mind. Soon the curtains parted.
Soon the previews came on, and down the aisle next to me,
in the soft flickering light of the projector, I saw a young girl
in a white cotton dress with a sash tied loosely around her
waist. She had a little boy with her, her brother, I thought,
and they'd stopped to let their eyes adjust to the darkness.
The boy had hold of her hand. She leaned over and whispered in his ear and then pointed to a row of seats just ahead
of me. The light from the projector lit up her hair, caught the
hem of her skirt and behind it the shadow of her legs as she
led the boy down the aisle. I thought of Bonnie Walker. I
thought of the letter that I wrote but did not send. I pulled
my legs tight to my chest, and over the noise from the movie,
the cry of horses and the sound of gunfire, I imagined myself
sitting beside the strange girl. I had my arm around her shoulders and they felt warm and strong and every now and then
she saw something on the screen that amused her and she'd
laugh and lean into me.

I didn't pay much attention to the movie that afternoon,
and when it was over, before the houselights went up, I left
my seat, and without daring to look back at the girl I hurried
to the lobby. Outside I put my hands in my pockets and
walked some more. I stopped at an arcade and played pinball

for a couple hours and lost every game. I just couldn't concentrate. I just didn't give a damn. Toward evening, I returned to our hotel room, where I found my father sitting in the dark at the Formica table in the kitchenette.

He rested his elbows on the edge, with his hands cupped loosely together. A cigarette burned between his fingers. There was a six-pack on the table, two of the cans already crushed and empty, and beside them a portable radio that he'd bought off the streets a while back from an old man who needed a few dollars. It was probably stolen, like the gun. But it was a good radio. Late at night you could pick up stations far away as Kansas. Country played on it now. I didn't recognize the song.

"Hey," I said, "you okay?"

"Where you been?"

"Around."

"I'm sorry I hollered. C'mere," he said. "C'mere, sit down."

He looked away from me to the burning tip of his cigarette, and I knew from that gesture alone that he had news and it wasn't good. I felt my ears grow warm around the edges.

My father pulled a chair out for me.

"Have a beer," he said. "You're old enough. I had my first when I was fourteen. Boosted it from my old man. I suppose you're no angel either." He paused, looking at the tip of his cigarette again, looking tired, looking vulnerable, looking older in the fading light that fell from the window. "I've been thinking, Bobby. I've been thinking a lot lately and a boy your age needs a real home. He needs his own room and three square meals a day and I don't see it getting any better for us, not for a while anyway." He dropped his cigarette butt into an empty beer can, then picked it up and began to roll it between his hands. "You ought to be in school. You ought to be learning things instead of pounding nails and sweeping floors."

"I'm learning things," I said.

"Not the right things. I mean algebra and geometry. I mean books."

"I don't care about that stuff."

"Someday you will," he said.

"You did fine without school."

My father laughed softly. He kept rolling the can between his hands, pressing in on its sides, slowly crushing it. "I don't know from one day to the next what to think of myself anymore. But I do know I could've done better for you and your mother and somewhere along the line I got turned around and quit caring. Hard luck, too much hard luck, I suppose, and the more I got of it the less I cared and that's the way I feel now and it scares me. Sometimes," he said, as he continued to crush the beer can so that the sides now had completely collapsed, "sometimes I wake up at night and lay there and look at you and I say to myself how beautiful, how beautiful and how you got to go back."

"I got nothing to go back to," I told him. "This is my home."

"Look around. This is no home. You had a hell of lot more going for you in Portland," he said. "I can't do for you what a father should."

"You're a good father," I said.

"No," he said, "I'm not. I wish I was, Bobby, but I'm not."

"If you want, I'll go back to school. It's no big deal. I'll study hard."

My cheeks grew warm now and inside me I felt the tears wanting to come up. I'll be damned, though, if I'd let myself cry.

"I'm not leaving," I said. "That wasn't part of the deal."

"What deal?"

"You and me. We stick together."

"We never had any deal, and if we did I'm afraid I have to break it."

I drank my beer. I drank it fast, opened another and did the same.

"Whoa now," he said. "You'll be drunk off your ass in a minute you don't watch it."

And I hoped that he was right. I crossed my arms over my chest, adamant in my belief that I wouldn't leave under any circumstances, all the while knowing that I really had no choice in the matter. He rose from his chair, and as he came around the table to me he leaned slightly to one side, righted himself and grinned.

"Look at us. What a pair. What a couple of stumblebums. Don't know who's the drunker, you or me on a few lousy cans of beer. C'mere, stand up."

But I didn't want to stand up. I didn't want to do anything but see how quick I could down another beer and start on the next.

"Up," he said. "Up, up, up."

He pulled the table back and then I felt his arms slip under mine, lifting me, and as much as I wanted to hurt him, to hit him like he'd taught me, hard and fast and straight to the chin, I rested my head on his chest. I let him take his hands in mine and I let his feet guide us both across the cracked and yellowed linoleum floor in the kitchenette. Patsy Cline played on the portable radio that was probably stolen.

"Crazy," she sung, sweet and slow. "I'm crazy, crazy for . . ."

The last of the light had drained from the room, and we were in darkness now. But we danced, drunk, my father and I, and as my head spun I felt the warm harsh breath of his whisper in my ear.

"Tomorrow. Tomorrow morning, Bobby, I have to put you on the Greyhound."

Years have passed since my father took me to the bus station in Seattle, bought me a one-way ticket to Portland and made damn sure I boarded. I've since found myself in dozens of other Greyhound stations around the country and every one of them, without exception, has been located in a part of the city where, after your ride sees you off, he wants to rush back to his car before something happens to it. Every time I set foot in one now, I recall the day my father tried to desert me, and how, had he been successful, my life might have been different. As for his own, I don't think my presence would've had any major effect on him, for he tended to do as he pleased, with or without me. Whether he sent me off for his own selfish reasons, however, or if he truly had my best interests at heart is another one of those questions that remains unanswered.

Our parting wasn't as emotional as I'd anticipated. The worst of it occurred the night before, so that by the time we got to the station the next day I was pretty much cried out. I also felt terribly sick to my stomach, with this constant pounding in my head from the beer I'd drunk. It was my first hangover, and I made a personal vow then and there never to touch the stuff again, as the repercussions, in this instance anyway, clearly outweighed the benefits. Of course I didn't keep that vow, but at the time I couldn't have meant it more. I boarded the bus lugging the same old suitcase and backpack that I'd taken with me from Portland and found a window seat across from a Vietnamese family. My father followed me down the aisle.

"Call me when you get in," he said. "I'll be waiting on you."

I was silent.

"You be good now."

More silence.

He bent over to give me a kiss good-bye, but I pulled away.

"Cut the bullshit," I said. "You don't need me, I don't need you."

Those may have been hard words to part on, but that's how it had to happen. I believe that he knew it, too. I believe he understood that there was no other way I could handle the situation; it was either meanness, the pretense of it or cry. So he left then, and soon the doors closed, the driver put the engine into gear and we pulled away from the loading area, dipped down the driveway and onto the street. If my father had stood at the curb waving to me, I didn't see him. I didn't bother to look.

Interstate 5 was the route. The coast was on one side of the road, and tall pine lined much of the other. It was a beautiful drive, though I couldn't have cared less. For I was beside myself now, full of anger and sadness, full of a whole host of emotions I didn't then and still don't know how to describe very well. I didn't want to go back to Mrs. Watson, though, that I knew for sure, and this was assuming that she'd even take me in again, considering that I'd robbed her favorite son, lied to her and ran away. My father hadn't taken any of that into account. There was a strong possibility that the next people I'd see when I arrived in Portland, after Mrs. Watson, Todd and Bonnie, were the police. I sincerely doubted that it would work out differently, and before the hour was up I got to thinking that I might be making one hell of a big mistake. The state of Oregon wasn't likely to open its arms and welcome me back into the bosom of its social welfare system. If they extended any sort of greeting, it'd likely be to the Boys' Ranch, or a youth center—by any name, a prison.

The bus made a stop in Kelso, a few miles short of the Oregon border, and I gathered up my things and got off. I decided to give my father one more chance. I decided that if he couldn't appreciate or recognize my return as an undifferentiated sign of my love and loyalty, and respond accordingly, then I'd go my own way and it wouldn't be to Portland.

It was a big test, certainly one that could backfire, and I knew that if it did I might well end up drifting from one town to the next. But it was a risk I had to run, for it didn't seem to me that I had many options.

At a market I bought myself some Oscar Mayer bologna, the smallest jar of Miracle Whip that I could find and a loaf of sourdough, and then I walked down to the Columbia River and watched the water pass while I made a sandwich and ate it. I ate two. Despite my hangover, which was slowly easing off, I was starved, as my father and I had skipped both dinner and breakfast. When I was finished I lay back on the rocks along the riverbank, closed my eyes, listened to the rush of the water and thought how it would be if I could just stay here, no worries, no nothing, just the river and me. But those thoughts passed quickly, and if I planned to get back to Seattle before dark I knew I'd better get on my way. It might take a while to catch a ride, and the chances of it only got worse at night. I put the bread, the rest of the bologna and the Miracle Whip into my pack, grabbed my suitcase and headed up to the highway.

I stuck my thumb out. Cars, RVs, eighteen-wheelers and huge logging trucks hauling timber blew past as if I wasn't there, leaving me in the wake of their exhaust. Once I spotted the highway patrol coming down the road, and I thought I'd had it for sure. I even considered running, but he shot by without so much as a look. I suspect that I was a pitiful sight, hungover, wearing a raggedy coat and lugging a beat-up old suitcase. If the situation were reversed, I'm not sure I'd stop for me. But eventually this guy in a Ford Fairlane with California plates took heart and pulled to the shoulder of the road about fifty yards ahead of me, and I grabbed my things and hustled over to him. He rolled down the window and I looked in. He wore his hair pulled back into a ponytail and tied with a rubber band, and it looked like he hadn't shaved in a few days, or else he was trying to grow a beard. I don't think he was quite old enough for that, though. It was spotty in places, thick around his chin but still sparse on his cheeks.

"Where you headed?"

"Seattle."

"I'm passing through there," he said. "Throw your suitcase in back."

"Great," I said.

It was already packed clear to the rear window with camping gear, a duffle bag, blankets, a cardboard box of record albums and a mess of other stuff I couldn't readily identify. But I managed to find room. He swept some old hamburger wrappers and a Styrofoam cup off the front seat, and I slipped in beside him and we pulled back onto the road. I suppose I should've been worried, getting into a car with a stranger, but he seemed friendly enough. I needed the ride and I didn't give it much thought, despite my father's many warnings about hitchhiking, and hippies in particular.

"They're all hopheads," he'd told me. "That's a fact. You ever want to grow your hair long, let me know and I'll buy you a pretty dress."

And my father wasn't alone in his opinion. I'd heard the men at Fanny's Bowl and Dine express similar thoughts, but I could never understand the logic, even allowing for the exaggeration, of confusing a man for a woman because of the length of his hair. As for the term hophead, it dated my father and his generation and betrayed his ignorance of a drug that was probably a hell of a lot less harmful than the booze he poured into his body on a regular, often daily basis. I had the opportunity to sample it myself that afternoon and make my own judgment. We weren't on the road more than five minutes when Doug, for that was his name, felt around under his seat and pulled out a joint.

"You get high?"

"Sure," I said. "All the time."

"This is good shit."

I'd never tried it in my life, and I wouldn't have known good shit from bad shit, but I was curious, I was ready to give it a shot and I didn't want to sound stupid. He lit it up, took a long hit and passed it to me. I knew enough to inhale it but holding it in was no easy feat, and my first few tries I coughed it up.

"You sure you smoked before?"

"Yeah," I said.

"Take it in slow."

I did as he instructed, successfully several times, and then I waited for something to happen. But nothing did, or at least I wasn't aware of it. I felt perfectly fine, though I was suddenly hungry again.

"Want a sandwich?" I said.

"Got the munchies?"

"Huh?"

"You're hungry."

"Starved," I said. "And I just ate."

He looked at me with stoned, bloodshot eyes and grinned.

"It makes you hungry," he said. "I told you it was good shit."

He laughed and I made us some sandwiches out of the last of the bologna and we ate them. Then we finished off the bread with huge gobs of Miracle Whip smeared on it because we didn't have any water or anything else to drink, and it was hard swallowing otherwise. Doug asked me how long I'd been on the road, how long I'd been out there thumbing, why I was going to Seattle, what was there for me, and though I normally didn't talk to strangers about my problems I discovered myself running off at the mouth. I told him about how my father was trying to get rid of me. I told him how at this point I was technically a runaway, and how if the old man could just see me now, with him, smoking a joint and eating Miracle Whip sandwiches, he'd go straight up the roof.

"You're welcome to come with me."

"Where to?"

"Canada."

"Going camping?" I said, because of all the gear he had in back.

He laughed again.

"You really are stoned, or you're living in another world. There's a fucking war going on, man, and you're next in line."

Slow as I may have been, I understood what he meant now, and I'm positive that despite my father's dismal record for upholding the laws of this country he would've strongly disapproved of Doug's decision and thought of it as cowardly. But I felt a certain camaraderie with him, knowing that we were both fugitives of sorts, running from the government. I respectfully declined the offer, and when he let me off in Seattle I wished him well, he wished me the same, and that's the last I ever saw of Doug. I hope he did okay.

I hope he's fine.

Occasionally, when I light up, I still think about him.

My father had cleared out. I found the door to our room unlocked, the closet opened and empty except for a few hangers left on the pole. The Murphy bed was pushed back into the wall, the dresser drawers were pulled out and bare inside, and in my father's haste he'd left the morning paper scattered on the floor. I cursed him. I called him every name I could think of. Then the fear set in, a fear that started in the pit of my stomach and worked its way up, so that it felt as if someone had a hold of my windpipe, and for a while there I had trouble breathing. Relax, I told myself. Think. I hurried down to the street, caught the bus and got off a block from Fanny's Bowl and Dine.

The sign on the roof, a huge bowling ball, flashed on and off in bright shades of red and yellow neon. It was Saturday night, and the Pacific West Brunswick Tournament was well

under way. The parking lot was packed and inside it was full
of smoke and noise and people. I made my way through the
crowd and into the diner, past the counter and back to the
kitchen. Dwayne must've had ten burgers on the grill and he
was sweating something fierce. Fat dripped onto the fire,
hissed and flared.

"Where's my father?"

"How should I know?"

"Because he's gone," I said. "He just cleared out his stuff
and split."

The fire flared up again. Dwayne stepped away from it.

"I don't know anything about that," he said. "But I did
hear you were supposed to be on the bus back to Portland."

"I got off."

"I can see that."

He flipped the patties with a spatula, fast, one after the
other. Then he went to the room where the time clock was
kept, and where the employees hung their coats, and came
back with an envelope. He handed it to me and I opened it.
Inside was the cash that I'd given him, a little over two hundred dollars.

"I meant for you to have this earlier."

"It's not mine."

"I never had any plans on keeping it," he said, "except
from your old man. Take it. You'll need it where you're
going."

"I'm not going anywhere."

"You're getting back on that bus. I'll put you on it myself."

I took a pencil from my pack, one that I used for my crossword puzzles, addressed the envelope and set it on the table.

"Do me a favor," I said. "Send it to Todd Bowman in Portland. Tell him it's from his brother."

"I didn't know you had a brother."

"Neither does he."

I picked up my suitcase and my pack.

"Where you going?"

I shrugged.

"If your old man doesn't turn up," he shouted after me, "you know where I live. I don't want you sleeping on the streets."

In the parking lot, away from the lights and the noise, I sat down and fought off the urge to cry. I didn't know what else to do. I didn't know what to think. Behind me, in back of the bowling alley, were railroad tracks, and as a train passed I considered jumping one of the boxcars and letting it take me someplace, any place. I didn't give a damn where. Because that's how I felt. I might've easily done it, too, for it was a long and slow-moving train, if my father hadn't happened along just then. He drove into the parking lot in the convertible, pulled into the loading zone near the front doors and went inside. I walked over to the car, threw my stuff in back and settled into the front seat.

It took me weeks just to piece together a small portion of what went on in the bowling alley that night while I waited outside in the parking lot. I still don't have a sharp fix on the details, but I have a pretty good idea of the gist of them, owing to my father's own account of how things occurred and from what I later learned from Melinda, whom he tended to confide in more intimately than he did me. I've also been accused of having an overactive imagination, a charge which I hold no stock in. I consider myself somewhat of an authority in matters concerning my father's temperament, his general demeanor and how, when desperate, he seldom made the right choice. It's all helped me to reconstruct events that I didn't witness, but to which, as a third party, I was inextricably linked.

My father told me that he'd only gone to see Fanny for an advance on his wages, what he felt was due him.

"Was that asking too much?" he said.

Evidently it had been. Since she'd already made out several checks, all for no small sums, and each carrying with it my father's promise of work yet to be done, I can understand Fanny's reservations in refusing to write him another. My father's notion of what was owed him likely differed from the facts, and by a large margin, I suspect. I see it like this. He went to her office, purportedly to ask for an advance on his wages, and to tell her that his son would no longer be in her employ. "I also wanted to return the boy's janitor keys," he said. But either he out and out lied about that part or else he simply forgot about them somewhere between politely asking for the money, then begging for it and finally, when that failed, demanding it. That he just so happened to be packing the Luger that evening was pure coincidence. According to my father, it was nothing more than a precautionary measure, given the recent situation with Bo Stenovich and the very real fear of a repeat encounter with the man. And that this night also just happened to be the night of the Brunswick Tournament, the biggest money night of the year, was again, in my father's version of how it all came together, or fell apart, completely without intent or design.

I pictured Fanny seated behind her desk in her office, just as I remembered seeing her the day that she'd hired me, when my father tapped lightly on the door. She asked who it was, he announced himself, and even if this wasn't the way it actually happened, it was probably something very close to it. However it might've occurred, her mistake was in letting him in precisely when she did, for she was counting up the tourney entry fees, at thirty dollars a head, with no less than two hundred competitors from all over Seattle, parts of Oregon and some from Canada.

It was a bad time for Fanny to deny him the advance, with all that cash on the desk, maybe the safe wide open, and my father likely interpreted her refusal as a blatant sign of greed, typical of the "money people." But it was an equally bad time for him to ask, considering that we'd left her bedroom open

to the elements two days before. To my knowledge no progress had been made on it since. Hanging some lousy tarps
couldn't keep out the cold, and I suspect, on the same token,
that Fanny saw those tarps as a sign of his ingratitude, or
laziness, and that she must've thought that she was being
taken advantage of, especially in light of all that she'd already
given him—clothes, a job, use of her car, the best meals. So
when he approached her about yet another advance, she'd
had enough and told him so. An argument ensued. It was
about this same time that Dwayne Washington, who had seen
my father enter the bowling alley and walk down the hall to
Fanny's office, finished cooking the hamburgers. He slipped
them onto plump sesame seed buns, piled some fries onto the
plates and informed the waitress that he was taking a break.
All he wanted to do was tell my father I'd gotten off the bus
and that he'd talked to me just a minute ago.

"He couldn't have gotten far," he said. "If you hurry you
might catch him."

At this point, however, I was the least of my father's
worries.

"Shut the door, Dwayne."

He looked at my father, then Fanny.

"What's going on?"

"Do what he says."

My father had lowered the Luger when Dwayne first came
in on them. But he raised it again now, from beneath his
jacket.

"Get on the floor," he said, speaking calmly, for they were
all friends of sorts, or had been until now. "Both of you."

Dwayne hesitated.

"Don't try any hero shit," my father said. "I'd like to part
ways with you still around to bitch about it. But if you rather
we didn't, I'd be glad to oblige."

I don't imagine that Dwayne responded much differently

than Todd Bowman had when I robbed him, with threats of the inevitable consequences.

"You'll go back to the joint for this," he said. "Except this time around they won't let you out. I'll testify against your ass. I'll tell them exactly what kind of man they're dealing with."

"I wouldn't put it past you."

" 'Lock him up,' I'll say. 'Throw away the goddamn key. He's rotten to the core.' "

"It'll be a cold day in hell when they catch Floyd Barlow."

"The way you drive you'll be lucky to make it out of the parking lot. Hopefully," he said, "the cops'll put you out of your misery before then and save the state a whole lot of time and money. I'll spit on your grave."

He literally spit at him then. My father pointed the Luger at his head.

"Maybe I ought to protect myself then," he said, "and put a bullet in that thick skull. I don't see how it's to my advantage to protect a man who's going to testify against me and spit on my grave." Then he raised his voice. "Get down, goddamn it, it's the last time I say it."

Clearly he meant business, and they both accommodated him. He tied their wrists behind their backs, using the telephone cord on Fanny and the strings from Dwayne's apron on Dwayne, and when that was done he gagged them. I hoped he tied the knots loosely, because the picture was ugly enough already, seeing them, in my mind's eye, as they lay face down on the floor. I hoped, as they strained and twisted against their bindings, that the only pain they felt was emotional, that their feelings, not their arms or wrists, suffered the injury, and that if it was any consolation they took comfort in knowing that they were still alive. My father was more dangerous than they or myself had ever thought.

It was a hell of a way to say good-bye to the very people

who had given him a break, who had befriended him and who, with that trust, he had turned around and betrayed. Had Dwayne been able to speak as he lay on the floor, bound and gagged beside the woman he cared so much about, I'd guess that he would've wagged his head and told her, straight from the heart, just these two simple words: I'm sorry.

The whole ordeal didn't take more than fifteen minutes. My father was in and out of there quick, and I knew as he came rushing back to the car, not running exactly but close to it, that he'd done something wrong again. He had a canvas bag clamped under his arm and his hand inside his coat. I opened the door for him. His eyes grew wide. He was stunned, all right.

"I'll be a son of a bitch. What the hell you doing here?"

"Waiting on you," I said. "What's it look like?"

"Goddamn it, Bobby, don't you ever listen? Get down, I mean *now*."

He threw the Luger under the seat and put his hand on my head and pushed, hard. Then he slammed the car into reverse, and with the accelerator to the floor he shot back out of the red zone, threw on the brakes, ground the gears trying to find first, found it and we lit out of the parking lot with the tires screeching and blowing smoke behind us. We hit the driveway hard and fast and the axles slammed against the body of the car and sent one of the hubcaps spinning across the asphalt with a sharp hollow ring. On the street we picked up even more speed. The wheels began to shimmy.

"Can I get up yet?"

"No."

"When?"

"When I tell you."

"Did you hurt anybody?"

"Shut up," he shouted. "Shut the hell up."

I stayed bent over in my seat until he made another turn

and backed off on the accelerator. When I sat up we were on a quiet residential street. Lights burned in some of the living room windows. My father glanced in the rearview mirror, and, seeing no one behind him, pulled to the curb.

"This is where you get out," he said.

"No way."

"I'll drag you."

"Try it. I'll scream so loud you'll have the whole neighborhood on your ass."

"You wouldn't dare."

"I'd be doing the police a big favor. They might even give me a reward. Hell," I said, "at least it'd be an honest dollar."

"Don't tell me about honest," he said. "When I go and put you on a bus and you lie and come back. I told you it wasn't going to get any better. I warned you, goddamn it."

He rested his head against the wheel and shut his eyes. He took a deep breath and let it out.

"I don't care if it doesn't get better. I'm sticking, thick or thin," I said. "I'm sticking to you no matter what." I rested my hand on his shoulder to console him, as he'd often done for me. The headlights of another car glanced through the cab, then passed us a moment later. "We better get going," I told him, "wherever it is we're going."

He raised his head and looked at me. He looked at me long and hard before he put the convertible into gear and got back on the road. I hadn't given him much choice in the matter, but then he didn't deserve it. We took Interstate 5 past Renton, turned off, and from there we picked up a dirt road, this dark and desolate one, and followed it a mile or so until we came to the edge of a cliff. My father flipped off the lights. It was pitch black without them, and dead quiet. Another pair of headlamps a short ways up the road flashed on and off twice.

"Grab your stuff," he said.

The other car rolled slowly toward us, and when it got

close enough I saw it was a Dodge Dart and that Melinda sat behind the wheel. She opened her door and scooted over for him so that he could drive. But before he got into the car he reached into his pocket, and in the faint light from the dome I saw him take out my keys, the ones from Fanny's that I'd given him to return for me. He reared back and pitched them over the cliff, and though I listened for them to hit on the rocks below, I heard nothing. I thought of Fanny. I thought of her bedroom and the plastic tarps, flapping in the wind, letting in all the cold. Melinda motioned for me to get in the backseat.

"I thought you were supposed to be on your way to your mother's?"

"I don't have a mother."

"Everybody's got a mother," she said.

"Mine's gone."

"That's not what your dad told me."

My father slipped behind the wheel just in time to hear her last remark.

"It's just a small matter of interpretation, honey. He's got a nice foster family back in Portland and I thought it'd be best if he stayed with them for a while."

"Jesus, Floyd, where's your heart?"

"I planned on sending for him soon as we got settled," he said. "It was only going to be for a few months."

"That's not what you told me," I said.

"Okay, that's enough out of both of you. Here I am risking my neck trying to make a better life for everybody and all I get is shit on."

"C'mere," Melinda said.

She put her arms around him and slipped her tongue between his lips, and he gripped her around the neck and pulled her closer as if he were trying to take her deeper into him, as if he wanted to swallow her up whole. They went on like this for what seemed to me quite a while. Finally she placed her hands on his chest and pushed.

"Not in front of the boy," she said, which struck me as odd, since she'd initiated it.

But they had no reason to worry. I'd already stopped looking.

"What's a five-letter word for gluttony?" I said, as my father shut the door and the dome light went out. "Beginning with *g*."

Cram, hog, devour, I thought.

Melinda turned in her seat and saw me at work.

"Gorge," she said.

"On what?" my father said.

"Whatever. Anything. *Everything*."

And she was right, though we were moving now, the road was bumpy, and it was too dark to write.

Thirteen

ACCORDING TO Melinda, who as an on-again, off-again law student knew considerably more about the criminal penal code than my father and I, he was now a triple threat to law enforcement agencies in Oregon and Washington, and because we had twice crossed state lines in a stolen vehicle, the FBI was also entitled to a piece of the action, if they chose to take it. In case that wasn't unsettling enough, she reminded my father that aside from the robbery of Fanny's Bowl and Dine, which netted us over six thousand dollars, he was an ex-felon in possession of a firearm, probably a stolen one, that he had used it in the commission of a crime and that he had skipped parole several months before. Those were violations enough, if the judge and parole board wanted to throw the book at him, to send my father back to Salem until he was eligible for his pension. The key, I thought, was for us to keep moving, since a moving target is harder to hit than a stationary one.

Had the police bothered to look for us that night, as I'm sure they did, their job was complicated not only by the switch of cars but by the fog, as was ours in putting Washington behind us. It was some getaway, too. I'd say that we averaged about twenty miles per hour. Along certain stretches of

the highway the fog was so thick that my father had to roll
down his window and stick his head out just to see the divid-
ing line. Every now and then the red taillights of another car,
or a truck, suddenly appeared a few feet in front of our
bumper and he had to throw on the brakes. Passing was dangerous, to say the least, but my father and Melinda were both
anxious to push forward, no matter the risk, and on one occasion, when he pulled out from behind a semi we almost ran
head-on into another car. All we saw were a pair of headlights
rushing toward us and the brief flash of the chrome grill. My
father jerked the wheel and sent us sliding across the seat.
The other car swerved and honked after it passed, in anger,
not in warning. It all happened in a second, but it scared the
hell out of me. Melinda, she just laughed.

"We had enough room to drive a truck through," she said.

"Yeah," I said. "No sweat."

She reached over the seat and poked me in the leg.

"Scaredy-cat."

"For good reason."

"Oh come on," she said. "I thought you were a tough
guy."

"If we're going to get caught," I said, "I'd like to be alive
for it."

My father spoke up.

"Don't even joke about that," he said.

"I'll say what I want."

Melinda sat forward in her seat, kind of huffylike.

"Your son's got a bad attitude, Floyd."

"Same to you," I said.

"Nobody's dying. Nobody's getting caught. Now both of
you," my father said, "knock it off. This is no way to start
the trip."

Still, for the next fifty miles or so, he didn't try to pass
again and I was grateful. With the fog came a heavy drizzle,

and even though I couldn't see much out the window I knew we were passing through the forest on one side with the ocean on the other. Because I could smell it. Because it was this odd blend of dampness, decay and regrowth, the scent of things green and yellow, of cedar and pine and big redwood, too, and with it the stench of seaweed rotting in piles on the beach.

We drove all night, stopping once in Medford to gas up, get some coffee and use the bathroom, then continued on toward the California border. The fog disappeared as we drove further inland, and at one point Melinda reached into the glove compartment, took out a Triple-A map and spread it open across her lap. I rested my elbows on the back of the front seat and watched her draw her finger down the red line marking the highway.

"Stay on Five until we hit Ninety-Nine," she said, "and we'll be okay."

"Where we going?" I said.

"On vacation," my father said.

"But where?"

"Vegas."

"You'll love it," Melinda said. "It's wonderful. No snow. No fog. Mark my words, in two days we'll all have fantastic tans."

"Or sunburns," I said.

"You're a real optimist," she said. "We'll have to work on that. We'll have to whip that boy of yours into shape, Floyd."

But I didn't care about swimming or getting a tan. I was worried. I was scared for what the future might hold for us, and if our encounter earlier with that oncoming car was any indication, it didn't look very bright. I curled up in the backseat and closed my eyes. Several times during the course of the trip I tried to sleep, but I couldn't. I couldn't get comfortable, I couldn't do a thing but twist and turn, and after a while I gave up on the idea and stared out the window, thought to myself what might become of us and listened to the hum of the engine.

We passed through Redding. We passed through Sacramento, where the weather was well over eighty degrees, and where we connected with Highway 99. Melinda pulled her sweater off, so that she was just in her T-shirt. "Kiss the nasty old cold good-bye," she said, as she rolled down her window. The warm air blew in my face, and I do admit that it felt good for a change. By late afternoon we'd put Fresno behind us and were headed across the desert for the Nevada state line. The weather, it only grew hotter and hotter.

"Doesn't this thing have an air conditioner?" I said. "I'm sweating to death back here."

"If it's not too cold, it's too hot," my father said. "I've never in my life known a kid who griped as much as you."

Melinda glanced back at me.

"Soon as we get to Vegas you can jump in the pool. There's not a hotel in town that doesn't have one and everywhere you go it's air-conditioned. I worked in Vegas two years and never broke a sweat."

"Where'd you work?" I said.

"Different places. Mostly the casinos."

"Cocktailing?"

"Dealing, honey. Craps. Poker. I can do a whole lot more than serve drinks."

It was a straight shot once we got onto Interstate 15, with not a whole lot to see except flat dry land, sagebrush and rock, and occasionally some mountains in the distance. Once we passed a billboard with a picture of a busty show girl with two fistfuls of hundred-dollar bills and her arms spread wide as if she were welcoming a lover. Beneath her it read: Vegas Is for Winners. Another sign, further up the road, said we only had eighty-three miles to go. Melinda kicked off her shoes and socks and put her feet up on the dash. She curled her toes.

"I lived in Reno, too, for six months."

"Is that a fact?"

"When I was nineteen," she said.

"Hawaii. Vegas. Portland. Seattle. Now, Reno. For a girl your age," my father said, "you've certainly done your share of traveling."

"I used to just pick up and go all the time. I mean everywhere," she said. "Europe, too. I've been to Germany and Switzerland. I've been to Italy. I've been to Paris, France. Then I met Bo and it was all downhill from there. Going to school, cooking and cleaning after that bastard, and he has the nerve to hit me. It wasn't the first time, either."

"Honey," my father said, "you'll never have to pick up after that son of a bitch again." He looked in the rearview mirror at me. His eyes were bloodshot from the long drive. "We pick up after ourselves, don't we? I've always said there's messy bachelors and clean ones, and Bobby and me belong to the latter. Is that the truth," he said "or is that the truth?"

"The truth," I said.

"We're a regular all-around cleaning machine. Baby," he said, as he reached for her hand and made a big act of kissing it, "this is just the beginning of one long vacation."

She held her foot up for my father and me to see, then wiggled her toes.

"What do you think, guys? Snow-cone pink or candy-apple red?"

"Red."

"Me too," I said.

"Can you reach me my cigarettes? They're right in my coat."

Melinda obliged him, then turned on the radio. She switched from station to station, getting mostly static before stopping on a church program. Organ music played. An evangelist spoke with a southern twang.

This is Dr. Joyboy coming to you live from the Church of Glory, twenty-four hours a day. Our mission knows no rest . . .

It didn't take my father long to get his fill of it.

"You mind turning that thing off?"

"I like it," she said. "You might, too, if you gave it a chance."

"I got my own religion, honey. Right here," he said, patting his chest. "I know when I'm doing right, and when I'm doing wrong. I don't need some crazy man telling me."

"You think you ever lived another life?"

"How'd that come up?"

"I don't know," she said. "Do you?"

"Not that I know of."

"I have," she said. "I used to be a man."

My father smiled. He reached over and patted her on the thigh.

"Looking at you now," he said, "that's a little hard to believe."

"It's true. But it was a long time ago. Like about a hundred years."

"You must have a hell of a memory."

"Don't tease," she said.

She rummaged through her purse and took out a bottle of nail polish. "I used to be a miner. A silver miner." She opened the bottle, and with her feet poised on the dash began to paint her smallest toe. The chemical smell was strong, even with the wind blowing through the cab. "I hit a big vein and I had all this money. I had two kids and a beautiful wife, too. But they left me. Of course that was before I made it." Melinda had small feet, the tips of her toes were perfectly rounded and pink, and the nail on the smallest was no bigger than a baby's, just the sliver of a nail. She carefully passed the brush over it, then licked the tip of her finger and wiped away a red speck from her skin. "One down, nine to go," she said. "I never got over my family. I wanted them back, but they up and moved, they were gone. I started drinking. Big time, serious drinking. Lost everything. I died in Taos, New Mexico, in 1896." She dipped the brush back into the bottle and steadied it over the next toe. "At forty-two," she said. "In a fire. It's the worst way to go."

On the radio the evangelist carried on about hell and redemption, vice and virtue. "Between you and Dr. Joyboy here," my father said, "I'm getting pretty depressed." He spun the dial. Rock and roll. But it didn't come in well. "What you need is a tape player," he said. "We don't get to Vegas soon, we'll have to pull over and buy one." Only there was no place around to buy anything, and it was about that time that the Dodge broke down. We were clipping along at eighty when the engine started bucking, missing and coughing, and the lights on the dash suddenly lit up.

"Goddamn it," he said. "Now what?"

We coasted to the side of the road. We all climbed out. My father opened the hood and we stood around and looked down at the engine while it ticked itself cool, as if staring at it would help.

"We should've kept the convertible."

"Sure," Melinda said, "that way we all could've stayed in Seattle. Try starting it."

My father climbed behind the wheel and gave it a shot, but it didn't even make a clicking noise. He pounded the wheel.

"I swear," he said, "if I don't have the worst damn luck with cars."

He got the map out of the glove compartment and spread it open on the trunk of the car. "There's a town up ahead," he said. "Shouldn't be more than a couple miles. I'll see if I can't get us some help." Before he got on his way he set the Dodge in neutral, Melinda steered, and we pushed the car further off to the side of the road so the highway patrol wouldn't see if it they happened to pass by. Then he tried to give Melinda a kiss, but she turned away, like this was all somehow his fault.

"Hurry it up," she said, "it's getting dark and I don't want to be out here alone. A place like this, you never can tell what might happen."

"Bobby's here to protect you."

"Yeah, a big tough fifteen-year-old scared of changing lanes."

"Hey," I said.

"Hell," my father said, "there's nothing around here to hurt you guys. You want, though, I'll leave the gun."

"I don't know how to use it."

"Bobby does. He's a crack shot."

"That's right," I said. "Anyone messes with us, I'll blow him away."

"On second thought," my father said, "maybe I better take the gun."

He left us there in the Dodge, off to the side of the road in the middle of nowhere. Cars passed occasionally, but we knew better than try to flag one down. Melinda sat with her door open, her legs crossed, one foot in the dirt and the other in her lap. She was painting her toenails again. I found a stick and jabbed at the ground. Above us long twisted clouds stretched across the wide open sky. The rest, the land, was desolate, it was barren. The colors were gray and yellow and that's all.

"I don't appreciate what you said."

"About what?"

"I'm not just a kid," I said. "I know how to handle myself."

"You do, huh?"

"I don't appreciate being patronized, either."

"That's a big word for a boy your age. It must be all those crossword puzzles. Very educational."

"For the record I'm sixteen, not fifteen, and I'll be seven-teen soon enough. Shit," I said, "you're not a hell of a lot older."

"Maybe not," she said, "but I'm a hell of a lot wiser."

"I've been around. I know about people and I know what my father sees in you. What I don't get," I said, "is what you see in him."

"Lots of stuff."

"Like what?"

"Like he *does* things. Like he's going places. He doesn't just sit on his ass all day, and he knows how to treat a woman, too, plenty better than most of the jerks I've known. And believe me, I've had my share. You don't know the half of it."

"I know one thing," I said. "We wouldn't be in this mess right now if it wasn't for you."

She stopped painting her toenails, and with her finger slipped a loose strand of hair behind her ear. The side of her face was still swollen from the beating, and now, in the middle of the desert, flustered and angry, she looked hard, she looked bitter, she looked old and she looked young, but she did not look so beautiful then.

"I hate to break your heart," she said, and she said it slowly. "But let's get something straight right now. If anyone goes it'll be you, and I wouldn't want that, Bobby. I think we both better do our best to get along."

I can't say her words shocked me, that would be lying, but they certainly didn't endear her to me. The hardest part was knowing that she was probably right. If any of us had to go our separate ways, it would likely be me, and at this point in my life I thought it wise to hedge my bets and keep quiet. Her time, as my father's father had once told him, would come someday, and it might well be before mine.

He returned within the hour, in a tow truck driven by a young man with a crew cut and a sunburned face. My father helped him hook up the Dodge. Then we all piled into the front seat and pulled back onto the interstate.

"I think it's electrical," my father said. "Could be the alternator. Could just be the switch. How long you suppose it'll take to get it fixed?"

"Can't tell," he said. "That's not my job."

"How about a place to stay?"

"We got a Best Western in town."

"Nothing nicer?"

"Not till you hit Vegas."

"Best Western okay with you, honey?"

She was looking pretty worn out and mad.

"As long as it has a shower," she said. "I just want to wash up and get some sleep."

Only a mile or so up the highway was a mountain range, and as we dropped over it, headed toward the faint glow of lights coming from a small town in the valley below, we saw a strange and marvelous sight. There were windmills everywhere. Dozens and dozens, maybe close to a hundred. They were set on long steel posts driven deep into the sides of the mountain and across the flatlands, too, and at the top of each was a huge propeller, like the kind you used to see on older airplanes, with blades easily twice the length of a car. They turned slowly in the wind, they turned silently on smooth oval hubs well greased, these odd-looking giants going round and round in the vastness of the desert, some of them fast, only a blur, some hardly moving at all. At the base of one I spotted a coyote. It was mangy, bony, and it had its tail tucked between its hind legs. For a long time we just watched the windmills go round, framed there in the evening sky, against the background of the long and twisted clouds fading into the darkness.

My father cleared his throat.

"Some sight," he said. "What're they for?"

"Irrigation pumps. Homes."

"Who'd want to live out here?" Melinda said.

Then it must've occurred to her that the young man had a home somewhere about.

"I'm sorry," she said. "I suppose some people like it. The privacy, the peace and quiet. No problem with traffic, that's for sure. And you have all these beautiful sunsets, too."

"Yes ma'am."

It wasn't much of a town, a Terrible Herbst gas station with an auto repair, a grocery store, a Fosters Freeze, two cowboy bars and a Best Western. The homes were located somewhere farther out in the desert. The young man dropped us off at the motel and said he'd have someone call us about the car just as soon as they knew what was what. We got our luggage out from the back and checked into a room under the name of Mr. and Mrs. Charles Tilton. I teased him about it later, calling him "Charlie" when he came back from the Fosters Freeze with two bags of burgers, french fries and shakes.

Melinda had just finished showering, her hair was wet, and she'd put on one of my father's T-shirts. It barely reached the middle of her thighs, and as she stood before the dresser mirror, drawing a brush slowly through her hair, I had to make a real effort not to stare. She noticed me in the reflection, but she didn't say anything, and I lowered my eyes. My father was busy setting the food out across one of the two double beds. His cigarette burned in the ashtray on top of the TV.

The call came after dinner, just before I fell asleep, and it wasn't good news. My father, with the sober look of concern on his face, cradled the receiver between cheek and shoulder, and nodded now and again as he listened.

"It's the fuel pump," he said when he hung up. "And they don't have any in stock. It'll take a day to get it and another to slap it on."

"Oh great," she said, "just great."

"Now, honey," he said.

"Don't 'honey' me."

"It's only a slight delay."

"This is really turning into a rotten trip, Floyd. I'm sorry I ever let you talk me into it."

"As I understand it," he said, "it was a mutual decision."

She went into the bathroom and slammed the door. My father, he just sat on the edge of the bed and massaged his temples with his fingertips.

"Every day," he said, "every day I lose more hair, and you sure as hell ain't helping it any." He raised his voice. "Hear me, honey? You'll have a bald lover on your hands, you don't come out here and make up."

But Melinda didn't take to his humor, and neither did I. I stripped down to my boxers, climbed into bed and blanked them out. That's how exhausted I was. But I didn't sleep for long. I woke several hours later with a jolt, as if electricity was running through my arms and out the tips of my fingers, and for those first moments I didn't know where I was. The lights were out and my heart pounded. My throat was sore and dry and I felt sweat slipping down the side of my face. The thermostat was turned up all the way, so that it was like a sauna in the room, so that you could hardly breathe.

As I lay in that strange bed in that strange room in a Best Western in the desert, afraid to move, to turn and look, I heard her moaning into the pillow, like the whimper of an animal, almost as if she were in pain, this guttural noise that seemed to rise from somewhere deep inside her. I could smell her too. I could smell them both, their sex and the sweat, the vague scent of perfume and my father's cheap cologne, and it made me dizzy. I shut my eyes tight and listened to the slap of skin on skin, the even slide of movement made easier with sweat, and the wet sounds of her as my father pushed. I made a fist under the covers, and each time I heard the kiss and slap of their bodies I drove it silently into the palm of my other hand. Harder, I thought. *Harder*. Give it to her. And as if they'd both heard my thoughts they did go harder, they did go faster and they kept at it, furiously it seemed, until at last the room was still and all you could hear was their deep, even breathing and the click of the thermostat finally shutting off.

I opened my fist, let the fingers uncurl. I tried to steady my breathing. I heard the rustle of sheets and outside, down the hall, the hum of the ice machine. Melinda whispered.

"Honey?"

"Hmmm?"

"I can't stay in this dump."

"It's only for a couple days."

"I swear," she said, "I'll go out of my mind."

Silence.

"You listening?"

Maybe he nodded. I don't know. I heard the flick and spark of his lighter, and a moment later I smelled the cigarette.

"I'm thinking."

"What's to think about?"

"I'm just thinking."

"Something like this never stopped you before," she said. "I mean it, I really need to get out of here or I wouldn't say it."

I heard my father rise from the bed, heard him slip into his pants, heard the sound that his belt buckle made as he fastened it. Then I heard the door open and briefly felt the cool night air on my face. Melinda rose a short while later. I had my back to her, so that all I saw was the shadow that her body made against the wall, and all I heard was the sound of her bare feet brushing against the carpet. Light from outside shone across the floor near my bed and I knew that she'd parted the drapes, that she was watching him. I wanted to look, to see her in her nakedness and freeze that picture in my mind. But I just lay there, motionless, feigning sleep, feigning ignorance until I felt her hand on my shoulder.

"Bobby?"

She shook me a little.

"Wake up."

I looked up, blinking, pretending that I was groggy. She wore my father's T-shirt.

"Get dressed," she said. "Your father's waiting on us."

I dressed and so did she, quickly, and in no time at all we were outside with our bags. He had found us the best car in the lot, a late-model Ford, a big Country Squire station wagon with the fake wood paneling on the sides, an automatic transmission and a luggage rack on top. There were some boxes in the back, an old, gray navy blanket, someone's suitcase and a pair of women's shoes. In the seat beside me was a child's booster seat.

"It smells terrible in here," Melinda said. "What's the matter with people?"

We drove through the empty town, down the long road back toward the interstate. It was almost dawn, and there were these wide strips of pink and orange rising in the sky. The windmills were pushing the colors up, mixing them together, all steel, silence and power. Melinda flipped on the radio. Dr. Joyboy again. Coming to us live twenty-four hours a day. My father turned in his seat and smiled at me.

"Happy birthday."

"It's not for a while."

"So you get your present early," he said. "What're you bitching about?"

I heard it then between the boxes, in a plastic traveling case with a wire door on the front. I took a look, I took it out. Inside was a puppy, the ugliest I think I'd ever seen. Its face was a mass of wrinkles, of layer upon layer of fat, loose skin and fur. The eyes, you could hardly see them, like marbles sunk deep into dough. Its tail had been cut, too, and the tiny stub still looked pink and sore.

"Don't say I forgot," he said. "Mind me now, you take good care of that pup."

I set it in my lap and it licked my hand.

"Did you hurt her?" I said.

"What're you talking about?"

"Fanny," I said.

"I wouldn't do that."

"Because she was nice to us," I said.

"Because she wanted something," Melinda said. "Don't put it past the old bitch. You say you know people, she was scheming on your daddy. She's just out for herself like everybody else."

Melinda pulled down the visor. It had a mirror on the other side, and she reached into her purse, this big bulky leather bag, and took out some lipstick.

"The last thing we need is a damn mutt," she said, as she made an O of her mouth and applied the lipstick, so that it sounded strange when she spoke, "especially such a godawful ugly one."

"That's not just any mutt."

"Who cares," she said, "if it's that ugly?"

"They breed 'em ugly," my father said. "That kind's worth money."

Ugly or not, I petted it, the loose skin and fat. I cooed in its ugly little ear while the windmills, on all sides of us, went round and round.

fourteen

ANYONE SEEING US in that big Country Squire station wagon as we blew down the highway that morning, our luggage in back and a puppy in tow, wouldn't have given us a second thought, though some may have questioned my father's judgment in choosing such a young bride. We were, for all outward appearances, just an ordinary family making a quick stop in Vegas to catch our breath and drop a few dollars into the one-armed bandits before continuing on, say, to the Grand Canyon. That that wasn't our real destination did little to quash my fantasy that it could have been, if my father hadn't robbed Fanny, if Melinda wasn't deserting her husband and if we weren't driving another stolen car. I figured we had an hour or two before the owner of the station wagon woke up, discovered it missing and phoned the police. By the time they took the report we'd be rid of the car, and with any luck our absence might go unnoticed until the auto mechanic called a couple days later. When we couldn't be reached he'd contact the motel clerk, who in turn would contact the police again once it was determined we'd skipped out on our bill. Then the process of piecing the puzzle together would begin, if it hadn't already, and considering the sloppy trail we'd left behind it didn't seem all that hard of a thing to do. This was supposing, however, in my father's words, "that cops had brains," and according to him he'd yet to encounter one that did. Melinda, he said, could attest to that firsthand. I didn't remind him that Bo and his cronies had done a good job of flushing them out before.

I could've spent my time worrying. I could've spent it bitching at my father, pleading with him to turn himself in, so we could straighten out this mess and get on with our lives. But in light of the consequences that was no longer a realistic alternative, for regardless of what he'd done, I certainly didn't want to see him sent back to Salem. Instead, I pushed those thoughts from my mind, and as false as it may have been I indulged myself in the image of us as some sort of family. Las Vegas was a wonderous sight from the highway after seeing nothing but barren land for the last ninety miles, and I shared in their excitement when it came into view with all its high-rise hotels and casinos. Though it was still early in the morning, heat waves rose from the desert floor, and through them it looked as if the buildings were wavering like liquid.

The first thing we did after we'd checked into a room at the Flamingo, and after my father had ditched the station wagon—where I don't know, but he came back in a Camaro from Hertz—was to buy some new clothes. "Unless," Melinda said, "you want to spend all night nickel and diming it at the Rainbow Club." She was, of course, speaking to my father, though I also benefited from the shopping spree. We went to The Broadway. We went to Neiman Marcus. We went to a pet shop, a drugstore and a few other places. Melinda bought a couple miniskirts, some bright red hot pants, a bell-bottom pantsuit, a pair of knee-high lace-up boots and several blouses. For my father she picked out some hip-hugger jeans, one pair of striped slacks and another plaid, two paisley shirts with wide lapels, a wide tie and a small pair of scissors "to keep your sideburns trimmed" because she wanted him to grow them out. Mutton chops were popular at the time. My new attire was decidedly less stylish, and not necessarily by choice. It consisted of striped T-shirts, one with a yellow happy face on the chest, two sets of khaki shorts, a pair of tennis shoes and some baggy trunks, "for all the swimming you'll do," as Melinda said. Her reference to swimming, along with the type of clothes they picked out for me, suggested that I wouldn't be accompanying them on their gambling junket this evening or perhaps any other, whether it was to the fancier casinos, a spot like the Rainbow Club, or just out to dinner.

I guessed correctly.

We returned to the hotel, where they quickly changed into their new clothes—Melinda, into one of the miniskirts, my father, into a hideous combination of plaid slacks and a paisley shirt. They left me with my bags from The Broadway, a new book of crossword puzzles, another called *How to Care for Your Puppy* and fifty dollars, which seemed like a lot of money just to hand over. My father was already warming up to the action and he hadn't yet gambled a cent.

"In case we don't get back in time," he told me, "buy yourself a big steak dinner. Food's cheap in Vegas, and there's plenty of it."

Melinda came out of the bathroom then. She turned in a circle for us.

"How do I look?"

"Terrific," he said. "Good enough to eat."

She did, too, in a miniskirt with her fine legs, replete with a blouse that laced up the front and showed off her bust. The pup, which had fallen asleep under the dresser, woke abruptly and sneezed.

"You keep that mutt off the bed," she said. "I don't want dog hair everywhere."

I promised her I would.

But I didn't hold to it long. The pup was an integral part of our makeshift family now, on the lam like the rest of us,

stolen from its owner, its mother and home. Except his greatest threat to safety was the other residents and hotel employees—maids, room service, the whole bunch—all of them
potential informers bent on tossing him onto the streets. I
couldn't have him whining. That simply wouldn't do. After
our second night alone, with all his whimpering, locked in the
bathroom and pawing at the door, I gave in and carried him
to bed with me. I couldn't have stood it either, curled up on
Flamingo towels in the darkness with a runny toilet and my
own stench for company. Besides, he was in need of comfort
and affection.

Its face matched exactly one of the pictures in the book,
and the caption beneath it read, "The Shar-Pei, once near ex-
tinction, was bred by the emperors of China." It was a freak
of sorts in its rarity, this puppy born ugly, with its mother
and father and all their kind before them, their history, their
entire legacy once on the verge of complete annihilation. Their
so-called noble lineage was no consolation, and even if I
didn't have the papers to prove it, I knew just by looking that
he was a purebred through and through.

I let him nestle his ugly little head in my armpit, between
pillow and sheet.

"Sleep," I said. "Sleep."

I wasn't concerned that my father and Melinda might have
ditched me. On one occasion, when I was out, I returned to
the room and found the shower still steamy, the cap off the
toothpaste and a pair of Melinda's panty hose drying on the
towel bar. On another occasion I found my father's suitcase
spread open on the bed and his pants and the paisley shirt
heaped in the corner beside the TV. A full roll of quarters, a
broken cigarette and seventeen dollars worth of chips from
the Aladdin were scattered on top of the dresser as if he'd
hastily emptied his pockets, or Melinda her purse, and in
their anxiousness to get back to the casinos, either forgot or

didn't bother to pick any of it up. Tucked under the base of the lamp, on the nightstand, was a note written in Melinda's fluid, ornate hand, "We're on a hot streak. Enjoy!" Beneath it was a crisp one-hundred-dollar bill.

Who knows what they did for sleep, if they did without it altogether or if they managed a few catnaps here and there while I was down at the pool or walking the pup on the outskirts of the Strip. I bought a leash for him, his own dog bowl and another better book specifically on Shar-Peis. The woman at the pet store was pretty impressed with him and confirmed my belief that he was the genuine thing. Real show-dog quality, she said. Worth up to fifteen hundred dollars. Sometimes more. I spent quite a few hours in her store browsing around with a wallet full of money, that other hundred still hidden in the sole of my shoe, and nothing better to do but walk around and kill time. I enjoyed taking in the different smells as I strolled down the aisles, of flea powder in the supply section, concoctions of cod-liver oil and powerful solutions of vitamins packaged in bright red-and-white boxes with pictures of fish, dogs and cats on them. I liked the smell of the birdseed, too, and the cool feel of it when I dipped my hand into the big fifty-gallon drum, clear up to my elbow, this tickling, sinking feeling all around my arm as if it were pulling me in, as if there were no bottom. I liked the brittle texture of the rabbit pellets, the smooth metallic feel of them against my skin and their rich green smell like freshly mowed grass, and I liked knowing that I could buy almost anything I wanted in that store. As I looked into the cages of puppies and kittens, tiers upon tiers of them the length of one wall, I considered that I had the power to set them free, if not all of them then at least a few, and they sensed it too, and the most desperate of them suckled and bit at my finger as they would their mother's tit. I could offer them a better life if I chose, and I fancied myself this rancher, with acreage for them to roam. Then the birds would catch my attention—parakeets, cockatiels, Mexican

Redheads and the enormous white cockatoo perched in the middle of the store, the featured resident, no cage but the walls surrounding us all, though its wings had been clipped and it could not fly. They chattered constantly, except for the white cockatoo, which now and then let out a terrible shriek that for several moments silenced them all.

The tropical fish were kept in the back of the store in a room all to themselves, where it was quiet except for the even hum of the pump motors and the bubbling noise they made inside the tanks and where, except for the soft glow of light in water, it was dark. The Siamese fighting fish were kept separated in small glass bowls, the size they hold goldfish in at the game booths at the county fair, and the woman said these were the prettiest of them all, but only when you put them together and they fought to the death, with their silklike fins flashing a rainbow of color. Otherwise the fins drooped, the colors were dull, and they were nothing to see. Most of the other fish had strange long names that I couldn't pronounce. Some stayed hidden under the rocks in the tanks, or in the hollow plastic feet of Neptune, and you rarely saw anything but their tiny, bulbous eyes. Still more swam lazily back and forth, waiting to be fed. When I left the store I felt somehow at a loss, and yet somehow relieved to put it behind me, the whining and the chatter, the cages and the cool darkness of the aquarium room, and once outside I'd suck the dry desert heat deep into my lungs until it burned.

In a vacant lot at the end of the Strip, away from the glitz, the tourists and the gamblers, I began the often frustrating process of teaching my dog the tricks and commands that I believed all dogs should know. It was the perfect place for lessons, quiet and free of distractions, this dumping ground for old mattresses, the rusty shells of abandoned cars, bent bicycle frames and the plastic remains of a Dough Boy pool. Sun shined on a cracked windshield and blinded you if you looked at it, and beyond that lay the wide expanse of desert.

I named the pup Sam for no reason other than that I liked the sound of it, and I tried to teach him to sit, lay down, shake hands and to stay when I turned my back and walked away. He was a smart dog, and it was less than a month before he mastered my simple commands, though he never did get very good at staying. Soon as I was out of sight, whether I'd crouched behind one of the rusty cars in that lot, or turned the corner around a building at some later point in the lesson, he'd come running. Of course I sympathized with him on this one, and after a while I gave up. The pup learned well enough what and when he wanted, so it wasn't my place to complain. I sneaked him back into the hotel the same way that I got him out, under my jacket. No one questioned the fact that it was too hot out to wear one.

Our room had a balcony that overlooked the pool and from it, six stories down, I watched the women sunbathing. When a particularly pretty one caught my eye I changed into my trunks, grabbed a towel, my suntan lotion and my book of crossword puzzles and the one on Shar-Peis, and rode the elevator down to the pool. I'd stroll along the edge of it, glancing up at the sun occasionally and pretending like I was looking for just the right spot to get that perfect tan. The books under my arm gave me an air of sophistication, or so I thought, and I had the towel draped over my shoulder in what I considered a masculine fashion. I'd stop and look around again when I was within range, and then, as if I were exasperated with my search, and as if I still hadn't the slightest idea that she even existed, I'd sigh loudly enough for all to hear and settle, at last, into one of the chaise longues behind her. I liked to stay one row back, so that without being noticed I could casually look up from my book from time to time and take in the smooth tanned skin, the breasts pushing against the bikini top, the small of the neck, the legs and the gentle curve of the ankle. I fantasized that one of these beautiful women would strike up a conversation with me, without the smallest effort on my behalf, and when she realized that I was mature well beyond my years she'd invite me up to her room where with patience and enthusiasm she'd instruct me in the art of making love. For the most part girls my own age didn't hold the same fascination for me. I lumped them together as gigglers, as innocents, as teasers who measured and doled out sex in terms of scoring, of bases, but who rarely allowed you that disreputable home run. I wanted the hands of experience. I wanted the full body of a woman, the deeper voice and the muskier smell. Ideally this *older* beauty, which now that I'm thirty-six years old strikes me as nothing short of ridiculous, would've been between eighteen and twenty-four. But instead of a woman, younger or older, pretty or not, I ended up having my first sexual experience with a man.

The act was not, as they say, consummated, though for my tastes it came plenty close enough. He called himself Mr. Ed and he laughed when he said it. But his real name was Claude Edwards and we met at the pool late in the afternoon on my third day alone at the Flamingo. He'd been reading *Don't Fall Off the Mountain,* the autobiography of Shirley MacLaine. Only a few minutes before Mr. Ed introduced himself, I positioned myself behind a terrific looking blonde, whose long slender legs rivaled those of Melinda. To my disappointment, however, she soon gathered up her things, slipped into her sandals and started back for the hotel. Mr. Ed occupied the chaise longue beside mine, and he was hip to my scheme. While I'd been watching the woman, and off and on working on a crossword puzzle, he'd evidently been watching me. He lowered his glasses along the bridge of his nose and peered at the woman from over the top of them. She was still within sight.

"Too bad," he said, "and to think you just got settled."

"Excuse me?"

"She *is* a beauty," he said.

I thought I'd been more discreet, but I acknowledged him

with a nod and then went back to concentrating on my crossword puzzle.

I needed a four-letter word for an Asian buffalo, and as I
considered the possibilities I listened to the water lap against
the sides of the pool. Above me I noticed two men standing
on their balcony a dozen floors up, sharing drinks and looking
out toward the desert. The sun would be setting in another
hour or so. Claude interrupted my thoughts.

"Enjoying yourself in Vegas?"

"I suppose," I said, choosing the word *suppose* over *guess*
because it sounded more mature, and that was my role of late.

"Where's your family?"

"Gambling," I said. "What else?"

"There's not much, especially for a young man. It's really
a playground for adults." He laughed, and that's when he
told me his name. "But everyone calls me Mr. Ed," he said.

Oxen, I thought.

The cocktail waitress came by as I was filling in the
squares. It was last call, for the pool bar anyway, and most of
the sunbathers had already left. Claude ordered a rum and
Coke and asked me if I'd like anything. A 7-Up sounded
good, and when the drinks arrived I put down my puzzle and
we talked. He told me he came to Vegas often, that he lived
in Scottsdale, Arizona, and after twenty years in the military
he'd retired, and now, with a full pension and no responsibili-
ties, for his two kids were grown and gone, he mostly traveled. Seemed to me he had a good setup.

Claude, or Mr. Ed, was a pleasant man with a gentle smile
and a soft voice. He was balding but handsome, with a long
face and long eyelashes, and when he laughed and reached
over and patted me on the knee I thought nothing of it. In
retrospect, I probably should've been suspicious, but I just
thought he was being friendly, as another man might when
he slaps you on the shoulder or cuffs you affectionately on
the side of the head. And like my ridiculous notion of older

women, I had this equally ridiculous impression of military men. It was GI Joe and John Wayne all the way. I was that naive. By the same token, I believed that only hippies and teenagers such as myself smoked marijuana. So it about floored me when, as I sat there rubbing lotion into my shoulders, this friendly fellow who called himself Mr. Ed asked me if I wanted to sample a joint of Acapulco gold. We couldn't very well light up at the pool, even if most of the people had left by now, so I followed him back to his room.

On the elevator he stood close to me so that our arms brushed together once, he smiled too, and though I should have caught on by then, I didn't. My experience with Doug had been a good one, and for all I knew this was how it was always done, this ritual of secreting yourself away with a co-conspirator, getting stoned and then wandering back into the real world with a foggy head, bloodshot eyes and a more pleasant perspective on life. His room was the same as ours, with gaudy orange wallpaper and twin double beds, between them a nightstand, and the two chairs had clothes draped over them. Because I didn't see it as my right to touch or move his stuff, I sat on the edge of the bed and folded my hands in my lap.

"Can I fix you a drink?" he said.

But the memory of my last hangover was all too fresh, and I respectfully declined the offer.

"Roll us a joint then. It's in the dresser, top left drawer in back of my socks," he said. "I need to take a quick shower."

I found it wrapped in a plastic bag with a package of Zig-Zags, and I set about trying to roll a joint without ever having done it before. It proved a formidable and unusally delicate task. The papers kept ripping, the pot kept falling out, and along about the fifth or sixth attempt I succeeded in making a thin, lumpy, hardly smokable joint. My lack of skill shamed and betrayed me for the amateur hophead that I was, and I would have gladly given it another shot, several if necessary, but by then Mr. Ed was out of the shower and ready to get high, among other things. He had on a rust-colored velour robe, with black piping along the lapels and his initials, CE, monogrammed on the breast. He sat beside me and we lit up and began to smoke. It was powerful stuff but less harsh than Doug's and easier for me to hold down. That numb, stoned feeling crept slowly into my head.

"I've been noticing you down at the pool these past couple of days. You seem lonely."

"Not so much."

"I used to be that way," he said. "But there's no reason. You're a very good-looking young man."

Fool that I was, I thought he was talking about women, and how because I was fairly handsome, at least in his opinion, I should've been able to attract one. The air conditioner kicked in and blew a steady stream of cool air through the room.

"I'm just shy," I said.

"I guess you know," he said, "that shyness is a sign of intelligence."

And I thought, as I grew more stoned, that Mr. Ed had made a profound observation about myself that others had long overlooked. Smart people tended to keep their mouths shut, they tended to listen and learn, and by default, if for no other reason, they were more intelligent than most. Later, when the marijuana wore off, I didn't think so highly of my little insight, but at the time it seemed revelatory.

"You really think so?"

"Oh," he said, "I *know* so."

Mr. Ed crossed his legs and the robe parted, all the way up to his thigh. Once again, however, I read nothing into it. It certainly was no cause for arousal, suspicion or alarm on my behalf, any more than it would've been to watch another man take off his shirt on a hot day, or stop along the roadside, unzip his pants and piss. Mr. Ed passed the joint to me and I inhaled deeply.

I thought of Doug, the vocabulary.

"This is good shit," I said.

He leaned back on the bed.

"The best," he said.

It was this posture, this studied pose, that first alerted me to the possibility that Mr. Ed felt anything romantic toward me. He sensed my apprehension, smiled and sat up.

"This your first time?"

"Getting high?"

"No, silly."

He took my hand in his and lifted it to his lips and kissed the back of it.

"Don't be nervous," he said.

I'd like to believe that I was in shock. But that's a weak excuse for not getting up and leaving right then. I let him untie the drawstring on my swimming trunks and drop to his knees.

I shut my eyes and let him go on like that, breathing in the cool air moving through the room and sensitive suddenly to the heat beneath my skin, sharp and tingling like a sunburn, until, in a stoned daze, I opened my eyes and saw the balding head of this middle-aged man bobbing up and down on me.

"It feels good," I said. "But I don't like men."

Mr. Ed kept at it, believing, I think, that if he only persisted I'd soon get caught up in the pleasure and forget who was giving it to me. I let him continue a moment longer, for the benefit of the doubt—his and my own—that maybe I *could* like it, that maybe I *could* enjoy it. I looked at the orange shag carpet. I looked at the picture on the wall, of a horse with hills behind it and the distant outline of a corral. I looked at the cheap thin drapes covering the sliding glass door and listened to the buzzing noise in my ears. But it just wasn't working and I told him so again, this time more forcefully, a clear, well-enunciated *"stop."*

And to show that I meant it I put my hand on his temple and pushed him away. Mr. Ed rose to his feet with considerable hesitation. Then he looked at me in disappointment, tightened the sash on his robe and went to the dresser. "Such a waste," he said. "You really ought to give yourself more of a chance. It can be fun." He began to roll another joint. But I'd had my share, for it was powerful stuff. With his back to me, which I took to be my cue, I pulled up my swimming trunks and quietly let myself out of the room.

By one that morning on our third day in Vegas, when my father and Melinda had yet to return, I grew disgusted and went looking for them. The Strip was crowded. Cabs and limousines cruised alongside pickup trucks full of loud young men, while the newly married—boasting out-of-state plates and streamers trailing from the rear bumpers—followed hundreds of others in Fords and Chevys in a procession of traffic that seemed to have no beginning or end. On the sidewalk women in furs and diamonds and high heels, their faces all made up, walked arm in arm with men equally well dressed. Drinks were free or cheap and the Strip was noisy with laughter and talk, and from the doorways of the casinos that I passed through came the sounds of bells and buzzers and the spit of coins on coins. Above it all burned the flash and pulse of neon, the big signs from the Aladdin, the Dunes, the Flamingo and Caesars. It was all brightness and fun in the way of an arcade, like the roller coaster, like the rush, this easy exchange of money. But what was laid waste in the night, the morning soon uncovered, if you cared to look behind the big hotels or in the back alleys where the locals, the hardcore and the losers dug through trash bins, slept or shared a thin green bottle of Thunderbird. And the women who only hours before might've been mistaken for the well-dressed single or married ones were now, as the sun rose, ducking into cabs, looking bored, tired and empty, their makeup worn, maybe a run in their nylons. The more determined and desperate working girls lingered on the corners, holding out hope that yet another customer might soon circle the block and stop.

I don't know how many casinos I wandered in and out of that night, but I went through them all. At the Dunes, just past the main doors, was a display of an old Packard riddled with bullet holes and carrying these wax mannequins made up to look like Bonnie and Clyde. They had these grotesque fake smiles, the kind some undertakers put on corpses, and they each held tommy guns. Bonnie had a pistol tucked in the waistband of her dress. On my way out I checked the parking lot for the rented Camaro; I checked all the parking lots of all the casinos. I checked the streets for it, too.

No luck.

By then it was daylight, and I widened my search to the smaller darker casinos where if I'd been smart I would've gone earlier. Because I found my father about seven that morning at this dive called the Gold Horseshoe, just a few blocks off the Strip. The place smelled of stale tobacco and some kind of industrial-strength cleaner that they used on the carpets, which were in dire need of replacement given the paths worn into them, the stains and the odor. Even the chrome plating on the handles of the different slot machines was worn to the dull gray steel.

He was at the crap tables with four or five black men who didn't look in any better shape than he did. His eyes were red, his shirt was unbuttoned at the throat, the collar dark with sweat, and he sported a couple days' growth of beard. Somewhere along the line he'd picked up a cowboy hat. I didn't see Melinda anywhere, and for a while I just stood there and stared him down, hoping, if possible, to shame him. Seeing him like this, all sweaty and tired and still going

at it, filled me with anger, an anger that I'd been feeling since
I left the hotel, but which until now I'd had no cause to vent.
My father, he just smiled, and that only made it worse. He
had a glass of bourbon in one hand and he was shaking the
dice in the other.

"I've been looking for you all goddamn night," I said. "We
gotta talk."

"In a minute."

"Right *now*."

"Since when," my father said, "did you start ordering me
around?"

He grinned. He looked at the men and shrugged as if to
say what can you do with a smart-mouthed kid like this? Then
he leaned over the table and let the dice fly. They smacked
against the backboard and stopped at eleven, which suggested to me that it was all on the up-and-up, for his loaded
pair of dice favored the number six. He let out a whoop and
shouted to the dealer.

"Let it ride."

Judging from his pile of chips I'd say he was up several
hundred dollars, and not to find him down or close to it
seemed a godsend to me. It was my intent to get him back to
the hotel, broke or flush, and seeing as how good fortune had
come his way I thought it wise to act quickly. At the same
time, however, being that I was underage and surrounded by
some very grim-faced gamblers not the least bit interested in
my personal crusade, I felt awkward and a touch scared.

I took hold of his arm. I spoke firmly.

"I'm sick of waiting," I said.

He shook me off.

"Get your paws off me," he said. "I'm on a streak and
you're messing up my stride."

"Don't blame it on me," I said, "it's been messed up for
years. You want to stay and watch it get worse, you go right
ahead, since that's all you seem to give a shit about anyway.

But I'm going outside. I'm giving you five more minutes, and if you're not out I don't want to say what I'll do. But you won't like it. I can guarantee you that."

Exactly what I planned to do if it came down to that I hadn't the slightest idea, but I thought I could figure out something of consequence in the next five minutes. I considered telling him I'd had my fill and that I was hitting the road. But I dismissed it for fear that he might not try and stop me. I briefly considered threatening to turn him in and justifying it on the basis that I'd be saving him from himself. But that was a line I didn't want to cross, largely because I was incapable of ever following through with it, and also because its mere mention, bluff or not, would only serve to widen the growing chasm between us. Fortunately, whether spurred by guilt, a capacity for which he seemed in short reserve, or horse sense—knowing when to walk before that fragile streak breaks—my father stepped out of the casino, wincing against the bright morning sun.

He tilted his cowboy hat so that it rode lower on his brow, then tucked in his shirt and lit a cigarette from the butt of another.

"Let's get some breakfast," he said. "I need something solid in my stomach."

He started walking, at first slowly, at first stiffly, as if he'd forgotten how it was done, and after a moment's hesitation I followed.

"You know, if I wanted a babysitter I would've hired one. You embarrassed me back there," he said. "I hope it doesn't happen again."

"Don't give me a reason," I said. "You think I like walking around all night looking for your ass, you're crazy. For all I know you could've been dead, you could've been busted. No," I said, letting my voice rise, "I can think of a whole lot of better things to do with my time."

"So do 'em."

"I just might, I just might start gambling and drinking twenty-four hours a day, too. Shit, if it's that much fun I don't see why I shouldn't get myself a good early start."

"Cut the wiseassing."

"Practice makes perfect."

"You don't need any work in that department," he said. "There was a school for smart asses you'd be at the top of the class. Melinda back at the hotel?"

"How would I know?"

"I'm just asking."

"I thought she was with you."

"Well," he said, " she ain't. We lost each other somewhere along the line."

I didn't say anything, though I was glad to hear it, and I hoped it remained that way. We crossed the street as the light dropped to red. I picked up my step for the cars, which were starting across the intersection, but my father didn't bother.

"You didn't spot her when you were nosing all over town for me?"

"If I did, I wouldn't tell you."

"How come every time I ask you a straight question you got to come back with some nasty remark?"

"At least you can depend on me for something," I said, "which is more than I can say for you."

We went on like that all through breakfast, and though I would have preferred not to argue, it did provide me with some semblance of comfort, knowing that my father was safe and that, even if we bickered, even if he was hung over and looked like hell, we were together. Afterwards, instead of taking a nap, we put on our trunks and went down to the pool, so he could get some of that sun he hadn't seen in days and shake that hard-earned casino pallor. Melinda had left no sign of having returned to the hotel, but my father wasn't overly concerned. He left a note telling her where we'd be and propped it against the lamp on the dresser.

"She'll be back when her money runs out," he said. "I'm just surprised it hasn't been sooner." His attitude seemed rather cavalier to me, and suggested that he'd fared well enough to cover whatever losses she likely incurred. But that might've been wishful thinking. For I was hard pressed to imagine that my father thought much further ahead than tomorrow.

"How we holding up on funds?" I said, as we settled into our lounge chairs. He set his back so that he could lie down. At the shallow end of the pool, a mother lifted her child up and down on the steps. He was about three years old, and he had the wide-eyed expression of shock on his face.

"Money," my father said. "That all you ever think about?"

"Now and then."

"Like about every other minute, I'd say. You're obsessed."

"Don't tell me about obsession," I said, "when you go chasing some woman all over the country."

"She's not just any woman, Bobby."

"I'm trying to be practical. We ought to get the hell out of here before you blow it all, if you haven't already. A moving target," I said, "is harder to hit."

"For your information I'm ahead a few bucks. And as far as moving goes, there's other ways than skipping town. I only took what was owed me, and if they want to persecute a man for that, by God, let 'em try. I've been taking it up the ass since day one and it's high time I changed positions."

His attitude, which I found at once frightening and reprehensible, was exactly what had gotten him into trouble. What struck me as even more perverse was that he'd somehow managed to convince himself that he hadn't done anything wrong. I told him that, too, that he had a shitty way of looking at things.

"You're changing," I said. "More and more every day, and it ain't for the better."

"Spare me the lecture."

He stretched out, yawned and covered his face with the cowboy hat.

The child at the end of the pool was crying now. His mother was guiding him into deeper waters where he had no footing. It must've seemed bottomless. The water was up to his chin, which he had pointed skyward, as if by sheer will he could lift his entire body out, and the look on his face had changed from one of shock to complete and utter terror. His mother kept saying, "There's nothing to fear, honey, don't be a coward. I'm right here." Except she wasn't. She kept giving him her arm, then taking it away, so that he sunk and rose, thrashed and pulled, swallowing water, then swallowing air.

I sat forward.

"That's enough," I shouted, because I'd had my fill of her. "Can't you hear the boy crying? Can't you see he's scared?"

My father sat up, too. The woman looked around, not knowing at first where the voice had come from. I caught her eye and we glared at each other.

"Hush," Melinda said, for she was there now standing above us in a bikini, with another woman as beautiful as herself. "Don't interfere." Then she smiled down at my father. "Floyd, I'd like you to meet Darlene. She's a dear, dear friend of mine."

Only he was in no mood for niceties.

"Where the hell did you run off to the other night?"

"Take it easy," Darlene said. "We've just been catching up on some old times. That's no reason for you to snap at her."

"Nobody asked you, baby," he said.

"C'mon, Floyd, show a little respect. Darlene just got me a job dealing craps, and since I figure you're flat broke or close to it by now, you ought to thank her *and* me." She tossed me a bottle of Coppertone, then stretched out long and sensuously on the chaise longue beside me. "Mind rubbing some of that into my shoulders, honey? Your father smells like a goddamn brewery and I don't want him touching me."

Darlene slipped off her robe and settled into a chair nearby. She, too, had on the smallest of bikinis.

"Melinda and I go way, way back." She paused. She laughed. "Soul mates. We first met in Taos, New Mexico, in 1893."

The boy in the pool went under again as I worked the lotion into the smooth, soft skin of Melinda's shoulders. When he surfaced he let out a terrible scream, and it occurred to me that he had just seen his life flash before him. Another time. Another world. Beyond him, on the far side of the pool, I spotted Mr. Ed looking for that perfect place to settle, and with him was a young Mexican kid. About my age, I thought, around a hundred years ago.

Once more, gently this time, the mother lowered her son into the water.

fifteen

IF THEIR FIRST encounter in another life strained credibility, their second was firmly grounded in the real world of the Las Vegas working girl. They had met at the Gentleman's Choice, where the services of hostesses, dancing partners and general companions of both sexes could be had by the hour or the night, with generous discounts offered for conventioneers. All major credit cards were honored. But where Melinda, in her past life, had made her fortune in the silver mines of New Mexico and lost it to drink, Darlene Whittaker learned from her friend's folly and applied the lesson in her next life. She was older than Melinda, though younger than my father, and after a half dozen years as a prostitute she turned her talents to real estate, got her license and landed a job with Century 21. As in the past, Darlene catered to the wealthier Las Vegans and out-of-towners buying vacation homes. Darlene's success in real estate proved instrumental in my father and Melinda's good fortune; that is, having sold houses to casino bosses and others high in their employ, she had the personal contacts to find her friend work quickly and, indirectly, as a spin-off, my father. I don't believe Darlene knew what they had planned.

Inside of a week, under the alias of Davis, we rented a fully furnished mobile home situated on half an acre off

Tropicana Avenue, near where the Liberace Museum was later built. It was there that our lives took on at least the appearance of normalcy, if only briefly, and given the recent turn of events that was good enough for me. There was a snailback trailer parked behind the mobile home, and I was excited about it, for my dog Sam and I now had a place we could call our own. If I spread my arms I could almost reach from one end of it to the other, but it was privacy, not size, that concerned me. It had electricity. It had an old air conditioner. It had a single bed and a tiny bathroom and two tanks, one for water and another for propane for the stove, on which I did most of my own cooking. The window over my bed looked out on the desert and offered an endless view of the Joshua trees, the yuccas and the purple sage. I had all kinds of plans on how to fix it up, with black-light posters, a lava lamp that glowed in the dark and strings of beads for the bathroom door that lay busted, torn from its hinges, around back of the trailer. There were cabinets, too, well placed all around, making smart use of every inch, like in a boat. In one cabinet I found an empty prescription bottle for nitroglycerin and that led me to believe that the man who'd once lived here had had a bad heart and that maybe he'd died in the bed I now slept in. If that was the case, I didn't think it was such a bad place to go, with the flat endless view of the desert and all its quiet. Wilfred, by the way, was a tidy man. The pots and pans were all well scrubbed and stacked neatly in the cabinet under the sink.

I couldn't have chosen a better place if I'd picked it out myself. The mobile home, however, I could take or leave. The ceilings were low, so that you felt like you were in a cavern, like you had to stoop when you really didn't, and in the kitchen area hung this crystal chandelier that dwarfed everything else in the place. In the living room, fake marbled mirror, cut in squares, covered one entire wall, and another was done in walnut paneling. But the thing that sold my father and Melinda on it, aside from the cheap rent, was the bedroom with its round bed and the dark blue velour canopy over it. Silver tassels dangled from the ends. At night, I often heard them making good use of that round bed, as sounds carried easily through the desert. The road outside our place was rarely traveled, it had only recently been paved, and when darkness fell it was so quiet you could hear a car approaching for a mile away. I soon got to where I could identify the make just by the sound of the engine, and if I didn't recognize it, say, as the rumble of a truck or the putter of a Volkswagen or the purr of Darlene's brand-new '71 Mustang, my heart sped up until it had passed. For as often as I lay awake listening to them make love, I worried that one night I might also hear the gravel in our driveway ticking under the wheels of a police cruiser.

In my estimation, it would've been smarter to put Las Vegas behind us, but my father and Melinda saw it as a city of hope and opportunity. Hard work would have its payoff, and I attribute my father's reserve, that is, not taking the edge he'd picked up in prison until he'd perfected his skills and better understood the many other aspects of gambling and sleight of hand, to his intelligence, Melinda's and their good sense of timing. In short, though I could have predicted the outcome of their efforts, as earnest and practiced as they may have been, they didn't leap blindly into their venture until Melinda had established herself as a loyal employee. In the meantime, my father seized the opportunity to further hone his skills, and when he wasn't hanging around the casinos, "studying and researching," as he referred to it, he was seated at the kitchen table or in the living room in front of TV, rolling a pair of dice back and forth between his hands, working hard to overcome his disability.

He soon accumulated a small library of books on gambling techniques in cards, but mostly craps. He bought *Gambler's Digest* the day it hit the racks. He bought several pairs of red translucent dice and a few yards of green felt, and each day he'd push the kitchen table up against the wall, gently smooth the felt across it and practice his throw for literally hours— until he complained, only half jokingly, of arthritis in his wrist. Hitting the right numbers was "all a matter of control," he said, and to prove it he'd demonstrate the whip shot for me, the slide, the drop and the pad shot, and another, his favorite, called the Greek. This last one was extremely difficult, but he could use it even hitting the backboard, or the wall in this case, where with the others you had to roll low. He also memorized long charts of numbers, those that were more likely to come up and those that were not, and in which combinations, and so bet accordingly. The lists, in length and complexity, seemed mind-boggling, and I couldn't for the life of me fathom how any one person could contain them all in his or her head. To relax, after a long hard morning of tossing dice, and before Melinda went off to work, they'd stretch out on these old lounge chairs in the backyard and take in the sun. My father always kept a cold beer at his side and this ridiculous-looking sun reflector perched under his chin. Melinda sipped a tall glass of gin and tonic, while she thumbed through the latest edition of *Cosmopolitan*.

While they worked on their tans and bided their time, and while Melinda continued to build the trust of her pit bosses, fellow stick- and floormen, I took it upon myself, as I had in the past, to situate myself in a place where I could observe them, and if possible watch out for my father when he made his grand debut. Melinda was dealing craps nights at Circus Circus on the Strip, and I applied for a position there as porter. They hired me on the spot, much to my father's consternation, but there was little he could do to stop me. It wasn't much different than my last job in that basically I cleaned up after people, only this time around they were gamblers instead of bowlers. I dumped ashtrays beside the slot machines, I picked up the plastic cups and the straws, mopped up spilled drinks and swept the empty quarter, dime and nickel wrappers from the floor, and occasionally I pocketed the change that someone had dropped. My shift began in the afternoon and I got off at nine at night, so even though my hours might not have completely matched Melinda's, they overlapped some. Circus Circus was only a couple miles from our place, and I enjoyed walking home through the desert at night when there was absolutely nobody around and it was cool out. The walk gave me time to collect my thoughts and put the day into perspective. The silence and vastness of the desert was a welcome relief coming from Circus Circus, its sloping roof made to look like a circus big top, and where inside the noise was great and the air reeked of tobacco. Above the ringing and buzzing of the slot machines, above the craps tables and spinning roulette wheels, trapeze artists swung from bars mounted to the ceiling, or a man on a unicycle balanced on the tightrope, and though I never tired of watching them I liked looking up at the stars, too, and into the darkness surrounding them.

I prided myself on doing a fast and thorough job. Few if any in the Circus Circus employ could outwork Bobby Barlow, and I hoped that my efforts would not go unnoticed. I was bucking for a raise, because at a quarter above minimum I didn't take home much after taxes, Social Security and all the rest. Even more, I wanted a promotion: my goal was to put in for a bellhop's position at the hotel, and because of the competition I figured I'd need a strong recommendation from my supervisor. The town operated off tips, and those guys made fifty or sixty bucks a day just carting suitcases up to people's rooms. I'd also heard tales that they occasionally received more from some of the most beautiful women that passed through Vegas. And I believed it. Bellhops were in a highly visible position. I befriended one, who said he might be able to pull some weight for me when the time came, and though that opportunity never materialized he did sell me my first lid of marijuana in the employees' lounge, just before I clocked out.

"It's dynamite shit," he said, as he clapped me on the arm, and slipped it into my pocket. I shook his hand, and as I did so, in the same gesture, pressed a neatly folded twenty-dollar bill into his palm. Slick, I thought. Professional. And right under the noses of a roomful of employees drinking coffee and talking.

I let him leave ahead of me, so it wouldn't look so suspicious, and to kill the few extra moments I studied the pictures on the bulletin board. They were mug shots, really, a dozen of them under the federal guidelines poster for workers' rights and minimum wages. They were the known cheats and hustlers about town, ones the dealers, stickmen and pit bosses were supposed to keep an eye out for. Ordinary people. Housewives. A guy in a baseball cap. Another wearing glasses. Just looking at them, no one could suspect, which was true of me and my marijuana, though I'd begun to let my hair grow and that was a dead giveaway to the older generation. Which meant that I had to take extra precautions if I planned to successfully carry on this business of dope smoking for any length of time.

My father and Melinda played a similar role with one another, that of total strangers, whenever he stepped up to her craps table and laid his money down. Being without two fingers, he wasn't the best at sleight of hand, but with Melinda in his corner he quickly overcame his handicap in a big way. I seldom had the opportunity to catch them in action, for although my shift overlapped Melinda's, my father generally made it a point to saunter into Circus Circus after I'd left for home, and when the casino was in the middle of its prime gaming hours. I don't know exactly when they first chose to implement their plan, I missed the grand debut, and I don't know how long they'd been at it before I had the chance to bear witness, but the first time I actually saw them at it occurred the same night that I bought the marijuana. I spotted my father at her table as I was passing through the casino, and when another gambler tossed and lost, he stepped up to the shooter's box, bought a hundred in chips and threw a twenty-dollar one on the table.

"Yo," he said. "On six."

She sent him the dice and I stopped, stood back a way and watched. He rolled up his sleeves, making a small act of it, turning the cuffs slowly, meticulously. The sleight of hand might've happened in the next moment, when he picked up the dice and let them fly, all in one swift movement. They tumbled across the table and came up six. There was a crowd around the table, for Melinda was a popular stickman, and they cheered.

My father swept in his chips, all but twenty, and bet fifty on six on the center. He blew on the dice, he shook them.

"C'mon now," he said, "be nice to daddy. I need a new Cadillac."

"Make sure they hit the backboard this time, sir," Melinda said.

"They hit."

"Barely. Raise 'em, please."

He gave her a dirty look, then let the dice fly. They flew across the table. Struck the backboard. Landed three up on both. Again the crowd cheered.

"Winner six."

"Let it ride."

The cocktail waitress brought him a drink, and he tipped her a couple bucks, then tossed a five-dollar chip outside the come line for Melinda.

"That's for you, baby," he said. "It's our lucky night tonight."

He bounced the one die on the felt. Snapped it up. He bounced the other. Snapped it up, too.

"Let's go," Melinda said.

"Patience now, I'm concentrating."

"Just shoot 'em, sir. You're not the only one here."

He shook them a few seconds, then let them fly. Once again the crowd cheered.

"Winner eleven."

He swept in his chips, placed a hundred-dollar bet, rubbed the dice between his hands and hurtled them across the table. This time they came up five, and the crowd was quiet. He picked up his take.

"That's it for me, darling. Let some other sucker have a chance."

At that my father left, no one the wiser, and an easy couple thousand richer. I didn't follow him out, again for the same reason I hadn't followed the doorman from the employee lounge, because of suspicion by association, and on my way home that evening I took a detour into the desert and tested the marijuana. Because I was still a novice in this matter of drugs, and because I suspected that the doorman might well have overrated the quality of his product—it seemed all marijuana smokers and dealers considered their stuff the very best—I let doubt get the better of me. When I didn't feel anything right away, I smoked another, and before I finished it the first kicked in and I knew that I was in for a serious ride. It was, as the doorman had warned, dynamite shit.

Going directly home seemed a mistake, but after wandering around the desert for a while the thought occurred to me that I was crazy. Both my sense of distance and direction were greatly out of whack. Walking took on a whole new dimension, requiring an act of considerable concentration in making sure one foot was securely planted before lifting the other. Because the ground, at alternating moments, could look far away and then, in the next, right in my face. I found myself thinking about all the rattlers around out here in the darkness, the diamondback, the furry tarantula, the armor-skinned Gila monster and his good buddy, the deadly scorpion. Normally the thought of poisonous creatures wouldn't have concerned me in the least, but in my present state of mind paranoia seemed altogether justified. Several hours must've passed between the time I prepared and smoked the stuff and when I eventually rediscovered the road, which I had lost sight of in my wandering. At one point, as I was headed home, a motorcycle sped by, and the high-pitched whining noise it made lingered in my ears long after it had passed.

Darlene's Mustang was parked in the gravel driveway. The lights in the kitchen and living room burned. Over the whining noise in my head, I heard music, an old Chuck Berry song. My plan was to head straight to the snailback and bolt the door, so that I could spend the remainder of the night in safety and seclusion. But I didn't make it past the driveway when the screen door swung open and my father stepped out onto the porch. He had a beer in one hand and a lighted cigarette dangled from his lips.

"C'mon in and join us," he said.

"I'll pass."

But my father would have none of that and did exactly as I feared that he might, which was to come down the steps and put his arm around my shoulders. There was no escaping now.

"I'm beat," I said. "I just want to go to sleep."

"Shit," he said, "you can rest when you're dead. When I was your age I could party all night and get up the next day and roof a whole house."

Sure, I thought.

We stepped into the house, into the light, and it was harsh on my eyes. Melinda and Darlene sat at the kitchen table, and Darlene had on this short skirt. Her legs were crossed, and I admired her knees and how her calves tapered down to her ankles small enough to close my thumb and finger around. My father had once told me that there were two types of redheads, those with freckles and those with a creamy, perfectly white complexion unmatched in all but the most fortunate, and Darlene definitely belonged to the latter group. She had a slender neck, she had pale blue eyes. She had a full damp mouth, too, that in my dreams I wanted to gently open with my fingers and then kiss. But even in fantasy I was hard-pressed to entertain that notion, for I sensed all too well that Darlene knew about young men like me, what lurked in our hearts and behind our polite smiles, and that there was a side of her that enjoyed the attention and at the same time re-sented it. The thought made me uneasy and for some reason left me feeling guilty, no matter my manners, no matter where I kept my eyes. I also had this sick feeling inside that she knew I was high, that Melinda did, too. My father, he was too drunk to notice, and even if he were sober I doubted if he could've told the difference. There was a bottle of tequila on the table, three shot glasses and a bowl of sliced limes, and Darlene took one, bit into it, winced and followed it up with the tequila. She slammed the empty shot glass down on the table.

"Look what the cat dragged in," she said.

My father still had his arm around me. He pinched the hair at the back of my neck.

"Time for a trim, wouldn't you say? It gets any longer we'll put a cute little red ribbon in it and call you Bobby Anna."

I knocked his hand away.

"Oh leave him alone," Melinda said. "That's the style now."

"Not for my boy."

"It's his hair," Darlene said. "He can do what he wants."

My father laughed.

"Not before he turns eighteen. Until then I'm in charge," he said. "You want a beer, son?"

"No thanks," I said.

My hair was getting long, it did cover my ears, but by no

means was it ready for any ribbon, and I resented my father for teasing me about it. But for this party of three I just smiled and excused myself into the relative safety of the living room. I figured I'd watch TV for a few minutes to make my father happy and ward off any suspicions Melinda or Darlene might've had about me being high, and then, when I'd sufficiently proven myself, and when they weren't paying attention, I'd slip out the back door. If that plan didn't work, I'd stick to my original excuse that I was just plain tired, which would explain my bloodshot eyes. Or I could say I got dust in them at work.

From the couch I could see into the kitchen, and now and then I tossed a glance their way. They were lining up another round and laughing. On TV, an old rerun of "The Untouchables" played, and Elliot Ness was staked out in his car across the street from an Italian restaurant. Inside, the gangsters held court over steaming bowls of cioppino. All wore bibs. One guy was sucking the meat from a crab's claw and talking out of the side of his mouth.

My father raised his shot glass.

"To Melinda," he said, "and her new job."

"Now that just leaves you," Darlene said. "I hear the boy's working too."

"I'm still on vacation, darling."

"What is it you said he did?"

"Carpentry," Melinda said.

My father corrected her.

"A class A finish man."

"That must've been a while back," Darlene said, "with those clean nails, with those soft hands. Tell me, Floyd, just how long you plan on vacationing?"

"Hey now," Melinda said. "I thought we were supposed to be celebrating."

Darlene threw back her shot.

"That's the spirit."

"Can you grab me another beer while you're up, honey?" my father said.

Before she could answer, however, Darlene cut her off.

"You don't look crippled to me. Why don't you get up and get it yourself?"

My father sucked in his breath.

"For the record, honey, I was *asking*, not ordering."

"I'm not your *honey*," she said. "I'm not your darling, either. I hate when men throw those words around like we're all a piece of meat."

"Baby," he said, "I get the feeling you don't like men *period*."

Then he made a show of getting himself a beer, rising slowly from the table as if it were a difficult task and taking several labored steps to the refrigerator. He gripped the door handle with both hands and pretended, as he struggled to pull it open, that it required great strength. "There," he said, when he finally had another beer in his hand. "Was that so goddamn hard?" Melinda laughed nervously, because I don't believe she'd ever seen my father behave quite like this. Darlene, she just poured herself another shot of tequila and ignored him. Myself, I returned my attention to the TV. It was an action scene, a real predicament.

Two more gangsters, these ones in a black sedan, pulled up behind Elliot Ness and boxed him in. He rolled out of the car and came up shooting. The battle was bloody, and given its timing made this ordinarily hollow spot in my chest knot with tension. I felt the couch give. Melinda had settled beside me.

"You hear any of that?"

"If you don't mind," I said, "I'm trying to watch the show."

"Don't be so rude. There's enough of that going on in the kitchen without you adding to it. It's the tequila," she said, shivering dramatically, as if she could taste it. "Nasty stuff, and it brings out the worst in people." She scooted closer to me, reached over and began rubbing my neck. "Fuel to the fire," she said. "Let's make your daddy jealous." I was embarrassed, I was tense, but I also enjoyed her touch. "Beats the hell out of me how they can drink that stuff straight. I don't blame you for getting high. I like pot better myself. But mum's the word. It'll be our little secret, okay?"

I nodded. My heart had quickened, as much from her words as her touch, and I don't think I could've spoken if I'd tried. For my mouth, already dry from the marijuana, had grown suddenly more so.

On TV one of the gangsters took a bullet in the back as he was running away. The camera dollied in for a close-up of the bloody mess. In the background another gangster took it in the neck. Another in the stomach. Bodies were falling everywhere.

"How can you watch this?"

I thought she was talking about all the violence, all the gunfire and bloodshed.

"Why this old black-and-white stuff," she said, "when you can see everything in living color now?" She patted me on the knee and rose from the couch. "Just keep me in mind for next time."

Over the wail of police sirens, as I started for the back door, I heard my father making fun of Darlene and Melinda. I believe he was jealous, though not on account of me. It had more to do with feeling left out, with competing with two very close friends, who aside from having once worked for the same escort service had in common a previous life in Taos, New Mexico, nearly a century before. He said he had one too, by God, now that he thought about it. It all came in a flood, it was all crystal clear.

"I was Pretty Boy Floyd," he said.

"In your dreams," Darlene said.

And fool that he could be, particularly when he'd been

drinking too much, he pulled the Luger out from someplace. Under his jacket on the counter? From inside a drawer? I don't know, but he had it.

"What the fuck you doing with that?"

"Got to dream."

"Put it away, Floyd. You're scaring her."

"Honey," Darlene said, "what scares me is you and your choice of men. Between this loser and your last, I'm surprised you're still alive."

I closed the back door behind me and headed across the yard to the snailback. But Sam, he was spooked, and he wouldn't let me by. I had him chained at the hitch and he snarled and lunged at me.

"It's cool," I said, "it's me."

I put out my hand and he snapped at it.

"Man, it's *me*."

He growled, he bared his teeth.

"Good boy. Good protector."

He recognized my voice then. His ears lay back, and he lowered himself to the ground and crawled toward me on his belly.

"Dumb dog," I said. "Don't even know your master. What gets into you?"

I petted him, and I would've petted him longer only I was in no mood. I let myself into the trailer and locked it and then stretched out on the bed and lay there wondering about my father, about Darlene and what she knew, what if anything Melinda had told her about him—prison, Portland or what we'd done in Seattle. I had seen my father in better times, and in moments of doubt like these I often called on them. Up until he'd gone to Salem I'd only known him to work, work hard, sometimes twelve hours a day, six days a week when his different bosses had let him, and even on Sundays it was tough for him to sit still. I thought about that and how, on that day my father laid claim to his death and dismemberment policy with Quality Life, it marked the beginning of losses much greater than a finger or two, no matter how you figured it.

I thought about it long and hard and I called on one of the earlier times when we were between apartments and living out of the Sleepy Hollow Motel near the highway. I used to walk home after school, but on the last day of class, when the teacher gave out the report cards, my father must have known something was up. Because he was waiting at the front gates for me that afternoon. "Don't look so glum," he said, "it's just a crummy piece of paper." This was first grade and I'd failed, but where another parent might have scolded his boy, maybe slapped him around, my father borrowed twenty dollars and bought me a Schwinn Stingray, almost brand-new, painted candy-apple red, with a banana seat. That night he taught me to ride it under the lights in the parking lot of the Sleepy Hollow. "Steer straight, pedal, and don't stop." He gave me a strong push, and I can still feel that wind in my face like I was flying, I mean soaring.

Way up there. High.

A rush, a real one.

Nothing like being stoned in a snailback in the desert on the outskirts of Las Vegas, Nevada. Now my old man was back there in the mobile home waving a gun around and talking the fool. "Got to dream," he'd said, and I remembered when it meant Tahiti. Mazatlán. Hawaii. And even though Vegas had been mentioned right along with them, it was only one out of four places and those weren't odds enough for me to sweat over. He had the cash for it fanned out across the kitchen table, taken from its hiding spot, that dark space beneath the refrigerator, the cobwebs and the dust. Twenties. Fifties. Hundred-dollar bills.

As I lay in bed I heard Darlene fire up her car, that roar of exhaust, followed by the spit of gravel against its fenders as she sped off down the driveway. The snailback faced my father and Melinda's bedroom, and soon after Darlene had left, the light in it came on. In their haste, or drunkenness, they didn't shut the drapes, and I watched my father take her into his arms, kiss her full on the mouth and undress her, slowly it seemed, much too slowly for me. They did all kinds of wonderful things to each other. Inhibition played no role, and though I felt it was wrong for me to watch I justified my voyeurism on the basis of ignorance. What better way to learn about lovemaking than observing two people whose appetites for it were keen and voracious, and who had no qualms about experimenting. They favored certain positions, but all in all their passion was unpredictable in terms of what it led them to do and for how long. To this day, one of the most vivid memories I have of Melinda Johnson is of her on top, her head thrown back, the cords in her neck taut, and the brush and sway of her long hair against her shoulders. The silver tassels on the canopy above the bed swung in rhythm.

I imagined myself in my father's place, as I had time and again. I imagined Melinda beneath me or pressing from on top. But now, when their bedroom light had gone out, I envisioned Bonnie Walker's face in her place. We were down by the Willamette River, stretched out on an open sleeping bag on a warm day, listening to the sounds the river made on the riffles and watching the trout suddenly rise to the surface, snatch a mosquito and disappear with it into the depths. We watched the rings they left in the water widen and fade, we felt a cool breeze on our faces, but I didn't get any more detailed about Bonnie other than how she lay on the sleeping bag in her bikini with her arms stretched above her head. We shared a bottle of Lancers and made love and afterwards we held each other and talked some and listened to the river some and drank the last of the wine. It was good, I thought, the way it could be sometimes, and I hoped that my fantasies would soon give way to the real thing and that one day I'd come to know the experience precisely as I had dreamed of it.

It was hours before I fell asleep, and the last thing I recall hearing was Sam jumping up and down outside the snailback. He was turning in circles and trying to nip at his tail, except he didn't have one anymore, some butcher of a vet had sliced it off soon after he'd come into the world. And his bark sounded odd, sounded strained, almost painful, almost human, like the garbled and anxious cry of a child lost in the darkness.

Sixteen

FROM THE VERY START, Darlene had my father pegged as a loser. In her eyes he was barely a step above Melinda's last pick of men, and that's not saying much in light of Bo Stenovich, who as a common wife-beater ranked among the lowest, most despicable sort of companion. She also seemed to know more about Bo than my father and I, which initially struck me as odd because she'd never met the man, but on the other hand, when I paused to consider it for a moment, it made perfect sense. Melinda and Darlene shared a long-running friendship that defied both time and distance, in this life by way of phone and letter, and in the other, I guess, by astral travel, projection, that mind-out-of-body experience or some sort of telepathy. Regardless of their methods or means of communication, it was from Darlene that I learned how Melinda and Bo had come to know one another. He had been her arresting officer on a prostitution charge, or, rather, he would've been the arresting officer if he hadn't tried to cut a deal with her. This was a few months after Melinda, bored, restless and embittered with her experience in the escort business, had packed her bags and left for Portland, hoping once again that a change of job and scenery might revitalize her.

Her life, like ours, had been a nomadic one, though on the surface Melinda's appeared considerably more glamorous. As a young, beautiful call girl, and one particularly adept in the pleasures of sex, she'd had occasion to travel with some of her wealthier clients. For a price, she would accompany them on their business junkets around the world—to Switzerland, say, to Germany, Paris or Hawaii, or maybe it was just for a weekend cruise with several business associates on the company yacht. No matter the itinerary, Melinda traveled as a legitimate companion and tended to her partners' needs in ways many of their wives would, although she steadfastly refused to cook for them, not for any philosophical reasons, either, but simply because she wasn't very good at it. The men, of course, who for the most part were middle-aged and desperate for things other than food, though given the paunches on many of them one might've suspected otherwise, were not overly concerned about her culinary skills. The arrangement was always the same. What was intimated prior to the trip was never addressed again, at least not in words. Alone in the hotel room on the morning of her departure or in the cramped quarters of the airplane bathroom thousands of feet above the Atlantic, if her companion was returning with her, Melinda would open her purse, and in it find an envelope full of cash and occasionally a note expressing fondest wishes, gratitude and friendship. They were always very generous.

Where Melinda had had the opportunity to see a good portion of the world, my father's idea of travel meant moving from one apartment, job or town to another. It was drifting all the same, whether it involved ten thousand miles or ten, and the sense of restlessness that spurred Melinda to leave Vegas and her best friend was the same sort of malady that affected my father and his constant pursuit of a different, if not better, way of life. In that regard, they were both one and the same, in this blind search for wealth, be it spiritual or material, and for Melinda, twice over, in this life and in her previous one as the silver miner who had lost what she loved most—her family, imagined or not. I know of no reason why or how they both wound up in Portland other than fate, but as my father would've put it, it's a dog-eat-dog world, and soon after she hit town hard times again befell her.

Though she secured a position as a receptionist in the law firm of Schwartz, Simon and Hansen, her salary was hardly enough to cover her bills, let alone support the lifestyle to which she was accustomed, and a few months later she took on a night job at an Oriental massage parlor to help supplement her meager income. Bo was on vice back then, he had a reputation for taking advantage of Portland's finest working girls, and Melinda proved no exception. The catch, more implied than overt, was that when he called on her the next week and asked for a "date," fully assuming that the term would be understood in the way that originally landed her in trouble, Melinda turned it around on him. She wasn't about to get screwed, figuratively or literally, and when he arrived at her apartment that evening, on his night off, she held him to the letter of his word. She answered the door dressed and made up for someplace nice, and before he could say anything she grabbed her purse and shut the door behind her.

"So," she said, "where you taking me tonight? I'm starved."

Bo wasn't one to push around, but then Melinda was an extraordinary woman, and in the short time that I knew her she generally got her way, as she did that night. They went out to dinner. They took in a movie. One good time led to another, and they were soon seeing each other on a regular basis—this all before my father happened into the picture and complicated their lives in ways perhaps best left, again, for fate to judge.

Bo's later attempts to reform Melinda might have at first appeared noble, earnest, flattering even, and at least on the surface motivated by love, but however well-meaning his intentions they turned sour fast. He had the temper of a child, and his idea of what a marriage ought to be was heavily one-sided in his favor. When she told Darlene that Bo had raised his hand to her, not once but on more than half a dozen occasions, she agreed that leaving the son of a bitch was the wisest thing that she ever could've done. This last bit of information about the beatings was revealed at poolside back at the Flamingo, when the bruise around Melinda's eye, though only a pale shade of yellow, was still plain enough.

"Forgive him," she said, "and it'll only get worse. I don't care what he says or how much he begs you to come back. Once they cross that line they're history. Believe me, I've been there myself. I don't understand why you didn't dump the bum sooner."

"Exactly my sentiments," my father said. "I've been after her to see a lawyer for six months."

"Excuse me," Darlene said, "but I think she's old enough to speak for herself now." Then, to Melinda, she added in confidence, "If this Bo character gives you any more trouble, I know some people who'd be glad to wise him up."

It's since been my experience that those who made that sort of boast were either mean drunks with delusions of power or certified psychotics, and even if they had the contacts to make good on the threat it likely would have ended in a botched job. But I believed Darlene Whittaker. That had been part of her world at one time, or the peripheries of it in any case, and she was neither a psychotic nor a vindictive, mean-spirited drunk. The casual way in which she extended the offer made my throat tighten.

"We can do without that kind of help," my father told her.

"That's awfully generous of you, Floyd, since you're not on the receiving end. Any other *man* would've evened the score by now."

"Bring him on," he said. "Any day. Any time. I'll kick his ass."

The intent was clear. He didn't want to be thought of as a coward, regardless of the fact that confronting Bo would've resulted in serious bodily injury to one or both of them. What's not clear was whether Darlene knew about our dark past and that by assisting Melinda she was aiding and abetting a misfit pack of fugitives. Considering how she already felt about my father, I didn't see the point in enlightening her further, and for my part I kept my lips sealed. In all fairness, however, her lowly opinion of my father should've extended to Melinda as well, for in terms of complicity she was certainly no innocent. It was only out of some vague sense of loyalty that Darlene hadn't passed judgment on her, too.

Their friendship ran deep, and it's safe to assume that they'd shared some good times together and some rough ones as well. All their dates couldn't have been with gentlemen; some must've had embarrassingly kinky or degrading requests, some must've been ill-mannered and less than attractive, and then there had to be others like Bo, whose misogyny took its form in physical violence. Those kinds of experiences could spark intense camaraderie between friends, and it's no wonder that they both imagined having lived a different life somewhere in the past. That they'd happened to share it together struck me as absurd, and when I expressed my skepticism they took immediate offense. To them, the chance of meeting in the real world was no more of a coincidence.

"Personally," Darlene told me, "I don't see the difference between discovering a friend in this life or another. Of all the places in the universe, how do two people, two soul mates, ever find each other? Come on, smarty, answer me that. You just like to *think* you have control."

"How I met your father," Melinda said. "That was fate. Can't argue that."

I could've, though I didn't.

"You know how I died?"

"In a fire," I said. "Like a witch."

"Sarcastic little shit," she said.

In the honorable tradition of my father, she tried to cuff

me on the side of the head, but she was much too slow and I easily ducked it.

Somewhere between imagination and fact, I believed, the truth rested. But I had little to go on other than my observations, and from what I witnessed Darlene was very protective of her friend. In the way of a big sister, she acted as if my father was taking advantage of Melinda, a young woman on the rebound, and his being so much older only heightened her distrust of him. To further compound the situation, Darlene resented him for not looking for legitimate work, and by having helped Melinda locate a job she'd indirectly contributed to my father's support. And that was never her intent. Her allegiance as a benefactor to this makeshift family of ours was really for her friend, and it was only by default that my father and I benefited.

Dealing craps was a highly coveted position among the casino employees, particularly at the fancier hotel casinos where the bets and the tips were often large, and there had to be dozens of other more qualified and experienced applicants ahead of Melinda when she put in for it. This wasn't a job you simply walked off the streets, applied for and got, and without Darlene's pull she would've had to take her place at the end of the line like anyone else. As with the rumor about doormen receiving sex in lieu of the standard gratuity, I'd heard similar tales about dealers, how they landed their jobs and how, in some instances, they spent their first two months paying off the contact, usually a floorman or a pit boss, if not with their bodies, then in dollars. And then there was no guarantee that the bum wouldn't fire you, so that he could run the scam all over again on another poor unsuspecting soul. However, this was not the arrangement with Melinda, and she kept every dollar she earned, and many more that she did not. Their streak of bad luck had finally seemed to run its course, and, as if the hex had been lifted from our shoulders, it was steak and lobster time for the next several months. All you could eat, too. The word, as Melinda had told me once for my crossword puzzle, was *gorge*. As in gluttony, as in cram, hog and devour. And that's exactly what we did.

Given the junk cars my father had driven most of his life, given all the run-down motels we'd lived in and the greasy foods we'd eaten, my father felt that it was high time we did it up in style. He bought a Cadillac Eldorado, used, but freshly painted and waxed, and for Melinda he bought a new pair of diamond earrings. They bought more new clothes, too, from Saks and The Broadway, and on Melinda's nights off they dressed up and went to dinner at the best restaurants and hotels, and afterwards they took in the big floor shows. Sinatra. Liberace. Wayne Newton, and Nudes on Ice. Naturally I was concerned about their newfound wealth, not so much how it was acquired, because I already knew that, but rather when they'd decide enough was enough and quit while they were ahead.

When I caught my father alone once I came right out and asked. He was sunning himself on the lounge chair in the backyard—if you could call it a backyard, for really it was just a barren plot of land with still more barren land beyond it. He had that sun reflector balanced under his chin, and his face was shiny with sweat and coconut oil. He was dozing and didn't answer me, not at first, anyway.

"Well?"

Nothing.

"Take that ridiculous thing off your face," I said. "I'm talking to you."

He opened his eyes and yawned.

"You're damn lucky I'm in a good mood or I'd just as soon grab you in a headlock and cut off that scraggly hair of yours. The longer it gets," he said, "the more you mouth off."

The hair bit, I thought, was simply another diversion, but I wasn't about to fall for it. I pressed my point, and because my father knew me as well as I knew him, that is, that I was stubborn and wouldn't leave him alone until he told me the truth, or begged off with a lie, he soon relented.

"First of all," he said, "it's none of your business how I make my money. You just be glad we got it. I know what's going through your head, and in case you doubt me, and I know you do, better think again. Your old man's a multi-talented individual who's only just begun to realize his true potential."

But that was book talk.

That was language he'd picked up reading about gambling, with chapters designed, according to the cover of the paperback on the ground beside him, to empower. Step by step. To unleash your inner potential.

"Knock off the shit," I said.

"It's no shit."

"Just tell me in plain English," I said. "When do you guys plan to quit?"

"When we have enough."

"What's enough?"

My father shrugged.

"Twenty thousand?" I said. "Fifty?"

"More."

"A hundred? Two hundred? You got to set some kind of limit and *stop*."

"Why?"

"You know goddamn well why."

"I don't want your advice and I don't need it, Bobby. Confidence," he said, "that's the difference between me a few months ago and me now. That's the difference between a winner and a loser. I could leave you with my own personal pair of dice right now and go into any casino on the Strip and walk out five minutes later with my pockets full of cash." Beside the book was a tall cool glass of gin and tonic, and he reached for it and took a sip. "With some tinkering, your old man finally worked out the kinks in the Barlow System. It was only a matter of time and fine-tuning." He set the glass down and grinned. "By the way, I got you something special the other day, but seeing as how you've been acting so high and mighty I'm wondering if I ought to give it to you."

"What is it?"

"You'll see. Maybe."

He leaned back in the lounge chair, positioned the sun reflector carefully under his chin again and closed his eyes.

True to his word, however, the gift was indeed something special.

I turned seventeen at Caesars Palace the night Bob Foster defended his light heavyweight crown against Hal Carroll.

Although I wasn't the boxing fan that my father was, I appreciated a good match, and this promised to be one, as Foster was one of the best light heavies ever to hold the title, and Carroll was a top contender, with twenty-seven fights under his belt, nine KOs, and only two losses early in his career. It had long been a dream of my father's, and to a lesser extent my own, to see a championship bout, preferably at ringside, which was precisely where we sat. The tickets cost a small fortune, or "an arm and a leg," as my father put it, waving them slowly beneath my nose as if they had an exotic aroma, as if you could eat them.

"But you only turn seventeen once," he added. "Enjoy it while you can, Bobby, because I'll tell you, it wears out fast."

Melinda went all out for the night and wore this red sequined dress, her new diamond earrings, and she had her hair done up that afternoon. Darlene loaned her a strand of pearls, and against her smooth tanned skin and that wonderfully slender throat they looked stunningly bright. My father rented a tux with a ruffled shirt, while I wore my first suit and tie. We shared a bottle of champagne on the way there, and as Melinda passed a glass of it to me in the backseat my father asked who we were rooting for.

"Foster," Melinda said.

"Same for me."

"He just might get his ass kicked tonight," my father said.

"Not likely."

"Nobody's unbeatable, Bobby."

"Foster's close to it. In his division, anyway."

"How much you want to bet?"

"Twenty," I said.

"Ooooh," he said, like he was impressed. "Mister Confident."

I put my hand over the seat.

"Shake."

"I hate to take your money."

"You backing down?"

I knew that would get him.

"Hell no, let's double it."

"For your own sake, Floyd," Melinda said, "you better stick to twenty."

Again he was betting on hope instead of the odds, but since both fighters were black the logic of his choice was slightly more convoluted. That Carroll was the underdog, for whom my father always had a soft spot, paled in light of the fact that Foster was a black *champion*, and to achieve, let alone maintain that kind of stature aggravated his racist sensibilities. Six months down the line, if Carroll won the belt, my father would be rooting for him to lose it.

It was something pulling up to Caesars in that big Eldorado, with a buzz on from the champagne, all the bright lights, the commotion and crowds. We were royalty that night; my father tipped the valet generously, the same for the usher, and when we settled into our seats the men around us couldn't keep from staring at Melinda. My father leaned over and whispered in her ear.

"They think you're some kind of star."

"I am."

"It's for sure you're pretty enough," he said. "Don't look now, but I think that's Ryan O'Neal over there giving you the eye."

"Big deal."

"He was good in *Wild Rovers*," I said, "with William Holden."

"I ought to go into acting," my father said. "I can ride a horse and I can shoot and that's more than you can say for most those Hollywood boys."

We were both something of aficionados when it came to westerns. My father had read most of Zane Grey and Louis L'Amour—I'd read a good third—and aside from a few lesser-known character actors, Clint Eastwood and John Wayne were our heroes.

As for Melinda's nonchalant attitude about Ryan O'Neal, or his lookalike, it was feigned, for throughout the preliminaries I noticed her casually glance in his direction several times and smile. And as for the main bout, it didn't last long enough, in my father's words, "to warm our seats." To his great disappointment, another underdog went down—Carroll was knocked out in the fourth round. From my seat I felt the vibration of his skull striking the canvas, and there passed a long sickly moment where I worried that it might be the end, the real one, for Carroll. He came around though, and the fans applauded.

On our way out, I jabbed my father in the ribs.

"Where's my money?"

"You'll get it."

"When?"

"Cough it up," Melinda said.

"All I got are hundreds. He'll just have to wait till I break one."

I meant no harm in razzing him, in fact I was trying to

cheer him up, for Carroll's loss as well as the twenty dollars
had badly sullied his mood, and it was only after he'd had a
couple drinks over dinner, and myself two Roy Rogers, that
he livened up again. We had prime rib at the Tropicana. Melinda squeezed his knee under the table.

"Sore loser," she said. "Sourpuss."

She winked at me.

"You're setting a bad example for the boy."

"I could've lasted longer than Carroll," he said.

"Double or nothing Foster gets his block knocked off like
he did with Frazier when he steps up to fight that loud-
mouth Clay."

I had no argument there, and by agreeing I reaffirmed my
respect for his boxing knowledge. That made the difference
between him hanging onto his sullen mood and letting it go.
But I also knew enough what was coming next. Without fail,
the mere mention of Muhammad Ali irritated my father, and
true to form, as if he'd rehearsed it, he picked up the cue
without the slightest bit of prodding from my end of the table.

"Ali," he said in disgust. "*Muhammad.* Ever met anybody
born and raised in Louisville goes by that? You bet your sweet
ass, you haven't. His momma named him Cassius and like it
or not that's who he is till the day he dies."

"By any name," I told him, "he's one hell of a fighter."

We could've gone on and on, but Melinda was fading fast,
and so we changed the subject. The evening proved a fine
one, one of our best, and I didn't press the matter of the
twenty dollars when, after dinner and the hundred had been
broken, he conveniently forgot to square up with me. I
would've been perfectly satisfied with my birthday, going to
the fights, going to dinner, I would not and did not see it as
my place to ask or expect anything more, but I was in for
another surprise, the big one, the main event, and it sent me
reeling as Foster had Carroll. Parked in the driveway of our
house was a powder blue Volkswagen bug, and around it was

big red ribbon, so that there was no doubt, as soon as I spotted it, that it was for none other than me.

"Oh man."

"That all you got to say?" Melinda asked.

"How about 'thank you?' " my father said.

"It's fantastic."

"Now that I don't know about. I was thinking of something more sporty. A Camaro maybe, a Firebird. But Melinda
and her long-lost friend thought you might like what those
hippies drive."

I overlooked the slight.

I believe I thanked him instead, thanked them both, although I don't recall having done so, because I was out of
that Eldorado before my father could pull up on the emergency brake. I made myself comfortable in the driver's seat,
gripped the wheel and stared out the windshield. It had an
AM-FM radio, a Craig eight-track, two big speakers and a
stick shift on the floor. There were a few tears in the head-
liner, but nothing some duct tape wouldn't fix. I guessed that
it was a '65, and I wasn't off by much. It was a '67, I discovered later on the registration. My father came around to the
other side.

"It's only a four-banger in back about the size of a Japa-
nese sewing machine. So don't think about going fast or you'll
burn this baby up. The keys are under the mat." He climbed
in and shut the door. "Don't forget your headlights."

Melinda came over to my side of the car and made a circle
with her hand.

I rolled down my window.

"Don't you look like a big shot. I'd join you guys but I'm
beat. Floyd," she said, "you'll really have to watch that boy
now."

She meant, of course, all the young women that I'd attract
with my car, and I only wished it was so easy. But I played
along, I smiled for her, and she returned it and reached into

the car, messed up my hair, laughed and headed into the house. As I had indulged myself in sexual fantasies, I'd often done likewise with cars, picturing myself behind the wheel of exactly this type, the classic Volkswagen, or an early model Peugeot, cruising down some nameless highway with a beautiful girl beside me, Bonnie Walker no less, and a bottle of wine on the seat between us. In my dreams I'd never felt anything resembling fear. The mechanics of driving came naturally, effortlessly, but now, seated behind the wheel with only a vague notion of how to operate the thing, I was scared. My hands suddenly felt clammy, and the very idea of driving, with all the switches, the blinkers, gadgets and lights on the dash, all the handles and moves to remember seemed overwhelming. Nonetheless, I mustered up my courage, sucked in my breath and at my father's urging turned the key. The car bucked forward, nearly throwing us through the windshield. The engine died. My embarrassment hung in its silence.

"The clutch, put in the *clutch*."

To ensure that I wouldn't repeat the blunder, my father worked the stick into neutral for me. Then he planted his hand on the dash and braced himself.

"Now try it."

After several attempts I succeeded, albeit in a jerky, spasmodic fashion, in backing out of the driveway. My father never wore a seat belt, as he contended that they were the cause of many a death, but on this occasion the fear of being trapped in fire must've seemed less threatening than my driving, and he securely strapped himself in, advising me, as we turned onto the road, that I'd be wise to do the same.

The desert wasn't a bad place to learn how to drive. There were few obstacles or distractions, no property to damage, no cars to collide with, and this particular road demanded no great driving skills, that is, it was straight, safe and boring, which for the time being suited me just fine. Once I got it into fourth gear—and that involved a good deal of metal grinding against metal, those spinning cogs refusing to mesh—my confidence grew in leaps and bounds.

"You're doing all right."

"Piece of cake," I said.

"My brother taught me," he said. "Same way I'm teaching you. I put in twenty-five and he kicked in fifty and we bought this old Edsel, beat all to shit, with a burned valve. Jesus, did it smoke. But we ran that baby up and down the state of Oregon the summer he graduated." He wagged his head. "I'm not sure what we rode harder, that old Edsel or the girls we came across. Luke was one hell-raiser."

"What else was he like," I said, "besides being a hell-raiser?"

"The best. Smart, too, like you. Only he wasn't such a wiseass."

"Think we would've hit it off?"

"I know it."

I gave it more gas.

We were flying. Fifty-five, sixty. Seventy. I turned on the radio.

"Now don't go getting all cocky," he said. "You never know what might dart across the road. Take your eyes off it for a split second and *wham.*" He slapped his hands together. "You're dead. Man," he said, "was not meant to be hurtled through space at seventy miles an hour in a box of tin."

"Relax," I said. "Everything's under control."

Though his admonishments had little effect on my heavy foot, the road soon went from being straight and flat to a gradual climb into a mountain range, and the engine started to bog down. It was by no means a steep grade, but it was a long one, and deceiving in the sense that because it rose so slowly, I didn't realize how high up we were until we were close to the top. The engine bucked, and my father ordered me to downshift, which I did quite gracefully, I thought. In the rearview mirror, the city lights glowed faintly beneath us, and to either side of the road, at the bottom of a considerable drop, lay the darkness of the desert floor. Third gear soon failed us, but where I'd downshifted before with ease, I encountered difficulty getting it into second, and again I was met, after much grinding of gears, with the dreadful silence of a dead engine. Two lights on the dash, one green and one red, flashed on. And the headlamps, which weren't all that bright before, grew even dimmer.

"Go ahead," he said, trying to remain calm. "Start her up."

I pumped the gas and turned the key but to no avail. I repeated the procedure several times, until my father hollered at me.

"You're flooding it, for Christ's sake."

That's when I felt this odd sensation that we were drifting backward. But because there were no landmarks by which to gauge our direction, I wasn't immediately convinced of it. Then I noticed in the rearview mirror that the city lights were getting larger, at first slowly, then more rapidly as we picked up speed. My window was open and the wind from it raised my hair.

"The brakes," he screamed. "Put on the brakes."

This, too, presented a problem, for my father's panic was catching, and in my haste to oblige him I mistakenly depressed the clutch.

We gathered more speed, and the intensity of his urging reached new heights.

"Brakes," he screamed. "Brakes."

Along the side of the road I spotted our first solid marker, a lone cactus, and judging by how fast it slipped back into the darkness as we rolled silently past it, our lives appeared in increasingly greater jeopardy. Furthermore, we seemed to be veering off the road, though I couldn't be sure of it since the headlamps were in front, and except for the distant city lights it was pitch black, going backwards. The tip-off, however, came when the smooth whirring sound of our tires on the pavement gave way to the unmistakable sound of pebbles ticking and snapping under the fenders. I'd estimate, and it's nothing more than that, just a ballpark guess, since throughout the ordeal I never looked at the speedometer, that we were going somewhere between twenty-five and thirty miles an hour. It was at this point that my father took control of the wheel, reached between the seats and yanked up on the emergency brake. The effect was dramatic, at once startling and yet, in those moments as the Volkswagen spun around and around, tossing my father and me from one end of the cab to the other—all of it occurring as if in a time warp, as if in slow motion—the effect, even in those critical moments, was one of tremendous relief. Once we'd finally come to a stop, he promptly cuffed me on the back of the head.

"There anything in that skull?"

"I'm sorry."

He cuffed me again for good measure.

"Sounds hollow to me," he said. "Thank the Lord there was nobody behind us."

I got out of the car in a huff, as I was shamed plenty without him rubbing it in, and I found when I attempted to walk that I was jittery all over, that my nerves were shot. One leg wouldn't stop trembling. Though I couldn't see it, I tasted dust in the air.

I walked around to his side of the car.

"You drive," I said.

But he didn't budge.

"I'm not the one who needs to practice. You want to pass that driver's test," he said, "you best get your ass back in here."

Either my father had an inordinate amount of faith and patience in me, or he was crazier than I thought. But owing to his belief that as in learning to ride a bicycle, when you fall you pick yourself up and try it again, he refused my repeated pleadings for him to drive us home. It was a good thing, too, because after such a close call with death I was willing to forsake driving forever.

Next to Sam, though, that Volkswagen became my closest friend, and before the week was out I'd completely tamed my fears and later passed the driver's test with flying colors. I bought a set of metric tools—open-end wrenches, extensions and sockets, which I kept cleaned and in order, from five millimeters up to twenty. I bought the Chilton's manual for my car's model and year and read it from cover to cover, studied the finer points closely and spent almost all of my free time tinkering with the engine, keeping it well tuned, and customizing the interior in preparation for my newest, most consuming pastime: long trips into the desert and the mountains. Outside the engine compartment I installed a cooling kit for the hotter weather; I mounted a five-gallon can of gas on the side in case of emergencies, and I always carried two one-gallon canvas bags of drinking water with me. I pulled out the backseat and put a sheet of plywood in its place, so that Sam and I could stretch and sleep when I decided not to come home at night. On my days off, I liked to explore the desert, to hike and collect rocks, to catch lizards and snakes when I felt like it and turn them loose. I liked to wander where there was no one around. I liked to take weekend trips to Lake Mead and blow off the afternoons swimming, or hike down around Hoover Dam and camp out where you weren't supposed to. But nobody ever hassled me. A forest ranger would've had to have been awfully ambitious to track down Bobby Barlow just to hand him a ticket, and the only other people I saw, and they were few and far between, didn't want to be bothered any more than I did. I fished, too, and caught my share of trout, gutted them, cleaned and cooked and ate them, all but the head.

I discovered service roads that weren't on any maps, and

though it would've helped to have a four-wheel drive, say, a
Willy's truck, in most instances I made do with my Volkswagen. If the road was too rough, I just didn't go down it, or if
it was only bad in a few places, and there were loose rocks
around, I'd fill in the holes and continue on. Time on these
outings was of little concern, and unless it was close to night-
fall I could take that extra hour or two to make a bad road
accessible. Even if I had no particular destination in mind, I
prided myself in my ability to get from one indeterminable
location to another, where others might've simply said "the
hell with it," turned around and taken the safer path home.
Then when I parked I'd go still further into the desert, or the
mountain, on foot with Sam, my sleeping bag, my backpack
and a change of clothes in it, matches, the Swiss army knife
my father had given me, my snakebite kit and enough food
and water to last a week, even if I only planned to camp out
for a couple nights.

My father wasn't too keen on the idea of me wandering
around the desert or the mountains alone, and I suppose he
could've forbidden me to do so, but since he wasn't willing to
join me, and I invited him several times, he really had no
ground to stand on. And so I kept to my ways, and the longer
I did, the more ambitious my trips became, so that eventually
I wasn't getting home with more than an hour left to jump in
the shower, change my clothes and run to work. Between my
job and camping, plus maintenance on my Volkswagen,
which required a great deal of it since the roads I traveled
were dusty, bumpy and hard, I saw less and less of my father
and Melinda.

I could've arranged it so that I took my breaks with Melinda, but she was well liked, there was always a group of
men flirting with her, and I'd gotten to where I enjoyed my
own company more, anyway, than I did others. When I
clocked out I was usually beat and headed straight back to my
trailer, maybe smoked a joint, made myself something to eat

and went to bed. I'd dream about my next camping trip, plan it out to the smallest detail and count the days before the weekend. As I carried on what I sometimes thought of as a kind of secret life with my marijuana, Sam and my travels, my father and Melinda continued with their team efforts, and though I watched them on several other occasions there's only one, the last, that's worth mentioning.

This was a weekday, a slower night, and the clown on the high wire didn't have much of an audience. A small crowd had gathered beneath him, but most of the gamblers just went on with their business like he didn't exist. My father and Melinda belonged to that group; they couldn't have cared less if a lion was running around loose in the place. I caught his eye from across the casino and I knew, without him having to say a word, to keep my distance. So I observed little up close, for his sake and my own, and I preferred it that way, to leave room for doubt, for possibility. There were several stacks of hundred-dollar chips in front of him, the crowd was cheering him on, and he was sweating, clearly more nervous than the first time I'd seen him. "C'mon, baby," he said, shaking the dice. "Bring it home to daddy." Then he let them fly, they hit the backboard and came up nine.

The gamblers cheered. But Melinda, she seemed confused as she paid off the bet. The boxman eyed her suspiciously. My father rolled again, and again they came up nine. Melinda started to pay him off, but he held up his hand and stopped her.

"Let it ride," he said. "All of it."

He pushed his stacks of chips forward. It was a big bet.

A win would've taken in somewhere around twenty thousand.

She pulled the dice in with her stick, about to pass them on to my father, when the boxman rose from his seat and snagged them from the table. The crowd fell silent. He held the dice up to the light and carefully inspected each one.

"Something wrong, mister?" my father said.

The boxman, a tired, sober-looking man with heavy bags under his eyes, dropped the dice on the table. They came up an even number. He dropped them again. Still no nine. Still no six.

"Let's go," my father said. "You're breaking my rhythm."

A pit boss approached the table then, and he and the tired-looking boxman turned to each other and conferred for a few moments.

My father spread his arms to the crowd.

"Everything's fine when we're losing," he said, "but soon as your luck changes the house gets all pushed out of shape. I don't need this bullshit. Nobody does. If you guys want," he said, stepping back from the table, "we'll take our money down the street."

"Do it," Melinda said, "I'm sick of your mouth. We're all sick of it."

"I got a right to gamble where I want, darling. Much as I want."

The boxman tossed the dice back on the table.

"Play 'em," he said.

She feigned disgust, or maybe by this point it was real.

"Just get him out of here," she said. "The guy's a jerk."

"I said *play 'em*."

Reluctantly, she ran the dice back to my father, but doing so had to trouble her. Because this time the dice were legit. Because there was big money riding on them. Because he had risked too much already. I can still picture him leaning over the table for that last throw. It's the same old moment frozen in time, the one when I tracked him down at the Gold Horseshoe after his three-day blowout when we first hit town. I hear the din of the slot machines, the bells, the keno announcers and the old ladies sitting on their stools, talking and laughing among themselves while they scoop up coins in plastic cups. He shakes the dice. He whispers to them. He rises slowly to his toes. His sleeves are rolled up to his elbows and he's perspiring. All that's the same, always, no matter how I try to envision it differently. There's that look in his eyes, that *rush*, when my father lets the dice fly from his hand, roll and tumble across the green felt. That, not the gambling, was the scary part.

Above me the clown on the high wire is dressed in a hobo's outfit, and he's juggling balls. He drops one, as in fact he always did, and then he pulls a flask out of his back pocket, takes a swig and staggers. Like he's drunk, like he's about to fall.

"Whoa," he says. "Whoa."

I'm standing next to this guy at the quarter slots, and he hollers up at him.

"Fall, you loser."

I don't know exactly how much my father had riding on that particular roll, on that particular night, but it was big money.

Lost. Fair and square.

Melinda swept in the chips and my father, always willing to give as well as receive, though not consistently and never in equal proportions, turned from the table and left, just another multitalented individual who had yet to realize his true potential in the city of hope and opportunity.

seventeen

I HAD THIS NOTION of myself, as my father had of himself, that is, one that veered radically from what he thought he was capable of accomplishing in the immediate future and what, in fact, he was not. For me, it was to see America while I still could, before obligations set in and the desire to travel, as well as the opportunity to do so, faded into the background of my life. Typically, those of my generation embarked on a cross-country trip after they graduated from high school, the luckier ones, college; they just put their day-to-day lives and future plans on temporary hold, packed up their stuff and split. With all those years of school behind you, it was a cause for cele-bration, a kind of last desperate blowout before you returned home to find the Selective Service knocking on your door. For Vietnam was still raging, its jungles, its villages on fire, de-spite the talk of our withdrawal. Though I'd only recently turned seventeen, and there was still a year between me and the draft, I often thought about my fate and what the future held in store for me, especially when I watched the late-night news and saw the long list of American dead or missing in action roll across the screen. The names were superimposed over Old Glory waving at half-mast, while our national an-them played in the background.

Then the commercials came on, maybe for panty hose, or

the one for Folger's coffee with Mrs. Olson smiling at the camera, and I blanked it out. After all, Vietnam was thousands of
miles away, and when I lit up a joint and inhaled deeply, it
seemed even further. My trips into the desert escalated in
terms of how far and how deeply I ventured into areas where
there was not a single living thing, no plants, no lizards or
snakes, no animals except myself and Sam. And if my Volkswagen had ever broken down, we never would have made it
back. But I liked the sweat that the sun drew from my body.
I liked the feeling that no matter what direction I walked in
I'd find nothing, that there was nothing, that this was government land, empty and flat and desolate, where even a nuclear
bomb could lay waste to nothing more than itself, and I was
its trespasser.

I didn't go to high school, so I couldn't very well take
pride in graduating from it, and the possibility of embarking
on a cross-country trip seemed as farfetched to me as one day
attending college, but I had the desert, and no signs, no
barbed wire fences could keep me from its emptiness. My
wandering often began before the sun rose and ended in
darkness, with the long hike back to my car—stoned sometimes, sometimes not. If I was high when I got home, I went
straight to my trailer, maybe read one of my father's Louis
L'Amour novels or worked on a crossword puzzle until I felt
drowsy enough to sleep. And if I wasn't high, and Melinda
and my father were out somewhere, as they almost always
were, I used the key they'd given me, let myself into the mobile home and rummaged through the refrigerator.

The pickings were usually slim, since they took most of
their meals in restaurants, but there was a fair to middling
chance that I might come across some good leftovers. Chi-
nese, or a couple slices of pizza still in the box, for instance, or
a chunk of lasagna wrapped in tinfoil. My father and Melinda
weren't big on cooking, and on those few occasions when we
shared a sit-down meal together, it was invariably a spur-of-

the-moment kind of thing, inspired by our mutual surprise that we all happened to be at the same place at the same time. My father viewed these occasions as an opportunity to embrace the traditional role of husband and father, which meant that we would barbecue, regardless of the weather or the time of day. We'd barbecued at ten o'clock at night before. We'd barbecued when it was storming out, my father and I huddled under the eaves of the house, wearing plastic bags on our heads and shivering against the cold. The rain sizzled on the hot coals. Our last dinner together, however, occurred at a more sensible hour on a Tuesday afternoon in warm but windy weather, the night after his big loss at Circus Circus, where his luck, his confidence and potential as a legitimate gambler had failed him at the most crucial moment of the game.

The night of the loss, when Melinda returned home, they had it out. I caught the fight as I was scrounging through the refrigerator for something to eat. My father was stretched out on the couch in the living room, drinking a beer and watching the late night news. Footage of the My Lai massacre passed across the screen, this ditch full of the twisted, mangled bodies of men, women and children, and then it cut to the anchorman in the news station. "Lieutenant Calley was convicted and sentenced to life in the murder of twenty-two Vietnamese civilians. . . ." Outside I heard Darlene's Mustang pull into the driveway, and soon Melinda came through the door in a huff. She threw her purse on the coffee table.

"That was really stupid of you tonight."

My father didn't even look up.

"Just leave me alone," he said.

"I don't know what the hell you were thinking, pulling a stunt like that."

"Let's talk about it tomorrow."

"We'll talk about it right now."

"There's nothing to discuss. I was winning on my own, no help from you."

"Honey," she said, "I don't like to disappoint you, but you couldn't do shit on your own."

"It was fair money, baby. Every goddamn last cent of it."

"What the hell's fair? You win and get out. Maybe you lose some the next night, you make it back and more tomorrow, but you don't go in there like some big roller and fuck it all up." She started down the hall to the bathroom, hollering as she went. "I don't want to see you at my table for a while, Floyd. I hope you got enough to carry you for a good couple months."

I don't think she let him sleep with her that night, or if she did she kept to her side of the bed, because the next day it was just more of the same. She'd gone to sleep angry, she awoke angry, and she remained angry most of the day. My father tried to make things good again by going out that morning and buying four redwood chairs and a beautiful redwood picnic table, with a bright yellow umbrella that mounted in the middle of it.

"Fire up the hibachi," he told me. "I'll run down to the store and pick up some steaks."

Though initially Melinda wasn't too enthusiastic about having a barbecue, she slowly warmed up to the idea, and while my father was off at the store she spent an unusual amount of time preparing the table. She covered it with a red-and-white checkered tablecloth, put out the plastic cups, the salt and pepper shakers and a stack of paper napkins, on top of which she placed a rock to keep them from blowing away. In the center, she set out a lazy Susan, the bowls on it heaped with chips, garlic dip and her own concoction made of canned clams, mayonnaise and sour cream. Finished, she reached for a few chips, stood back and admired her work.

"Doesn't it look nice?"

It was an idyllic picture.

"Sure does," I said.

She popped a chip into her mouth and tossed another to Sam, who was sniffing at her feet, then she went back into the house to make her special marinade.

My father returned soon afterward with a case of beer, some steaks, two pounds of potato salad and a package of paper plates and plastic forks, so that we didn't have to worry about washing dishes later. By then I had the fire going, burning slow but steadily, only that wasn't good enough for him.

He held his hands over the coals.

"Call that a fire? Throw some more of that stuff on it," he said, "and let's get this show on the road. I'm starving to death."

"Give it a few minutes."

"It's going out."

"It is not."

"Who's the cook here? I was barbecuing before you took your first step. Give me that shit. I'll show you how it's done."

In order to break the wind, I'd put the hibachi close to the porch just before the fire had died down, and I advised him, as I passed him the lighter fluid, to do likewise.

"It'll be okay."

"You're not supposed to do this," I said. "It tells you right on the can."

"Don't believe everything you read, Bobby. They just say that to cover their asses in case some moron blows himself up and tries to sue. Anyhow, I'm only putting on a little."

His notion of a little varied wildly from my own. He doused those coals as if he was putting them out with water, and they steamed and hissed like it, too. He struck a match.

"Stand back now," he said.

He tossed it into the hibachi at the very moment that Melinda stepped out onto the porch. She was balancing a bowl of potato salad in one arm, and in the crook of her other our steaks, fully marinated, in a glass baking pan. "Who wants a beer?" she said, cheerfully, just as a great ball of flame burst into the sky and momentarily engulfed her.

All two pounds of our potato salad crashed to the steps. The glass baking pan miraculously survived the fall, but the steaks, soaked in Melinda's special marinade, landed in the dirt. Sam was on them in no time.

"Grab that goddamn dog," my father hollered, "before I kill it."

I took Sam by the collar, and it seemed, for a second anyway, that the worst was over. Melinda had escaped unscathed, and the fire had died out quickly. But the look on her face, one of shock, even horror, hadn't changed in the least.

"You're all right," my father told her in a firm but soothing voice. "It's okay now, honey. There's no reason to get carried away. Things like this happen every day. I'll just run back to the store and we'll start all over again."

Food, however, was no longer the concern. She pointed her finger. Her voice rose in pitch.

"Floyd!"

At first I thought that she was leveling the finger of blame at my father, that she wasn't about to let bygones be bygones so easily, that there was hell yet to pay for all but catching her on fire. It was the heat on the back of my legs, for I was wearing shorts, that informed me otherwise. My father and I turned around at the same time and both bore witness to the stunning sight of the brand-new redwood picnic table swallowed in flame. Smoke curled up from under the bright yellow umbrella, like a mushroom in motion, billowing outward.

My father screamed at me.

"Don't just stand there, for Christ's sake. Get the hose. *Move.*"

I responded quickly and efficiently, but speed alone was not enough. By the time I returned the umbrella had caught, too, and because it was made of vinyl it gave off this hideous, toxic smell, and the smoke was black with thousands of the smallest of fibers aflame and floating in the sky, like snow-flakes on fire. There was really something quite beautiful about it—in the power of its heat on my face, in the curves of smoke and flame and how the shapes twisted and changed in the wind, with a faint hint of blue at its tips. But my father didn't share my sense of aesthetics, and when he noticed that my efforts to put out the fire were, at best, distracted, he yanked the garden hose out of my hands.

"Gimme that," he hollered. "This isn't a goddamn lawn you're watering."

Where I failed, he succeeded, and in a minute he had the blaze under control. All that remained of the umbrella was the blackened skeleton of its aluminum frame and a single tassel dangling from a thread. The chairs were untouched but the redwood table was charred from top to bottom, and the plas-tic cups on it, the plastic forks and the plastic dishes in the lazy Susan had been reduced to grotesque lumps of smolder-ing putty.

Melinda just stood there on the porch and stared at what was left of the table. Then she looked down at her feet, and for a long time she stared at the potato salad on the steps. Then she stared at the steaks in the dirt, where Sam had re-sumed his meal with extraordinary vigor. My father and I waited in silence for some more telling reaction from her. He still had the garden hose in hand, and a puddle grew fast at his feet. Suddenly the table made a creaking noise as if the nails were slowly being wrenched from its spine, and assisted only by a gentle wind it collapsed into the dirt, scorched um-brella frame and all.

"Hey," my father said, "we'll get another one. Hell, we'll buy a couple." He glanced at his watch. "We got to go right now though. The stores close in another hour."

"Forget it, Floyd."

"Honey," he said, "don't let something this little ruin our day."

"Little?"

"It's only a table."

"You almost set me on fire, you almost burned down the goddamn house."

"Baby," he said. "Honey," he said. "C'mon, don't exaggerate."

But it was plain enough that Melinda had had her fill, and instead of focusing on the bright side, of seeing the potential humor in the situation, she chalked it up to just another fun-filled family afternoon gone awry. She stormed into the house and slammed the screen door behind her. Sam hadn't helped matters, either. Throughout it all he hadn't missed a beat on our steaks, and he kept making these gluttonous, slurping noises. My father kicked at him, missed and cursed.

"Goddamn mutt," he said. "Get it out of my sight or I'll barbecue its goddamn ass."

Goddamn seemed the word of choice for both him and Melinda that afternoon. In her case, though, the harsh language suggested darker, more insidious complications than those prompted exclusively by anger. Fire scared the hell out of her. Had my father listened to Melinda more closely earlier on in their relationship, in particular when we were en route to Las Vegas, today's bout with a barbecue out of control would've jogged his memory, as it had hers, and consequently he might've had a more sympathetic reaction to what, from his point of view, seemed an insignificant event. It was irrelevant whether or not Melinda had actually had a past life that ended gruesomely by fire, so long as that's what she believed, and she did. With a passion. "I got a right to my beliefs," she'd told him, when he'd teased her about it one time. "You can't take that away from me, Floyd. I was *there*." He avoided an argument by changing the subject, getting up and making her a drink, but this time around his patience and understanding seemed in short supply. Tensions escalated when he followed her inside and blatantly accused her of getting worked up over nothing. It was, after all, "just a fucking picnic table." Melinda, in turn, told him to go fuck himself, because she wasn't fucking him tonight. Then she locked herself in the bathroom.

He pleaded with her. He pounded on the door. But she wouldn't open up.

"Go on, get the hell out of here," she hollered. "Go get drunk like you always do."

"You drive me to it, darling."

"I hate you when you're like this."

"I can't say I feel a great deal of affection for you either right now."

He came into the living room and grabbed his coat from the couch.

"Cool off," I said. "She'll get over it."

He reached into his pocket, took out his money clip and thumbed through a thick wad of twenties. Though I knew I had little chance of stopping him, I figured it was worth a shot.

"Why don't you stay home for a change? We'll get some Kentucky Fried Chicken and come back and watch TV. I'll drive us to pick it up," I added. "I've gotten a lot better at it."

"I might be mad," he said, "but I'm not crazy. I ain't getting in that death trap with you again." He shoved the money clip back into his pocket and then, characteristically, attempted to reverse the blame. "If you started the fire right in the first place none of this would've happened. Fix yourself a sandwich," he said. "I'll see you later."

"Where you going?"

"Not out to eat," he said, "I can tell you that. My appetite's shot to hell."

He started toward the door.

"Mind if I tag along?"

"You couldn't keep up."

"Try me," I said.

He stopped and looked me up and down, as if on the one hand he was measuring me against a younger version of himself, and on the other, because I didn't fare well on the first account, he weighed the difference in pity. I still came up short.

"I don't think so, Bobby. You're too green around the edges yet. Give yourself a couple years, and then we'll cut loose."

He had misinterpreted my intentions, though I made no effort to correct him. I didn't necessarily want to go out drinking and carousing with him. Instead, I saw our roles for the evening, as I had before and increasingly more so as time had passed between us, in the complete reverse. He was the child. I was the parent. And it was my responsibility to look after him as best I could, particularly in a volatile situation such as this, when he was more vulnerable to trouble than normal. However, if he insisted on keeping me at arm's length, there was nothing that I could do to stop him from going out. No advice in the world would affect his plans, and I was left to hope that his better, more sensible side would prevail if he found himself in a tight spot. Hope was a small consolation in light of his past record, but it was all that I had. The possibility of my father winding up in a brawl, or worse, was considerable, for when he was mad *and* drunk his mouth worked overtime, and without a great deal of searching he often encountered someone who wanted to shut it for him. Yet I trusted him to come home late that night or early the next morning, smelling of whiskey, as drunk as he was full of remorse and desperate apologies. For me. For Melinda. Through their bedroom window, through the drapes, I had seen the outline of my father's shadow, this dark, nebulous figure seated on the edge of the mattress beside her, with his head down, with his hands in his lap, I imagined, and though

I couldn't always hear them I knew what it was about, I knew what he was saying because I had heard the words myself, all those excuses before.

I never doubted the sincerity of his apologies. I never questioned the depth or earnestness of my father's guilt. It was, instead, his inability to understand the importance of that thing that he had damaged. I wrestled with it, too, my anger, my guilt and my love, and I concluded, without ever being able to articulate precisely why, where or how, that it came from a place remote from experience and that it over- whelmed, that it took me by surprise and won out, hands down, every damn time. I waited up for my father that night, hoping that any hour, any minute, he would wander in with a sheepish smile on his face, acting humble in his drunken- ness and inquiring about Melinda, who shortly after he'd left gathered up a stack of *Cosmopolitans* and retired to the bed- room early. Or, quite possibly, he might come home playing it high and mighty—maybe he'd met up with some other angry husband and they'd come to agree, in a moment of drunken revelation, that the more shit you take today, the more you got coming down the pipe tomorrow—so that by the time he pulled into the driveway he'd be all worked up. He'd twist the story around until it sounded as if we had literally dragged him out of the house and double-bolted the door be- hind him, and now that he was back we both better treat him right or else. I could already hear him stomping around the living room and carrying on about how you don't know what you got till it's gone, and how, the more he thought about it, we owed *him* an apology, and if we said it just right he might be willing to forgive and forget. Just this once. Next time around, it was the big good-bye.

I would've gladly welcomed that scenario or the other if it meant having him home. But he didn't return that night. He didn't come back the next morning, either. By then my anger and disappointment had given way entirely to worrying, not so much because he had split on me, but because when he'd left he was in a bad state of mind. I decided that if he wasn't back by tomorrow, I'd start looking for him. I'd check the casinos. I'd peek into the bars. I'd sneak through the nightclubs, and if I could get past the door I'd slip into the strip joints and justify it on the basis that all avenues, all possibilities deserved my complete and thorough investigation. Other than that, I didn't know what else to do—it wasn't as if I could enlist the services of the Nevada Police Department and file a missing person report. Melinda was worried, too, though not enough to let it interfere with her plans for the afternoon, and I didn't begrudge her for it, either. She and Darlene were going to pick up Melinda's check at Circus Circus, then go out to lunch and do some shopping.

"I'm not letting him screw up my day," she said, as she stood at the living room, looking for Darlene's Mustang to come down the road. Her purse was on the couch, within quick, easy reach, and she had her arms crossed over her chest. She wore a white sleeveless blouse, heels and a black skirt.

"You can tell him not to wait up for me tonight. I might be home late, then again it might be tomorrow. This shit can work both ways," she said. "Your old man just better not bring home any diseases."

"He's smarter than that."

"Shows how much you know. That sweet little innocent prom queen can give you the clap just as sure as a whore. The least," Melinda said, "the very least he could do is call. I mean really, what am I supposed to think?"

I resented her use of the term whore as derogatory and dehumanizing, and as ironic and hypocritical in light of the fact that not so long ago prostitution had been her main source of income, and that her best friend had profited from it as well. But I didn't have the time or inclination to point this out to her, for outside, in the driveway, came the sound of a horn—a quick, friendly blast—and in the next moment she'd grabbed her purse and left me to my own devices. I watched her slip into the Mustang, turn to Darlene and laugh at something one of them had said. Darlene smiled and waved to me before they backed out of the driveway.

I was scheduled to work that afternoon, but as I was clocking in one of the pit bosses came into the employee lounge carrying a black folder. He took a snapshot from between its pages and tacked it up on the bulletin board alongside the others. One of the dealers, shoving money into the candy machine nearby, glanced over at him.

"Got another live one, eh?"

"Take a good look. This son of a bitch almost walked out of the Rainbow Club with eighteen thousand last night. It's the same punk that was playing at Melinda's table a few nights back—the one missing two fingers. From what I understand," the pit boss said, as he stepped away from the bulletin board, "he just lost himself a third."

And there was my father among his newly adopted family with this fake, though familiar smile plastered on his face.

I immediately got on the phone and called the county hospital. He was there all right, under the alias of Davis, but they put me on hold until they could locate his nurse. I waited. I twisted the telephone cord around my fist.

"Your father," she later told me, "was in a very bad fight."

The condition in which I found him when I arrived at the hospital made me queasy, light-headed and momentarily sick to my stomach. His left hand was wrapped in white gauze, and his face was swollen up. Those ribs that weren't broken were badly bruised. His lip was split, both eyes were blackened, there were teeth marks on the bridge of his nose, a wound that required seven stitches, and a mean gash on the side of his head that required seventeen more. I counted them while he slept, from my chair beside his bed, while I waited for him to wake up. His nurse told me that beneath the bandage on his left hand he was missing a finger, that it had been cut off, crudely, and that he was lucky he hadn't bled to death.

I wanted to get the Luger and hunt down the bastards who had done this to him. There had to be more than one involved, considering the viciousness of the beating, and I'd make them line up and kneel, shove the barrel in the mouth of the first bastard, pull the trigger, then do the others. To this day, I still have that dream and it hasn't softened over the years. To this day, I also can't stand hospitals, the smell of antiseptic and sickness, for it all recalls the image of my father's face, bloodied, swollen and misshapen. It clearly hurt for him to speak, but when he woke up and focused on me through the thick, swollen flesh around his eyes he managed something close to a smile.

"How you doing?" I said.

"Terrific. Never felt better."

"You sure as hell don't look it."

"It's what's inside that counts," he said.

"The nurse told me that's pretty busted up, too. I hear you lost another finger."

"It'll grow back."

"Yeah," I said. "Right."

"Son of a bitch tried to bite off my nose. I had to save one or the other. You ought to see what those assholes look like now. Your old man didn't take it lying down."

"That supposed to make me proud?"

"It should count for something."

I shook my head.

That he had fought back valiantly didn't console me in the least, and though I wanted to avenge my father, though I imagined it intensely while he'd slept, playing the murder scene over and over in my mind, I knew that I'd never realize it even if I had the chance.

"What happened?" I said. "You can start from the beginning."

"I didn't think you cared."

"I got a right to know."

"It was just another case of plain old bum luck," he said.
"I don't want to talk about it."

He tried to sit up, but it hurt too much.

"Where's Melinda?"

"Out shopping. With Darlene."

"You don't mind," he said, "I'd appreciate if you'd let her
know I'm all right."

"I'll see what I can do."

"Don't inconvenience yourself," he said. "I know how
busy you are."

He raised his hand slowly to his temple, to the place
where the hair had been shaved to the scalp, and lightly drew
a finger along the stitches.

"There's seventeen," I said.

"Feels more like a hundred. Damn," he said, "my head
hurts."

I was careful, as I rose from the chair and sat on the edge
of the mattress, not to put my full weight down on it and
cause the bed to dip or shake and discomfort my father un-
necessarily. Still, he winced, and looking at him in his sorry
state made me want to do the same, but I kept a straight face.
It was one thing to joke about his condition, but an altogether
different one to actually show, physically, through some telling expression, what he must've already known well enough,
that he was not a pleasant sight to behold.

"Damn you," I said, "you really got yourself into it this
time." He nodded, and I took his hand in mine and pressed
it gently against my side. "At least you didn't lose it on the
same hand, and that nose of yours was ugly to begin with."
That made him smile, and I felt a tightening in the back of
my throat.

"Do me a favor."

"Sure."

"Run pick up my Cadillac. It's parked off the Strip, across from the Thunderbird Motel. Spare key's under the front right fender," he said. "The way my luck's been running somebody's probably already ripped it off."

Later, on my way out of the hospital, all I felt was anger and disgust. Certainly I blamed him. Certainly I knew he'd brought it on himself. But I don't believe he or anyone deserved that kind of beating, not over money. I got in my Volkswagen and just sat there for a long time with my head on the wheel.

Retrieving the Cadillac presented a problem in that I could only drive one car at a time, which meant that I would need Melinda's help, and I doubted, when I told her what had happened, that she'd be willing to do my father any favors for a while. I drove past the Thunderbird Motel, and his Cadillac was there across the street from it, up the block from the less glamorous casinos. I wouldn't have wanted to leave my car overnight around this place, either. Insofar as it hadn't been stolen, his luck had held fast, but he had again come up short sometime earlier. The right rear fender was smashed, the taillight shattered and the wires exposed. I pulled up alongside it, got out and looked through the front window. He hadn't even bothered to hide the bottle of Jack Daniels on the seat— a fifth of it, two-thirds empty. I thought it might be another night before I had the chance to drive the Cadillac home, so I felt under the fender for the magnet box with the spare key, unlocked the door and shoved the bottle under the seat, grabbed the coat he'd left in the back, then checked the glove compartment. In it I found the Luger, and I wrapped the sweater around it and put it in my car for safekeeping. Then I locked the doors and got on my way.

I didn't expect Melinda to be home; it was early yet, darkness had just fallen. But on the kitchen table there were two glasses, the ice in them still melting, and in the ashtray rested one of Darlene's thin long cigarettes, the filter stained with her red lipstick and the other end hardly smoked before it had been stamped out, as if she'd been in a hurry. Down the hall, I heard the shower running in the bathroom.

"I'm back," I shouted.

I waited for an answer, but there was nothing except the sound of the water striking against the porcelain. I called out again, and this time when she didn't answer I thought of leaving, for it wasn't as if I was looking forward to breaking the bad news. Instead I crossed the living room to the hallway and looked down it. The bathroom door was open a few inches, no more, and through the steam, through a space in the shower curtain I saw her leg, the dime-sized mole on her left thigh and a flash of her ankle as she worked soap over it.

"Bobby," she said. "That you?"

"Yeah."

"Would you be a darling and get me a fresh towel?

"There's something I got to tell you."

"In a minute," she said. "Bring me the big fluffy one, with the palm trees on it."

I went to the linen closet, got it for her and came back.

"Here it is."

"Could you bring it to me?"

"I'll just set it on the floor," I said.

"Don't be silly. You couldn't see anything through these curtains even if you tried."

I heard the water go off.

"Bobby?"

"Yeah?"

"Hurry it up," she said. "I'm freezing."

"Aren't there any other towels?"

"They're all in the wash. Just bring me a goddamn towel, would you? I don't want to get the floor soaking wet."

"Okay," I said. "Okay, okay."

I kept my head lowered and held the towel out as I stepped into the bathroom. Soon as I crossed the threshold, however, the door slammed closed behind me. Melinda wasn't in the shower.

"Look," she said. "It's not like you haven't seen me before. I know you've been watching. You been watching a long, long time."

"Oh Jesus," I said.

The only thing she had on was her diamond earrings.

"Now what's that you wanted to tell me?"

For the longest time, despite my efforts, I couldn't get out a word.

"If it's about your father," she said, "I already heard when I went in to pick up my check. Your daddy's the talk of the town."

"He's beat up bad."

"Want to dry me off?"

"I don't think that's such a good idea."

"This is it," she said, "you won't get a second chance. I've had it with your father's bullshit."

Leaning in, slowly, Melinda pressed her lips to mine the way I'd watched her do with my father so many times before. Her hair was wet and in the cool thickness of it, like a nest around our faces, I inhaled its scent of shampoo and dampness. She moved her hands around my waist and pulled me to her. The towel, it fell to the floor. But as much and for as long as I'd wanted Melinda Johnson, for all those times I'd imagined her beautifully, gloriously naked in my arms, I couldn't have been further away. The window was open, and from over her shoulder I looked through it, and there was nothing beyond or between us but the darkness and the desert. There were no borders. No beginnings. No end. Outside, Sam tugged against his chain and barked.

"Somebody's here."

"It's nothing."

"I *swear* it."

Melinda took my hand and guided it.

"It's all in your imagination," she said. "Living alone in that snailback too long is bound to drive a young man crazy."

My breath, she sucked it right out of my lungs.

eighteen

MY FATHER'S earlier contention regarding the loss of my foreskin, and how it would have a numbing or deadening effect on my future sexual pleasure, proved highly inaccurate. In fact, it was just the opposite, though his notion of circumcision as conspiracy took on a whole new meaning for me, in so far that I now understood, intimately, the term betrayer and all its many offshoots. Traitor. Judas. Deception. And dishonesty. I would've liked to blame Melinda, and in some ways I'd be justified, for she most certainly initiated the advance and in doing so sealed our fate as conspirators in a scheme that, if uncovered, would cause irreparable damage to our relationship with my father, as they had done with Bo before. Except it's not like I couldn't have run. It's not like I couldn't have summoned up every thread and fiber of my willpower and pushed her away, as impossible as that may have seemed at the time, given the testosterone level of your average, red-blooded Amercian seventeen-year-old boy. If there's blame to be placed, I'm as responsible as Melinda, whether I choose to believe it or not.

The love that we made was in no respect gentle, as I had imagined it with Bonnie Walker, as I'd dreamed of my first time—down by the Willamette River on the soft pallet of a sleeping bag, unzipped and spread along the bank, its cotton insides warmed, like our bodies, from the hot afternoon sun. This was hard and fast and bordering on the violent. This was full of sharp angles, cold porcelain and fluorescent light, urgency and fury. Though it was powerful and good in its own way, I was left with what I deserved, with what was as inevitable as the act itself, and that thing was guilt—a pounding, crushing sense of it that wouldn't let me eat or sleep or think of anything else, and then in a flash I'd find myself hot and feverish and aroused all over again. I had become, without even knowing it, too much like the man I saw in my father, that reckless, compulsive side of him that robbed without regard to consequence. Like the things he'd stolen from others, himself and me, the time I spent with Melinda became another part of the past, unalterable and beyond reclaim, like those vague memories of my mother, whose picture I kept in my wallet and whose resemblance to Melinda was considerable. For the longest time I couldn't look at it without feeling an overwhelming sense of guilt, shame and loss, a loss that far transcended that small sleeve of skin, or even my innocence.

The emotional beating I gave myself can't compare with the physical one that my father experienced, but by way of time, in terms of days, at least, the two closely corresponded. It wasn't the kind of news that made the paper. It wasn't anything you told the police about, either. But it was exactly the sort of news that got around town fast to all the casinos, boxmen, floor managers, pit bosses, stickmen and dealers. I understand that the snapshot I saw of my father, the one posted on the employee bulletin board alongside the others whose manipulations of the house odds had earned them this dubious honor, also graced the pages of a larger portfolio. It had a black cover, and it was routinely circulated around the casinos whenever a new member had the misfortune of joining the club.

The story, from what I gathered, went something like this.

Feeling bold and reckless, a condition no doubt aggravated by the fight with Melinda earlier that afternoon, and after polishing off nearly a fifth of Jack Daniels, my father had gone to a casino hoping to recoup the money he'd lost the night before playing by the house rules, and successfully introduced a pair of loaded dice into a high-stakes craps game. That mistake almost cost him his life, in addition to destroying whatever team efforts my father and Melinda might have had planned for the future, once the heat had passed on his earlier blunder. I suspect that he wanted to test himself, to prove he was capable of working without Melinda, but slipping a pair of loaded dice into a craps game of any caliber required no less than the tacit consent of a second party in the casino employ, or incredible finesse and skill on behalf of the solo hustler. And getting them out of the game was even tougher, for as soon as lots of money had been won all eyes were on you, and if you ever needed a friend in the right place this was the time for it. I'd seen my father practice the move at home, one known as the palm switch, which typically occurred in the process of picking up the dice to throw them. The loaded ones are hidden in the palm, trapped between the base of the thumb and the edge of the hand, and when the casino pair are picked up their places are reversed, all in one move, as the fingers curl in. It's harder than it sounds, and if you know what you're doing it's even harder to detect.

As for this particular game, the details I supply are based on my general experience from working at Circus Circus and seeing what went on, and I would go so far as to say that all craps games are the same in one regard: they attract the most boisterous, obnoxious and foolish of gamblers. If there's commotion at a casino, look to the craps tables. Shooters are the shouters. Shooters are the sort who blow their whole paychecks on a single roll and then flip out when they lose. Drunk or not, I'd give my father the benefit of the doubt that when he entered the casino he at least had the sense to check out the different tables and look for signs of inexperience on behalf of the stick, and to see if the pit boss was preoccupied elsewhere, maybe flirting with one of the blackjack dealers who didn't have anyone at her table. Then, when the conditions were right, he swaggered up to his mark and placed the first of one too many bets to follow. The table was crowded— mostly with men, though I imagine there might've been a couple women, too. The stickman was young, looked green, and the boxman looked bored and tired, maybe riding out the last blurry hour of his shift. My father bought a hundred in chips and threw twenty on the table.

"Yo," he said.

The stickman set the bet.

Typically my father rolled up his sleeves, making a small act of it, turning the cuffs slowly, meticulously. It was a gesture designed to do two things: call attention to the loss of his fingers, and, by so doing, if only subliminally on the part of the stick- and boxman, dispel any possibility that he might be a cheat. For he must've had the dice already palmed when he did it, and for a man with this kind of handicap to roll up his sleeves, and slowly, and in the process conceal a pair of loaded dice, should've convinced even the most skeptical that no sleight of hand could have occurred, not in that moment, anyway. And from then on he didn't give them reason to suspect, other than in winning too much. His hands never left the table, they never left sight, and he finished each throw palms up. When he made the switch was anyone's guess, though undoubtedly it happened in the blink an eye early in the game, between picking up the house dice, and in the same instant letting the loaded ones fly. It all had to be done in one quick smooth move.

"Yo," the stickman said. "Winner."

The crowd cheered. One guy whistled, another hooted, and a loser cursed. My father slapped the edge of the table and let out a whoop, as if he was as surprised as them. Just another lucky drunk. He swept in his chips, all but twenty, and bet fifty on six in the center.

Nine to one odds.

He blew on the dice, he shook them.

"Here we go," he said. "Bring it home. I got mouths to feed, baby, and an angry woman."

The dice tumbled across the table. Hit the backboard. Landed three up on both.

"Winner six."

My father let out another whoop. Again the crowd cheered.

"Let her ride," he said, flashing his best smile.

He bounced the dice on the felt, as he often did, and snapped them up, shook and tossed them.

"Winner eleven."

By now my father must've had two or three thousand on the line, and that should've been enough. That should've been the time to pack in it and get the hell out of there. And I suspect the thought crossed his mind. Only he was drunk, that part was no act. Only he was enjoying himself too much, and although the money was easy and good it had gone beyond that—where the game, the rush and power of the con was all that mattered. By now, too, the pit boss would've heard all the commotion and sauntered over to the table.

I see the boxman as bored. I see him thinking about getting home to his wife and kids, and who for the first couple rolls might've attributed my father's wins to nothing more than a hot streak bound to break the next time around. But when it didn't, he had to wake up, lean forward on his elbows and narrow his eyes. My father would've noticed that. All the gamblers would've. And it should've made him nervous, and it probably did. Maybe this is the time, up eighteen thousand without a bum roll, that he decided not to push his luck any further—to get the house dice back into the game, sweep in his chips, cash out and split. It was here, however, in getting the dice *out*, that his limited talents failed him.

The loss of his two fingers, which had contributed, at least in part, to his choosing a life of crime, and which on this occasion had served to further those crooked aims by distracting attention, now clearly had him at a disadvantage when it came, once again, to manipulating the dice in the palm of his hand. He suffered the extreme embarrassment of dropping one at his feet, with two still on the table. The man beside him looked down at the floor, then backed away. The laughter and cheers died and suddenly it was silent. The boxman rose from his chair. The pit boss came out from around the table.

My father could've run then, he could've walked even, however briskly, for the door. But I have a feeling that he was as stunned as the rest, and he paused, and that's all it took. House security was on him in no time, and against his will, claiming there had been some mistake, he was escorted upstairs, questioned, then taken outside and turned over to two very large men whose positions had no official title, though their duties were rigidly defined. And they did their jobs well, more efficiently and effectively, say, than if they had simply turned him over to the local police, who beyond arresting my father for this crime and those of his past had no personal stake in teaching him a lesson that he wouldn't soon forget. They drove a Lincoln Continental. My father sat in back, sweating, scared for his life.

The driver glanced in the rearview mirror.

"How'd you lose your fingers?"

"In a sawmill accident," my father told him. "Back in Portland."

"That's too bad."

"You learn to get by without them."

"In the Family," the driver said, "that's the sign of a thief."

The other guy turned around in his seat. He had a Polar-
oid with a flash.

"Smile," he said. "Give me a big, big smile. We're going
to make you famous all over Vegas."

The flash went off as the Lincoln slowed to make a turn
somewhere deeper into the desert. They bounced along a
bumpy, desolate road for a while, then came to a stop, and
the two men climbed out. One went around to the side and
opened my father's door, but he wasn't exactly anxious to
get out.

"C'mon."

"We here already?"

"Stop talking," the other guy said, "and let's get it over
with."

"Listen, guys, I don't know what they're paying you, but
if you're anything like me, with a wife and a kid and house
payments and all that, it's never enough."

"Get outta the car."

"Why don't we just say we came out here," my father
said, "you did what you had to do and that's that. Look
around. Who's going to know?"

One of them reached into the Lincoln and pulled him out,
and knowing my father and what he saw coming, as soon as
he was on solid ground he probably whirled around and laid
into them. Of course it was a futile effort, and in no time they
were punching and kicking. I saw the end result, and these
guys were vicious. I also suspect that at some point during
this beating he managed a stinging blow straight to one man's
nose, and that that accounted, as retribution, for the stitches
in his own. It must've been an odd sight, this hood baring his
teeth like an animal, then lunging forward, covering my father's nose with his mouth, almost like a kiss, and biting into
it. As he lay in the dirt, bruised and bleeding, one of them
pulled out a knife. The other stepped on my father's hand.

"Move," he said, "and I'll cut your fucking throat."

The details of the blade pressing into the skin, and the crunching sound it must've made when it hit the white of bone was all I could fathom without getting sick to my stomach. How, in that condition, he later dragged himself back to the highway was no less of a miracle than his chance encounter with two young marines driving back to their base that night and catching him in the glare of their headlights as he crawled along the side of the road. If not for them, my father may well have bled to death out there.

"But I guess it just wasn't my time," he told me the next day, when I visited him again at the hospital. "The good Lord saw fit to spare me, Bobby." And I saw fit not to question him on his newfound faith and upset him any more than he already was. The notion of God rarely entered our conversations, and I suspect that whatever gratefulness he felt toward the good Lord would last about as long as it took for him to get well, give or take a day or two. The doctors wanted to keep him for five. Which meant that he had three to go.

On the way up to his room, I stopped at the gift shop and bought the newspaper and a copy of *Popular Mechanics*. I knew he would've enjoyed *Playboy* more, but I doubted if the clerk would've sold it to me and I didn't want to try. I dropped the magazine and the newspaper on my father's lap.

"Where's Melinda?" he said. "How come she hasn't come to visit me?"

"Busy, I guess."

"Hell of a note."

I thought it was, too, though I didn't have the heart to tell him, for I could hardly look him in the eye. We'd take it one step at a time. First, and most importantly, he needed to get better, get back on his feet, and so far as what happened between me and Melinda I prayed that he'd never find out. The guilt nauseated me, as much for what I'd done as for Melinda, who was supposed to love my father. I doubted if she did. I doubted if she ever had. I doubted if it was a concern.

"Here I am laid up in the hospital and my woman can't find the time to check and see if I'm dead or alive. Not even a goddamn phone call," he said. "She got herself another man already?"

His words cut close, and the guilt, with its companion, remorse, hit another high.

"Not that I know about," I said.

"It's not like she'd tell you."

"She did ask about you."

"That's real sweet of her."

He reached for the glass of water on the nightstand and took a drink.

"I think she's been hanging out a lot with Darlene," I said.

"That bitch."

"She's not so bad."

"Like hell, the woman puts thoughts in her head. Miss Liberation," he said. "I can't stand that shit. And your hair," he added, as if the two thoughts were somehow connected. "When you gonna get it cut? You're looking more and more like a damn hippie every day. Before you know it you'll be smoking pot."

"Don't worry about me," I said. "You just concentrate on getting better. We have to move on soon as you're out of here. I should've told you before, but they got your picture hanging up at Circus Circus and who knows where else."

He grinned, and when he did I noticed that he'd lost a tooth toward the back of his mouth. Between that, his missing fingers on the right hand, the one on the left, and his receding hairline, he was wasting away before me. The years hadn't been kind.

"I'll be damned," he said. "Is that a fact?"

"It certainly is."

"I always wanted to be famous."

"There's all kinds of famous guys locked up at Salem," I said.

In the next bed, an older pasty-faced man lay snoring. My father nodded at him.

"Think I got it bad, that poor son of a bitch played it clean all his life. No booze. No cigarettes. For what? Cancer of the lungs."

I looked at my watch.

"I have to get to work," I said.

"Melinda on tonight?"

"Far as I know."

"Tell her to call me," he said. "I have some apologizing to get off my chest."

"Sure."

"Don't forget now," he said.

"I won't."

"Thanks for the magazine."

"Sure."

"Say, you pick up my Cadillac?"

"I'll do it tomorrow," I said. "Promise."

I left then, and at work that evening I looked for Melinda, but she didn't show up. I checked her time card, too; it hadn't been stamped, and on the previous night she'd clocked out three hours early. At first I thought she might've quit, seeing as how all the money my father had stolen just happened to come from her table. She must've worried that the pit bosses and the boxmen would make the connection and fire her, or something worse, along the lines of what they did to my father. Then I got to thinking that if she split right away it would only confirm their suspicions, if indeed they had any, and knowing Melinda I doubt if she would've risked that. More likely she left work saying she felt sick and called in the next day with the same excuse. It's hard to figure. But I hung around awhile after my shift and she didn't show up. I don't know what I would've said to her, anyway, or if, as in the case with my father, I could've even looked her in the eye.

The past few days of worry and restlessness had worn me down to nothing, a walking corpse, and I had no plans other than to head home, feed Sam and then try and get some sleep. Whenever he heard my Volkswagen pull into the driveway he'd start jumping up and down, yanking against his chain, whining and barking like crazy, and he wouldn't knock it off until I set him loose and let him dance around me, nip at my heels and lick my face. I expected the same tonight, I welcomed it, but when I turned off the headlights and climbed out of the car it was pitch black and dead quiet. No moon. No stars.

"Sam?" I called. "Sam?"

Nothing.

"Sam?"

I got down on one knee next to the snailback and felt around the hitch for him. "C'mere, you dumb mutt," I said. "Come out from under there." He was gone, though, chain and all. I didn't know how he could've gotten loose unless somebody let him, and finding him in the desert, especially at night, would've been impossible. Sam was a damn good dog, but he hadn't been blessed with a keen sense of direction. Lost in the heat for a day or two and he'd be one dead pup. I rattled his food dish, hoping he was close enough to hear it and come running back. I whistled. I called out twice more, and I was considering walking into the desert a ways or so, calling from there and seeing if that made a difference. Then a voice came out of the darkness.

"The dog's gone."

I froze.

"Who's that?"

Bo held a flashlight under his chin and flipped it on. How the shadows played on his face, it was like he had no eyes, just these empty black holes. My heart sped up. I felt the blood pounding in my ears.

"Where's Melinda?"

"In the house, I think."

"I checked inside," he said. "She's not there, and all her clothes are gone."

"I don't know anything about that."

"Where'd she go?"

"I told you, I don't know."

"How about your old man?"

"He left us," I said. "Up and split a month ago."

"Bullshit."

"No bullshit."

"I got nothing against you," Bo said. "Just don't fuck with me. Don't ever fuck with me or I'll bury you with your old man. Nobody'll find you in this desert, it'll be like you never existed." Then to dramatize his point, as if he hadn't made it firmly enough, he hit me. With the flashlight, I think—it was harder than a fist, anyway, and in the dark I didn't see it coming. It knocked me to the ground. "I been driving all night, and I don't have any patience for this shit." He leaned over me, so that I was staring up at him. Even if I couldn't see him well in the dark, I still made out that thick fat neck, like a linebacker's, the outline of his beefy shoulders, all muscle and head, with those two black holes for eyes. I could hear him breathing, too, and I caught the smell of whiskey. "Listen," he said, as he slowly drew the butt of the flashlight down my forehead to the tip of my nose. "I don't know what she told you about me and I don't care. I know I fucked up. I did her wrong, I admit it, but we all make fucking mistakes, you know what I mean? You got to forgive."

I knew what he meant, if not exactly at least in general, though I wasn't clear on why he was telling me all this, unless in his own confused, desperate way he needed to convince himself that he was somehow a changed man now worthy of

Melinda's affections. In any case, I wasn't about to debate with him and run the risk of having my skull split open, and I nodded my support. When I thought about it later, he and my father didn't seem to be all that different.

"Yeah," I said, "I know what you mean."

"She's all I care about, man. She's the only bitch I ever really loved and I've been going crazy since she left. I got to find her. We got to talk and work this out. I love the bitch, man." Repeatedly referring to Melinda as a bitch seemed a strange term of endearment, and certainly not one likely to win over many women. But again, I didn't see this as an appropriate time or place to take issue with him. He held the flashlight above my head and spoke softly. "Now tell me," he said, "where do you suppose she could've run off to?" If I could be of any assistance to him, short of informing on my father, I'm afraid that I felt obligated, largely because of the threat of severe physical harm, but also because I frankly didn't feel any great sense of loyalty to Melinda. And though she'd been kind to us in many ways, I believed, as I had from the very beginning, that my father and I would've both been better off without her.

"She might be at her friend's place," I said.

"Who's that?"

"Her name's Darlene."

"Darlene Whittaker?"

"Yeah."

"Shit," he said. "That whore's crazier than your old man. She's been trying to bust me and Melinda up since we met."

I volunteered the next piece of information, that is, that Darlene Whittaker lived in an adult community called the Club Oasis, off Sahara Avenue and surrounded by a golf course.

"You messing with me?"

"No," I said. "Honest."

"I'll be back if you are."

At that he disappeared back into the darkness, and seconds later I heard a truck start up in the desert. I felt my cheek, then rubbed my fingers together. They were slick with blood. "Asshole," I muttered. I waited until he was on the road before I ran to my car, hopped in and hightailed it to the hospital. The main doors were locked. I pulled on them. I knocked. But the lights in the lobby were all out; it had to be after midnight, and there was no one around to hear me, not even a janitor. So I had to run all the way around the building to Emergency, and I'll be damned if it wasn't locked, too. A nurse passed down the hall and I pounded on the glass. But she wouldn't even look my way. There was a red button next to the door and I leaned on it, hard, until finally this old security guard showed up, sipping a cup of coffee.

"What's the problem?"

"I need to see my father."

"Visiting hours ended at eight."

"It's an emergency," I told him. "He might not make it through the night."

And in a way, I thought, it was true.

"Talk to the nurse," he said. "She's at the end of the hall."

He let me by, and it's a good thing he did, because I would've pushed past him if he hadn't. At the end of the hall, however, I made a detour and rode the elevator to the third floor and hurried down it. The doors to the other rooms were open and all were dark inside, except for a bed lamp here and there, or the green and red glow of the small lights on the monitors. All was quiet, too, except for the steady electronic hum of the machines and somewhere the ugly thump and hiss, thump and hiss of a respirator.

The old man with cancer was curled up on his side, holding his stomach. My father's bed was stripped to the mattress, and his things on the nightstand—the pitcher of water, a roll of Tums and the glass—were gone. The magazine I'd given him early that afternoon rested at the foot of the other man's bed. I put my hand on his shoulder and gently shook him.

"Excuse me."

"Huh?"

"Excuse me, sir."

The poor guy didn't seem to know where he was at first; he was groggy and high on something, morphine, I guess, and for a while he just stared up at me with this vacant look in his eyes.

"The guy in the next bed," I said, "you know where he went?"

"The contractor?"

I didn't know what bull my father had told him, but I went along.

"Right," I said.

"He checked out this afternoon. The doctors wanted him to stay, but he wouldn't listen."

"He say where he was going?"

"No," he said, "I don't think he did."

I left then and drove by the Thunderbird Motel. His Cadillac was gone. I went by the house, too, and it wasn't there, either. It was a downward spiral, and since things were rapidly going from bad to worse, I figured he went for broke again.

The Club Oasis reminded me of the River Towers, where it all began, though this complex looked considerably more expensive. The sign out front showed a picture of a sexy woman in a bikini sitting on the edge of the pool, dipping one foot in the water while a young man with a towel draped over his shoulder stood staring at her in the background. Beneath the picture, in bold letters, it advertised a heated pool and spa, marble Roman tubs, wet bars, ceiling fans, a full eighteen-hole golf course and a community gym. I'd only been to

Darlene's place once, when I went with Melinda and my father to drop off a birthday present, and even though all the condominiums looked the same from outside, I remembered the exact one because its front porch overlooked the ninth hole. It was also particularly easy to locate because my father's Cadillac was parked in the driveway beside Bo's truck. I pulled up behind them.

All the lights were on in the place, and Melinda was hollering, although I couldn't make out the words. I heard Darlene screaming, too, and I went to the window and looked between a space in the drapes. Bo had my father down on the floor in the living room, and he was beating on him. Melinda and Darlene, both in their bathrobes and slippers, were huddled next to the couch. Melinda was crying and Darlene held her. My father was in no condition to fight, high on painkillers, with seventeen fresh stitches in his skull, bruised and broken ribs and another lost finger, which had begun to bleed heavily, the white gauze bandage growing red with it. It simply wasn't an equal match, in light of Bo's size, weight and muscle, his occupation and love of violence. I had no choice but to come to my father's aid and quickly before Bo inflicted greater damage, and seeing as how I was no bruiser myself, and that it wasn't to my advantage any more than his that I get beaten to a pulp, too, I ran back to the car for the Luger.

In my father's words, if the door had been locked, he would've been up shit creek. But either he or Bo had kicked it in sometime earlier, because the doorknob was busted so that it couldn't close, and the chain latch had been snapped. Inside, the living room was a wreck. One of the legs on the coffee table was broken. The couch lay on its side, and the telephone had been ripped out of the wall. From Bo's belt, under his baggy sweatshirt, which had ridden up his back in the fight, hung a pair of cuffs and a holstered .38.

I cocked the Luger.

"Let him go," I said.

Bo looked over his shoulder. He had his knee in the small of my father's back.

"Put the gun down, Bo said."

"Get off him," I said.

"You want to go to prison with your old man?"

"All of you," Melinda screamed. "All of you, get the hell out. Leave me alone."

"Honey," my father said, "I'm doing the best I can with two hundred some pounds of shit sitting on top of me."

Bo reared back to hit him again.

"Don't," I said.

"Put it down or I'll ram it up your ass."

Bo had my father with his face pressed into the carpet, but my father managed to turn his head and look at me.

"Bobby," he said. "It could go on like this all day. Just shoot the punk in the leg and show him we mean business."

"Which one?"

"Left or right. What's the difference?"

"Why not in the head?"

"We don't want to kill him."

"He already belted me once," I said. "Now he wants to ram a gun up my ass. He wants to send us both to prison. I don't see why we ought to go soft on the son of a bitch."

"The boy's got a point," my father said.

"You're crazy," Bo said. "Both of you."

I aimed at his head.

"Like father, like son," I said. "Let him up or I'll blow you away. It don't matter to me any more than left or right."

Bo let him up, and when my father got to his feet he unsnapped the holster and took the .38. If I hadn't put a scare into Bo, my father certainly did. Just as Bo had done to him back on the Willamette River, going on four years now, he jammed the barrel under his chin. I really thought he might pull the trigger, too. He was high, I could see it in his eyes, and he was crazed enough to do it.

"The girl's been through a lot of bad shit," he said, using the same words, or ones close to it, that Bo had used on him in their first formal introduction, "and assholes like you just keep dragging her back down. Come around again, I'll blow your head off."

Then he ordered him into the kitchen and, taking Bo's cuffs, locked him to the handles of Darlene's big double-door Frigidaire.

"Motherfucker," Bo said.

"Bobby," my father said, "hand me that wash towel over there."

I did, and he gagged him, though not without a struggle. When the job was done, we went back into the living room. Melinda was still crying, and a big part of me suddenly felt sorry for her. I saw this moment as a vulnerable one for all of us, and I deeply feared that the worst was far from over. She only had to open her mouth, and in several words she could've betrayed us both, as we had my father.

"Hop in the car, honey."

"She's not going anywhere," Darlene said.

"I'd appreciate you minding your own business and letting her talk for herself," he said. "Baby, you staying or going? We can't wait long for your answer. You got to make up your mind."

"Get out," Darlene said. "Get *out*."

It was nothing long. It was nothing drawn out. And I knew what Melinda's decision was without her having to say it. And she didn't. They just looked at each other, and finally he caught on. It was a heartbreaker of a moment, with everybody staring at him, everybody suddenly quiet, and him just standing there toward the back of the room, all beat to hell and doped up, both eyes blackened and teeth marks and stitches in his nose.

I took him by the arm.

"C'mon, let's go. She ain't coming."

Melinda managed a weak smile. "You take care now," she said. "Both of you."

But I don't think my father heard her, because he'd shaken me off by then and headed out the door. I hurried after him, because I didn't want him driving in his condition, and I beat him to the Cadillac. "I'll drive," I said. "You do the navigating." He pointed us to Highway 95. Straight through the desert. For the longest while we just listened to the engine and the purr of the road running beneath us. The days had grown shorter, the weather cooler, and come night the desert was downright cold. The land was flat and empty and the sky pitch black except for the headlights of the Cadillac stretching before us, like we were driving into nothing. I shivered. I reached for the heater switch.

"It's broken," my father said.

"How come we always end up with cars that don't have heaters?"

"Quit complaining."

"I'm just stating a fact."

"We had one. That Chevy Nova in Portland, from the Safeway."

"For one whole day," I said. "Big deal. The rest of the time we've either been freezing or sweating our asses off."

My father rested his arm along the top of the seat and sighed.

"That was really something you did back there. I suppose I ought to thank you."

"Yeah, you should."

"Tell me, were you really planning to shoot that son of a bitch?"

"It wasn't even loaded," I said. "I took the bullets out."

He got a kick out of that, as I expected he would.

"You're kidding?"

"Nope."

"You know something, Bobby, you're all right, you're

okay. You and me," he said, "we'll make a fine team. This vacation ain't over yet." He opened the glove compartment and began rummaging through it. "I had a bottle of Jack around here somewhere," he said. "A couple shots sound in order about now."

I'd stowed it under the seat, and when I felt for it I found it all right, along with Sam's chain. I suspect that the expression on my face was one of shock, but my father didn't notice and I said nothing. I just passed him the whiskey. He took a bottle of painkillers from his pocket, shook a couple out into his hand and swallowed them with a shot.

"You're not supposed to mix that stuff. It says right on the label."

"Don't start on that again, we both know what happened last time around." He took another drink. "If I remember right," he said, "after you held up that hot dog stand you asked for a shot, and I wouldn't let you. That was a while ago, though, and you're plenty wiser now." He offered me the bottle. "Go on, take a swig. All that green's gone around the edges. It's time we cut loose."

I passed on it with a wave of my hand.

"We got a long way to go and that shit makes me sleepy," I said. "But I'm curious about something."

"What's that?"

"My mom."

"What about her?"

"You never did say why she left."

"It had nothing to do with you, if that's what you're worried about. We got by well enough without her, anyway."

"That's not what I'm asking."

"I fed and clothed you and changed your diapers. Me," he said, "not your mother. What more do you need to know?"

"Why'd she leave?"

"Since when did that matter?"

"Since lately."

"You want the truth?"

"Yeah," I said. "The truth."

"She met this marine at some bar and ran off with him. That's your mother, son. I wasn't her first, and by God I'm sure I wasn't her last. She was barely eighteen when she had you, and babies just didn't figure into the picture. Neither did I. But I raised you up, goddamn it. I did my best."

I didn't know what to say. I didn't know how to feel. The road ran on and on and after a while the whiskey and the pills took effect and my father covered himself with his coat and slid down in his seat and closed his eyes. I put the cap back on the bottle and set it on the seat between us. Come dawn, along this desolate stretch of highway, we came across a gas station. A strong desert wind had kicked up and it rocked the sign. I pulled up to the pumps. I nudged him awake.

"Give me some money."

"What?"

"Some money," I said. "We need gas."

"I'm a little short."

"You must've got something for the dog."

He sat up straight.

"Now don't go getting all pushed out of shape. It's just a mutt and we needed cash for the trip. I was only thinking of us."

"Stop bullshitting me. Stop bullshitting yourself." I was mad and getting madder. "You quit caring about us a long time ago. The money," I said, "how much you get for stealing my dog?"

He nodded toward the backseat. There was a cardboard box there that hadn't been yesterday, and in it was a half dozen or so cartons of Marlboros.

"You're looking at most of it. I was figuring we'd stop at a bar and sell 'em. Shit," he said, "the grease monkey here might even buy a couple or trade for a tank of gas."

I got out of the Cadillac. I had six bucks in my wallet and the two fifties I'd saved still in the sole of my shoe.

"You planned on ditching me again, didn't you?"

"Hell no."

"You don't have to lie anymore," I said. "You okay to drive now?"

"What're you talking about?"

"Better see a doctor about that finger, too," I said. "You don't want to get gangrene and lose the whole goddamn hand."

"It was just a *dog*, Bobby. We'll buy you another one when we hit Reno."

I pulled off my shoe, took out one of the fifties and gave it to him.

"This ought to get you there," I said, "if you don't stop anywhere along the way."

"What're you gonna do? Where you gonna go? Open your eyes, damn it, there's nothing out there for you."

I looked around me. Outside of the gas station there was nothing but desert, sagebrush and a strong cold wind blowing from the east. The attendant started toward the car, wearing a parka with the hood up and his hands tucked in his pockets.

"I'll find something. Hell," I said, "maybe I'll cut my hair and join the army. I hear they'll take you at seventeen."

I turned and began to walk. My father's voice caught in the wind. "Bobby," he shouted. "Bobby . . ." But I kept on and on, that day and for several months to come, and in my travels I saw a good deal of the country. Idaho. Montana. Colorado. Texas and Kansas and a half dozen other states. I made it as far south as Georgia, where my father's aunt lived, but no one seemed to know where my mother had gone, she was barely a memory, and even if I've long since given up the search, in my mind I often return to that place in the desert.

There was no obstruction but the sky that day, no shade or cover, and nowhere left to hide. The land rolled up toward me, endless and distant, breaking like a surf, and in its desolation there was the promise of a new beginning. I would go on to make a fine soldier. I would see battle. I would see the end of the war, the wreckage and loss, and later, as if in another life, a gentle woman and the birth of our two sons. Dust rose from the desert floor and spun around itself, and though I knew nothing for certain, I believed that if I only walked fast enough I'd find myself somewhere in the middle of this storm.